Praise for
K.M. TREMILLS

———— ·· ◖●◗ ·· ————

"K.M. Tremills is the gold standard for strong, independent and feminine heroines. *Blue Moon* is the start of a wickedly clever trilogy!"

— Kathryn Cottam, *The Shoemaker*

"K.M. Tremills writes with passion and understanding about a young woman's rite of passage. *Blue Moon* is a compelling tale!"

— Elizabeth Stanley, *Dark Path Chronicles*

"I fell in love with these vibrant characters. *Blue Moon* is a delightfully dark blend of quirky, flirty, sarcastic, and charming."

— Vanessa Mayville, Vanessa Mayville Designs

"*Blue Moon* is a witty, fast-paced novel with wonderfully written characters that immediately drew me into their story. I can't wait to meet them again in the next book!"

— Laura Wrubleski, Designer

———— ·· ◖●◗ ·· ————

"*Messenger* is an absolute treasure and fascinating story. The storytelling and the cast of characters are unique and make the novel a true joy to read."

— Renee Alarid, Designer

"The ancient wisdom in the engaging story of Gabriella comes through in the eloquent words of K.M. Tremills. *Messenger* can be read on many levels all of which are entertaining."

— Jen Clarke, Institute of Play

"*Messenger* is brilliant … a fantastic journey that steps into a realm of mysticism and fantasy. K.M. Tremills causes the reader to ponder their own beliefs."

— Barb Weston, Inner Focus Holistic Healing

"Well-written and entertaining. The pacing fast and smooth. *Messenger* gets it all just right."

— Joe Gazzam, *Uncaged*

ALSO BY K.M. TREMILLS

Messenger
Queen Isabel (A Great Lands Tale)
Three Short Tales of Red
Fabled: 17 Tales You Think You Know

BLUE MOON

Book One in the Fated Series

K.M. TREMILLS

Blue Moon

Copyright © 2014 by Kate Tremills

www.kmtremills.com

Cover concept by Roberta Cottam
Cover art and book design by Laura Wrubleski

Print Edition: March 2015
ISBN: 978-0-9921042-3-8

Kindle Ebook Edition: March 2015
ISBN: 978-0-9921042-4-5

Kobo Ebook Edition: March 2015
ISBN: 978-0-9921042-5-2

Published 2015 by RavenHeart Press

For the lovers of magic.

*May you find joy and delight
in the mysteries of the world.*

MYTHOLOGICAL MAGIC AND MYSTERIES

AKASHIC RECORDS Library containing the life events of every being in the universe.

APHRODITE Goddess of love, beauty, pleasure, and procreation.

APOLLO God of sun, truth and prophecy, healing, plague, music, and poetry.

ATHENA Goddess of wisdom, courage, inspiration, civilization, law and justice, warfare, mathematics, strength, strategy, the arts, crafts, and skill.

BELLADONNAS Beautiful women with clairvoyant ability whose seductive talents can be alluring or devastating.

BELTANE Celtic fire festival in early May that marks the beginning of summer.

CENTAURS Liminal being with a human torso and a horse's body.

CHIRON Centaur known for his wisdom, healing, and prophecy.

ERIS Goddess of chaos, strife, discord, contention, and rivalry.

FATES Three goddesses who weave the thread of mortal and immortal lives according to eternal laws.

FURIES Goddesses of justice and vengeance who punished wrong-doers by driving them mad.

GAIA Great mother of all. Goddess of earth, one of the primal elements who first emerged at the dawn of creation, along with air, sea and sky.

HACKERS Intelligent beings that exploit or explore the mutability of code, objects, or social structures.

HADES God of the underworld, dead, death and the hidden riches of the earth. Also the name for the abode of the dead.

HEKATE Goddess of crossroads, entrance ways, magic, witchcraft, knowledge of herbs, night, crescent moon, ghosts and necromancy.

HERA Goddess of women, marriage, sky, and starry heavens.

LILITH Goddess of heaven, dark moon, fertility, agriculture, and owls.

MEDUSA Goddess of serpents, death and rebirth, dark moon, divination, healing, magic, and sex.

MOUNT OLYMPUS Native home of the Greek gods built after the Titan war where humans are not permitted to set foot.

PALLAS ATHENA Another name for Athena. Athena took the name of goddess Pallas after causing her death, placing the name of her fallen sister before her own.

PANTHEON The collective of gods and goddesses. Also the name for a temple dedicated to all of the gods and goddesses.

PARIS Prince of Troy, chosen to settle a dispute between Hera, Athena, and Aphrodite, over the apple of discord, a golden fruit inscribed to the fairest.

PERSEPHONE Goddess of spring, innocence, maidenhood, vegetation, and the underworld.

PROMETHEUS Titan that aligned with Zeus in the Titanomachy, war between titans and gods, then later defied Zeus by returning fire to humans.

SHAPESHIFTERS Beings that can change appearance and navigate different levels of consciousness, dream, waking states and the astral plane.

SIRENS Winged beings with the power to enchant and charm with their songs.

SOPHIA Goddess of wisdom, creation, grail, earth, and heart.

SYLPHS Elemental beings of the air, mercurial and intense, associated with dreams, sky, birds, and all aspects of air.

VALHALLA Domain for warriors who die in battle and are carried to Odin's hall by the Valkyries.

ZEUS God of sky, thunder, weather, law, order, and justice.

PROLOGUE

On that night, a full moon rose in the sky.

Full of portent and beauty, the gods and goddesses kept a close eye on New York. This was the night their chosen one arrived. The one who would change the fabric of reality.

Until now, the gods chose to play by the rules. Allowing Fate to dictate the landscape, while Choice spoke up when a little finesse and magic was needed.

But the world had changed. A mortal was rising to challenge all that the gods had built. A man bent on bringing immortals to their knees and humanity to perpetual servitude.

And so, three sisters were tasked to bring forth one who could confront this dark force.

The immortal realm watched as the sisters poured magic into the streets. Pulling and pushing the weave of the intricate fabric of life. Working the threads until they achieved the right warp. The subtlest of shifts. The slightest adjustment. They guided their chosen one to arrive. Unsure and unsteady.

The time had come, the sisters knew, for humans to reclaim their gifts. Gifts not so different from the gods. Vision. Connection. Creation. But the mortal ones had not believed in magic for many centuries. They were rusty, doubtful, and even resentful.

Nevertheless, the world needed their particular kind of magic. The stars had aligned. The gods had spoken. Ready or not, the humans were asked to embrace the power that would bring them back into alliance with the gods.

Under the light of a sacred blue moon.

CHAPTER ONE

Helen stepped off the elevator. She wasn't sure what drew her here. She had followed an instinct. Luring her up sixty-one floors to the top of this glass sky rise.

She stood for a moment in the entryway.

Gazing around, she absorbed that no man's land between elevator and business. Imagining how many people passed through this space. Matching what they wore to the finest details of the wallpaper, the door frames, the frosted glass. She smiled. Knowing these were the tiny specifics most people blurred past in their day.

For Helen, each detail was a clue. A fascinating mystery to be solved. She knew that someone had chosen each item, no matter how banal, to give an impression. To set a mood. Every thing selected to intimidate or welcome, depending on the business at the end of this passage.

Helen knew she stood on a bridge between worlds.

On her last birthday, Helen had created a game to follow any pull her instinct presented with enough force. No matter where it took her or how much talking she needed to do. She promised to follow.

Usually it involved picking an unsuspecting business or

event, seeing how far she could get and how much she could find out. She gathered as many clues as she could before she opened their door, then kept the game going as long as possible. Other people went to movies. Helen invented her own little plots.

She knew Manhattan had millions of people, but it could be a lonely place at the best of times. Never mind expensive. So she created a fun source of entertainment to get to know the city, while meeting people she would never run into in her normal life. Not that Helen was remotely normal.

She had been on her way to a housewarming party with no intention of detouring into an Upper West Side skyscraper. Helen strode extra fast when she was forcing herself to a destination. She didn't like parties much, especially ones where she had to bring a home-oriented gift, but she reluctantly admitted they were a place to meet friends. Or potential job prospects.

She would have gone straight past the building had she not spotted the Logan & Associates logo. The moment she saw it, she felt a spine-tingling chill, and stopped in her tracks. The chill was her sign that there was something special about the place. Something mysterious.

Helen couldn't explain it. But she suddenly had to know who Logan was and why he needed associates.

She found herself pulled into the lobby by a curiosity so strong she would have sworn someone was tugging her blouse. The building was remarkably quiet. She looked around but did not see a soul in the lobby. Even the security guard was strangely missing from his desk.

Helen didn't question her luck. She headed straight for the

elevators, quickly checking the building's directory for Logan &
Associates before disappearing through the elevator doors.

Now that she stood in front of their logo, emblazoned on the
wall, Helen wondered what could have possibly enticed her up
sixty-one floors.

Their conservative emblem announced their importance
like a law firm yet with too much flair to be such a practical
enterprise. Sparkling silver, the logo's material implied expensive
services and the size laid claim to the entire floor. Yet the name
was so banal, she would almost assume they didn't want anyone
making the trip.

*What kind of company offers high-end services to a limited
clientele,* Helen wondered as she moved her gaze from the logo
to re-examine the entryway. She suddenly picked up on the
missing washroom. And the lack of art on the walls.

They aren't looking for exclusive clients, Helen thought,
they don't want clients at all. Or, at least, she corrected herself,
they don't want anyone who isn't invited.

Helen smiled. Jackpot! And the chill shot up her spine. Just
like when she saw their name. If she needed any confirmation,
she had it. There was something mysterious about this place.
Which made her game all the more exciting.

As she turned her gaze to the office behind the glazed glass,
she wondered how to play this. The best approach was to let the
receptionist take the lead. Helen preferred to be in charge, but
when the dance was this unscripted, she knew to follow where
other people loved to show the way.

Luckily, she had dressed for the party. Most days, she would
never wear pants that required an iron, let alone a blouse discreet

enough to be worn to a job interview. She glanced down at her flirty blouse, and shifted the shoulders back to adjust the plunge down her chest. Well, almost discreet enough.

Helen shook off her doubts and pushed open the glass door. She wasn't surprised to see the waiting area empty. But she had expected a receptionist. Not seeing anyone at the front desk, she moved lightly yet confidently into the quiet space.

As she moved past the simple, modern furnishings and the non-descript glass table, she was no closer to figuring out what this place was. Luckily, she spotted a pile of magazines in the far corner of the waiting area.

Helen was a pro at figuring out a business within five minutes of seeing their reading material. She walked straight past the front desk, around the edge of the waiting area, and reached toward the stack tucked in the corner. As though no one expected them to be read at all.

"May I help you?" a voice asked in an unhelpful tone.

Helen practically jumped out of her skin. She whipped around to see the receptionist leaning out from behind an absurdly large computer monitor, looking far from amused. Helen wondered whether this woman was really a receptionist or a guard dog with her finger poised on an alarm button.

Helen smiled effortlessly and stepped toward her opponent. She didn't actually care what the woman's real job was. Helen reveled in the challenge. Hostile receptionists were like a rite of passage. If she hadn't piped up, Helen would have been disappointed to move past so easily.

"Why, yes," Helen began, approaching the front desk.

Helen's eyes swept over the clean, sharp lines of the white

barrier between her and the reception area. The chest-height obstruction said much more than anyone else might imagine. Discretion. Restraint. Secrets.

Where others noticed simple elegance, she saw protection and suspicion. Logan & Associates didn't want anyone sneaking up on their receptionist and catching a peek at her work. Helen smiled innocently and leaned in to create an air of intimacy with the cool guardian of the front desk.

"I have an appointment with Mr. Logan," Helen said, glancing over the barrier at the immaculate desktop. Not a sheet of paper in sight.

The receptionist gazed back without flinching. Then asked, "Which one?"

"Senior," Helen responded quickly.

She had no idea where that answer came from. Helen cursed her fast tongue.

Why did she say Senior? She should have opted for Junior. Helen always had better luck with younger men. Between her playful tone and complete lack of interest in their opinion, they couldn't help but be drawn to her.

"Your name," the receptionist demanded.

"Helen," she replied. "Helen Troy."

"Take a seat, Miss Troy."

As she perched on a white leather chair, Helen was nervous, but excited. She had secured an invitation inside this secret place. Not only was she going deeper into the labyrinth but she was officially rescued from her party.

Who knows, she laughed to herself, *she might even get a job out the deal.*

While she waited, she picked up one of the neatly stacked magazines. Intrigued to find an interior design magazine on the top. She glanced around surreptitiously as she flipped the pages.

No way this is a design firm, she thought. *Not a stitch of art. No minimalist yet pretentious furniture. No discreet yet oh so obviously placed awards for clients to notice.* She gazed down at the magazine. *Unless this is meant to distract me from whatever horrible problem I have by gazing at harmless, pretty pictures.*

Helen looked up, trying to catch a glimpse of the inside workings of Logan & Associates. No one walked by. No one showed up for appointments. No one called. She was alone with the sullen receptionist.

She began to wonder if anyone worked in this place. The more she wondered, the more the quiet grew unsettling.

Helen's mood shifted. She no longer felt excited. She felt vulnerable. She was alone in a strange office with one exit. If anything went wrong … she glanced up at the door. Thinking about how quickly she could get to the stairwell.

Wait. Had she seen a stairwell? Or just the elevator? She wondered. *Skyscrapers had to have a fire exit. It must be code. But she couldn't recall seeing the door. Or the bright red Exit sign that lit the way in case of fire.*

Helen admonished herself. She was getting worked up over nothing. She must have missed it. Her instinct had never steered her wrong. That intuitive pull had landed her all kinds of amazing jobs, apartments, and even the occasional fun affair.

But she couldn't shake the feeling that this place was strange. Like whatever they did here was definitely *not* a game. And that feeling clashed with her reason for doing anything.

By her twenty-seventh birthday, Helen decided she'd had enough drama to last several lifetimes. That night, after many drinks, she swore on an invisible stack of bibles that she was never taking anything seriously again. Not love. Not money. Not even life itself.

As far as she could tell, life was some elaborate game played by the gods. Where dice got tossed and you had no say in the numbers that showed up. Helen had lost that toss too many times in twenty-seven years.

She was playful by nature. But she decided it was time to up the stakes — so her game was born. If life was a crapshoot, she was going to have as much fun as possible. Helen wanted to play life full-tilt, following her intuition. Life was for living. Not for getting attached. And definitely not for staying in one place too long.

Nope. Helen was about as far as you could get from every other twenty-seven year old on the shores of Manhattan. Most twenty-somethings with enough chutzpah to get to this island, and afford the rent, were filled with more ambition than one human being had the right to carry. The very thought of it made her nauseous.

They were determined. Helen gave them that. Determined to climb any and every wall presented. To what aim, she had no idea. Their pathological need to prove themselves seemed just as random, and infinitely less fun, than her decision to let her intuition take her wherever it damn well pleased.

When she committed to her game, Helen was so excited she made the mistake of telling people at parties. She loved the idea of letting life lead the way! Pure adventure. Letting go of the reins. She was sure people would be inspired or at least intrigued.

Not so. The response she typically got was horror, confusion, or a blank stare. Not one ounce of curiosity. Not one person wanting to tag along and give it a try. She had expected more of people in New York. Especially the artists.

Somehow, her lack of ambition did not make her intriguing. Helen discovered that it made her suspicious. Like she made the whole thing up just to trick them and steal their gold when they weren't looking. Though she had ancestors who might have done that, she wasstill insulted.

Helen felt a twinge. Someone was staring at her. She turned to see a young associate waiting. Eyes flitting from Helen to the floor then back to Helen. She cradled a pad of paper in her arms like a shield and had a nervous energy that made Helen think of a startled fawn.

The jumpy associate did not ease her fears. Helen figured the young woman was naturally twitchy. But for some reason, Helen had a feeling she made the little fawn extra nervous. And the longer she waited, the more uneasy the associate grew. Helen had to decide. Either she was in or she was out.

They stared at one another for a very long moment.

When Helen thought the young woman was poised to bolt, she stood up and smiled. Then gave a quick nod.

The associate sprang forward down the hall without as much as a glance back. Either she had no interest in an introduction or she figured she would never see Helen again. Helen wanted to ask questions, to gather as much information as she could before getting launched into the interview.

But the fawn kept a far enough distance to discourage

conversation. Helen shrugged off the awkwardness of being led without a word and used the time to look over the unusually silent surroundings.

She walked past stretches of secluded cubicles. Not so unusual, though Helen found herself a bit surprised to see people. She half expected the place to be as deserted as the lobby. Despite the number of diligent employees at their desks, not a peep was made. Only the hushed rhythm of keys tapping and papers shifting.

When she tried to make eye contact, not a single head glanced up. Every face stayed glued to the task at hand. Her presence was of no interest. Or they had too much work to worry about the new recruit.

Giving up on human contact, Helen caught sight of the tall windows above the cubicles, displaying the sun falling over the skyline. No matter which way she turned, her view was filled with light gleaming off elegant skyscrapers and landmarks. From this height, the city took her breath away.

But then, she had fallen in love with New York at first sight.

A fact that might have worried her ... for a few reasons. First, she had promised never to fall in love. And second, she was no romantic. As nostalgic as she sometimes felt for eras like the 1930s with their sensual approach to life, she knew romance was a fantasy. Even with a city, love affairs brought trouble. Setting you up for overblown expectations and crushed dreams. She preferred to follow the whims of her heart. Not someone else's.

Lucky for her, New York never stood still. If a place could be more restless than Helen, it was Manhattan. The city was always shifting, always changing. She had picked the perfect relationship. Like being with a new lover every night.

The associate stopped abruptly. Catching Helen off guard. She stopped as the young woman stepped aside, to the right of a heavy-looking wooden door. Helen waited. Thinking the fawn might lead the way.

But the young woman just stared. Blinking at Helen, like she should know what to do. Helen smiled and stepped toward the door. Glancing at her guide for any clue she had guessed wrong. Nothing.

So Helen reached her hand out to grasp the doorknob. Turning slowly. Wondering, for a brief second, whether she really wanted to go through with this.

The latch clicked. And the associate bolted. Springing away in the flash of an eye. Leaving Helen alone.

Fair enough, she thought. *Into the deep end we go.*

And she pushed the door open.

CHAPTER TWO

As Helen's eyes adjusted to the change in light, she felt like she had stepped into another world.

Dark and plush, surrounded by ancient books and even older paintings, this office spoke of eras gone by. Not the modern, minimalist décor outside. Every wall was filled with books, though she could not make out the titles. The light cast from the standing lamps was too soft to illuminate the spines. Surrounded by clues, Helen couldn't make use of a single one.

She stepped forward carefully. Wondering if she was disturbing the older man at the desk. She assumed he knew she was here, but his attention was focused entirely on his papers. Not flickering for a second in her direction.

Helen wondered whether her intuition had steered her wrong. *Maybe her wires got crossed,* she thought. *Why would it lead her to this strange office where no one talked? To this old man in a library?*

Doubts swirled in her mind and threw her off. The strange feeling that hit her in reception returned and she wondered how quickly she could reverse out of this office. She could say she got the appointments mixed up. Yes. That might work.

Helen didn't like backing out on her game. She had

promised to see every intuitive hit through to its resolution. The whole point was to take risks. But this place gave her the chills. Her nervous system was on high alert. And not in a good way.

There's a first time for everything, she thought. *The sooner she made her way out that door, the faster she'd be on the streets of New York.* Helen shifted her weight to take a step back.

At that moment, he looked up. And locked her in his gaze.

"Helen Troy. My final appointment."

His confidence threw her. Her mind was spinning. *What was going on? Why was he playing along?*

Usually she had to talk her way into things. Not have doors magically open where they didn't exist. Her bravado faltered.

Helen took a deep breath. Reminding herself that men like this had no idea what their schedule was until it was presented. He was flying blind. He assumed that what was in front of him was accurate.

The lightness of the game returned, and Helen suddenly felt herself again.

Why was she taking this so seriously? The office was quiet on a Thursday afternoon. Was that really so strange? Besides, she much preferred the risks of this harmless diversion to the dangers of a party filled with judgmental couples.

Helen took three long steps toward him and presented her hand. "Yes, sir. Very nice to meet you."

Logan Sr. gazed at her over his dark-rimmed glasses. He did not offer his hand or respond. He simply took her in.

The scrutiny put her at ease. This was more like it. The stony stare. The questioning body language. Though, as she sat down, she saw that he actually wasn't doing either.

He was assessing her. Openly, yet discreetly. Like she was a piece of art.

She waited. Knowing that the next move was not hers. If she jumped in too quickly, she would expose herself as a fraud and an amateur. Making herself available for someone like Logan Sr. to toy with until he got bored. Though, as she held his gaze, she doubted he was the toying type. That role likely belonged to Logan Jr.

This man had a stare like an eagle. Fierce and piercing and not missing a flicker of movement. Helen simultaneously felt a thrill of excitement and cautioned herself. If she was battling an eagle, she needed to reassess her approach.

Eagles had an incredible sense of timing. They waited for hours until the right moment appeared to swoop down and seize their prey. Infinite patience combined with a swift instinct to attack.

As uncomfortable as it made her, Helen waited. She even allowed the corners of her mouth to curve upward gently in a smile. Sending the message that she was enjoying this little game.

She had entered the arena. There was no backing down. She must match this man, move for move. How could she resist? Rarely was she given the opportunity to go toe to toe with this steely an opponent.

Helen no longer cared how many chills rippled up her spine. Or how her feet danced to run as far away as possible. Her curiosity was piqued. She had to find out what this place was. And who sat in front of her.

As much as she called this a game, the rush of adrenalin and the pursuit of prey were addictive. Once she committed to the pursuit, she could not let go.

So, Helen found herself in a silent test of wills with a man who undoubtedly had more experience that she did at outwaiting opponents. She realized, however, that she had the advantage of not being at the whims of time.

Helen had no commitments. No appointments. Not a single person waiting for her. Aside from the party's host who would shake her head and assume Helen had dodged another invitation. Helen could wait all night.

In that one realization, Helen evened the scales. She relaxed back into her chair. Smiled. And waited. Seeing the shift, he finally broke the silence.

"I presume you are here for the assistant position," Logan Sr. stated.

"Executive Assistant," she countered, knowing that if you bluff, you go all in.

"Of course," he stated. Not taking his eagle stare off her for a moment.

Helen smiled, politely. A less experienced player would assume the interview had not begun. But she realized that the interview had started the moment she was presented with the closed door to his office.

Each step was a test. Each moment a possible chance for her to fail.

So she sat. Eying him curiously. Awaiting a question. The longer she sat, the more she became convinced one was not coming. She suddenly realized she would not hear a single question in this interview.

She could not help but smile. How brilliant. Test by silence.

The surest way to crack a weak-willed person was to subject her to silence. Sustain a wall of quiet that leaves her swimming in the ocean of her own doubts. Her shadows. Her personal undoing.

The purest test of whether a woman had the stamina for the game.

Shadows? Stamina? Helen shook off the gladiator metaphors and reminded herself this was meant to be fun. Playful. A silly distraction on the road of life. A personal challenge, not a match to the death.

Yet, she sensed that entering this room had somehow shifted her game. Brought it to another level. The feeling shook her.

Helen struggled to stay playful, as doubts swirled up from the corners of her mind. *What tide of fate had led her to this room? Who was this man? What did he want from her? Was she in danger? Why did he not speak? This was not normal!*

Yet something about this game, this test of wills, felt familiar. Far in the corners of her psyche she felt a strange sensation. Like she had been put to this test before.

What are you talking about? Helen chastised herself. *You've never been challenged to a duel of silence!*

But even as she thought it, Helen knew that was untrue.

She would not let this old man rattle her. Even though she sensed the depth of his honor. They had barely shared a handful of words, yet Helen was drawn in. Trusting him. Wanting to ask him the questions.

Helen dug her fingers into her thighs. A reminder to stay focused. She kept her lips locked in silence. And would not allow her doubts, or this strange pull to connect, to get the better of her. Though the mood had shifted and she may not recognize the playing field, she must assume the rules were the same.

So, she waited.

CHAPTER THREE

Logan Sr. knew full well this young woman — Helen — if that was even her name, did not have an appointment.

He had no idea why his staff had brought her to his office, disturbing the end of his afternoon, and forcing him to pay attention to this pretender. He presumed they were too afraid to admit they made a mistake. And so, foolishly brought this confident *Helen* right into his domain.

As they sat across from one another in silence, he realized something magical was afoot. Logan focused his attention beyond the surface. Time had shifted. A connection was forged. *Whatever lured Helen into his office was not the real reason she was here. Or was it?*

Logan was startled. Surprise was a strange sensation for a man who had been in his line of work this long. *No.* Logan couldn't bring himself to believe it. And yet, he knew. Helen was the answer to his prayers. Or, more accurately, his request.

Though, truth be told, he struggled to recognize what the Fates saw in her.

She did not look like someone who could carry a torch into the depths of darkness. Logan narrowed his gaze. Assessing her with an increased intensity. Helen shifted slightly in her chair, sensing his ferocity. But, admirably, did not reveal any discomfort.

Logan sensed she had ended up in his office on a lark. That fit his dismissive assessment of her generation. A judgment that, he admitted, was unfair due to his frustration with his own son.

Despite his bias, Logan was gifted at assessing character. And he knew Helen was one of those young people who simply wanted to play. She had no interest in the pain, torture, and cruelty of the world. Or helping those who suffered at the hands of malicious intent. Life was her personal ocean; each wave designed for pleasure.

Logan had no time for such dalliances. And though this Helen and her patient silence were growing on him, he wondered how long it would take for her to crack and present a reason to doubt the Fates' choice.

This was not heresy on his part. He had doubts about a lot of people and their abilities. Humans were incredibly fallible. *As were immortals*, he added judiciously. Proven by the fact that, as happened more often than one would assume, the Fates made wrong turns in directing a person's destiny.

Logan restrained a sigh. Such were the challenges of his position. He had worked with the three sisters an infinitely long time. And, as talented as the Fates were, they got distracted. Occasionally sending a person on a wild goose chase only to realize, partway along, that they had forgotten the reason for the hunt.

The sisters quickly corrected the error, shrugging it off as a detour bound to happen when you managed the lives of several billion people. Unlike air traffic controllers, the Fates didn't get stress leave. So mishaps were part of the job.

Logan watched Helen. Her attentive, relaxed posture. Her kind and amused smile that wavered only occasionally. He realized she probably thought he was testing her. He supposed that was true, now that he knew who had sent her.

For all his dismissive judgment, he was impressed with her silence. He sensed she was not naturally patient. So her ability to wrangle her own tongue revealed an inner strength he might have missed. She was focused when challenged, able to force her demons into submission while waiting out her opponent.

These were all admirable qualities. And might show some promise in the sisters' candidate. Though as much as Helen might think he was outwitting her, he was really outwaiting the Fates. If he gave them enough time, the sisters would realize and — this was his true test of patience — admit their little mistake.

Fitzgerald Logan the Third was too long in the tooth to waste time on false hope. Particularly when caused by whimsical immortals suffering from increasing bouts of attention deficit disorder. While his reckless son might find that kind of thing amusing, Logan had more important things to do.

If this young woman was being presented as a serious candidate — *not* for an Executive Assistant position — then he intended to wait until the Fates were absolutely sure.

Logan softened a little. As stern as he held his face, and as steely as his practiced gaze appeared, he felt bad that he had to subject this young woman to a test of silence.

Even if his primary intention was to reveal cracks in the Fates' logic, the result was to place Helen's character in a pressure cooker. The longer he sat across from this playful young woman, the more she grew on him. Quietly winning over his heart with her patient, lighthearted smile.

He would much prefer to find out a little about her. Ask her questions. Inquire as to her origins. Yet, here they sat. Without a single word exchanged. Not that he disliked the test. By far, this one was his favorite. He simply had not intended to lock this innocent woman in its jaws. Her trial was purely coincidental.

He paused. Coincidental.

In his line of work, there was no such thing. The Fates might take a wrong turn, but they did not brook coincidence. They had released plagues of locusts on people for suggesting less. Coincidence reeked of amateurs. When you've pulled the cosmic puppet strings for as many millennia as the Fates, *no one* called you an amateur.

Eccentric, certainly. Forgetful, maybe. But definitely *not* an amateur.

As Logan sat in silence with this lovely, young woman — and Helen was beautiful — he began to wonder whether they were both being subjected to a test. This rankled him. He was too old for tests. He had proven his loyalty infinite times. Steering this ship through choppy and unpredictable waters. Dealing with changes and challenges his predecessors never dreamed of, let alone mastered.

Helen shifted in her chair. Looking uncomfortable, verging on pained. She caught herself, but Logan noticed. She had not winced once until he grew distracted and lost control. Could it be that she felt his anger? That his absent-minded fury had caused her pain? Or at the very least, doubt?

Those tricky witches! He thought. Admonishing himself for using the "W" word. Yes, they wielded immense power and magic beyond any mortal's understanding. But the sisters resented any reference to them as conjurers hovering over a bubbling pot in the woods.

Logan shook his head in amazement and wonder. He admired their finesse. He'd worked with the sisters a long time and, still, he had taken almost an hour to realize what was happening.

This was not a test of silence. This was the bonding test. Far from slipping up, the Fates had put Logan and Helen in this room together to test their alchemy.

Not their chemistry. That was a *much* different test. Though the sisters were far from prudish and would not be above pairing a senior gentleman with a woman far too young for current mores. He knew this was not that test.

The alchemical test was designed to provoke reactions between two people. Ultimately, to comprehend how they would manage the flow of power. Logan knew the first level of the test was whether either party perceived the flow. If they were sophisticated enough to notice, the next level was whether they could each master their current when the pull or push of the other person fluctuated.

So when Logan lost control of his temper, Helen faced an internal struggle provoked by the wave of his attack. No matter that the anger was directed at the Fates or that he questioned his worth, not hers. The feelings rippled in Helen's direction, setting off a chain reaction. Provoking an internal battle to master her reactions, based on the assumption that his anger was aimed at her. Had she responded, the test would have escalated.

Far away in the nether reaches, he swore he heard laughter. Logan refrained from grumbling. *Clearly, we are never too old for a test*, he thought. *And never too familiar to amuse the ancients.*

He ignored the laughing sisters and turned his attention to Helen. Regarding her with a different gaze. For Helen to warrant the alchemy test, the Fates considered her a significant player. In point of fact, they hadn't brought another candidate to his office in, well, centuries.

Helen Troy had caught the eye of the goddesses of timing. And was about to play a role she had never seen coming. *What made this young woman special? What traits did she possess that he could not see? Did she come from a unique lineage? Or was she naturally talented in areas not bred into the classic bloodlines?*

"Be not afraid of greatness," Logan said. "Some are born great. Some achieve greatness. And others have greatness thrust upon them." Logan loved the Bard. That man understood timing. And the Fates. Despite portraying them in such a stereotypical —

"Excuse me?" Helen asked.

Her question startled Logan. *Had he spoken out loud?* When he saw her confused expression, he realized he had. After such a long silence, she was puzzling out why he led with Shakespeare.

"Twelfth Night," he stalled, attempting to sound like the mishap was intentional.

"One of my favorites," she replied.

Helen shut her mouth. *What just happened?* She wondered. Helen never confessed anything true during the game. She kept her real feelings hidden. Walking away was easier and cleaner when nothing of your true self was invested.

But the surprise of his words and, she admitted, her growing attachment to this mysterious gentleman provoked her honest response.

They relapsed into silence. Staring at each other with a shift in understanding. Something deep and unfamiliar was afoot. Their roles as they understood them were being revised. As their connection deepened, Helen's and Logan's fates were being woven together in a new pattern.

One neither of them recognized.

CHAPTER FOUR

The sisters enjoyed their work. Few would imagine they ruled their roost from the Upper East Side. But, really, if you could run the universe from anywhere, wouldn't you prefer to be in a place with style and infinitely delicious baked goods?

Clarissa smiled. Peering into her cup of jasmine tea. She preferred to scry using unconventional methods. She didn't need a clear glacier lake or a wide bowl with fairy water. No, she loved to watch her subjects in her cup of tea.

True, she was the one who made the most *errors* as the mortals loved to call them. But she believed wholeheartedly in improvisation. Pulling the cosmic strings should be an art rather than a mechanical show with no finesse and even less pleasure.

Clarissa felt and saw the universe as music played by an orchestra. She was the concertmaster, directing the way. Lifting them up with the melody ... leading in an infinitely beautiful song.

Humans often mistook the Fates as the Conductor. Certainly, she was flattered. But as important, and immortal, as she was, Clarissa was merely one instrument among many. She felt the power of the conductor surge through her, guiding her fingers as she pulled the strings of her instrument.

Stella, the oldest sister, was infinitely less amused by Clarissa's approach to her work. Stella was a traditionalist. She found Clarissa's methods offensive, if not downright heretical. The sisters had a reputation to uphold.

If the Board of Immortality decided they had been playing too fast and loose with the patterns of the universe, the sisters could kiss goodbye to job security.

Stella scowled and searched the little café for interlopers. There was always some ambitious new goddess nipping at their heels, wanting a crack at running the show. They never understood the hard work and coordination required.

The role of the Fates was far from some glamour-filled power gig, Stella grumbled to herself. The new ones always saw the flash and not the sleepless nights. Assuming they could do better with less, not imagining that running the universe took stamina and a thick skin.

When things went wrong — or really, when humans in their short-sighted view believed something had gone wrong — all fingers pointed to the Fates. No one ever said, "Thank you, Fate" when everything lined up beautifully.

No, Stella muttered silently, irritated by every mortal sipping a cup of tea or offering a cupcake to her beloved. *Humans take all the credit for those little endeavors. Maybe they toss the occasional crumb of gratitude up to the Conductor. Maybe.*

But when life went sideways, you could lay money on who got blamed.

Ironically, those were the moments that took sharp attention and keen reaction. When humans got it into their heads that life needed to be fixed, that's when Havoc arrived. And that girl loved to make a mess that took centuries to clean up.

Stella frowned, sipping her cappuccino, and casting resentful looks at patrons in the little shop. After Prometheus made the idiotic choice to hand them fire, human beings never got the hang of using it. They'd been burning their fingers ever since.

She wasn't even sure why they had been given free will. She had been too young at the time to vote, but she would have firmly been in the No contingent.

All it took was one rogue human to run amok with their intricate plans. Thinking he could make things better than the Fates — three women who had been ruling destinies since time immemorial. Multiple timelines went off track and valuable resources got used up to set things right.

And, above all else, Stella believed in doing things right.

Jenna, the middle sister, admired both of her siblings. Each was strong-willed and believed her way was the best way. No matter that they had worked together long enough to see there were infinite ways to tackle a problem. Her sisters were resolutely stubborn.

As the middle child, Jenna was like a bridge between two lands. Always finding a way to connect their different territories. Her job was to keep a close eye on them to ensure the balance of the forces. Forever making peace offerings and smoothing ruffled feathers.

"Croissant?" Jenna offered the plate of French pastries to Stella, then to Clarissa. "Pain au chocolat?"

She attempted to soothe her headstrong sisters with sugar and butter. They had refused to speak to one another since their most recent disagreement that morning.

Stella was not amused that they were working outside of their comfortable and secure penthouse apartment. She insisted their decisions needed protection from the unpredictable noise and distraction of the people they were directing. They risked a security breach. The whole thing was unorthodox and dangerous.

Clarissa, on the other hand, had been complaining for weeks about being cooped up. She needed a change of scene and her work was suffering. As much as Jenna knew precision was important, there was also harmony and beauty. And Clarissa was the master of those gifts.

Jenna smiled as she saw the light return to Clarissa's eyes and her body relax. More than the other two sisters, Clarissa loved being among the mortals. She drew inspiration from them. She was the artist in the family and watching the humans make messes on a regular basis fueled her.

Clarissa insisted no one would know what they were doing. To the mortals, they looked like three elegant women having afternoon tea in exactly the neighborhood where three old sisters would do such a thing. Though the sisters donned whatever illusory appearance suited their purpose.

On this occasion, Jenna had thrown her tie-breaking vote behind Clarissa. Infuriating Stella, who grabbed her coat and gloves and swore she was "not going to take the blame if anything went wrong."

Jenna tried to calm Stella's reaction as they hurried to catch Clarissa. The moment she had Jenna's agreement, their youngest sister had exited the apartment and was repeatedly pushing the elevator button. Anticipating her freedom, like an eager five year old.

"Surely the gods would not take offense at going out for macaroons and a decent pot of tea," Jenna insisted. But Stella simply harrumphed and turned her back.

As the elevator doors opened, Clarissa jumped in, turned and announced, "What is the point of living in New York if we can't take advantage of the plethora of inspiration at our doorstep?"

Stella stomped into the elevator, crossed her arms, and fumed. Refusing to speak to either of them. Holding that stance until well into the second round of sweets.

Jenna sighed, sipping her cup of tea and trying to enjoy the change of scene. Stella and Clarissa had been butting heads for millennia. One pushing the envelope and the other insisting the rules existed for a reason. Stella reminded Clarissa on a regular basis that the rules were as much for their protection as for the foolish humans. After all, they weren't the first triad to hold this exalted position.

Jenna distracted herself from the sibling feud by gazing at the loving young couple in the far corner of the cafe. They played with each other's hands and ignored the desserts unless they were feeding them to each other. Each one enraptured, lost in the wonder of the other's eyes.

She could see the waves of heat and passion pulsing outward from their little reality, burning like a bonfire at Beltane. And Jenna understood why Clarissa needed a change. All they did these days was work. They rarely got a break to go outside, let alone have fun.

Jenna thought wistfully about the irony of their position.

Humans obsessed about control. A position the Fates held every day. Yet all Jenna wanted was freedom. The opportunity to leave responsibility behind and not need to control one more life or destiny.

She lost herself in a fantasy that was becoming all too familiar. Jenna pictured herself jumping into a cascading waterfall in Brazil under the light of the rising sun, then whisking over to the Andes to climb their sheer peaks in the afternoon. Reveling in the beauty and joy without a moment's thought for anyone else.

That would be Heaven on Earth.

"Jenna. *Jenna!*" Stella's voice snapped her from a glorious reverie.

"Yes?" Jenna replied, focusing on Stella. Practicing centuries of patience in one word.

"We do not have time for your daydreams," Stella said. "We are on a deadline. One we promised Zeus."

"Zeus is an overblown pencil-pusher," quipped Clarissa. Causing Stella to turn scarlet and Jenna to giggle.

"Do *not* encourage her," barked Stella. Drawing attention from a few tables.

Stella lowered her voice. Hissing her tension at the other sisters. "If we don't hit this deadline, there will be hell to pay. And whether or not Zeus actually deserves his administrative position," she glared at Clarissa, "he has the ear of Pallas Athena and can make life very painful for the three of us."

"Pallas knows better than to listen to a word from that hothead's mouth," Jenna mumbled. Surprising all of the sisters — herself most of all.

Clarissa howled. Laughing wildly, her head fell back and her voice cascaded into the corners. As her tidal wave of glee shook the café, patrons stood, yanked bills from their wallets, and fled.

The owner stormed out from behind the counter, ready to demand that the three sisters leave; when she stopped in her tracks. The abandoned tables held heaps of money that were easily three times the bill.

Startled and speechless, she assessed the bounty. Counting how much more she made from one little outburst of laughter, never mind that the tables were open for more people to sit. She lit up like a Christmas tree.

Glancing at the sisters, the owner disappeared behind the counter; moving faster than the day she opened. She peeked to make sure the sisters had not left, and prepared a plate of her most exquisite handmade chocolates.

These were the special chocolates that she labored over all morning. The ones she set aside for the mayor and his wife when they arrived at the end of the day.

She fixed her hair, checked her apron, and carried the chocolates personally to Clarissa. Lowering the delicate plate filled with her personal pride to the table, the owner smiled graciously.

"The lavender is my favorite," she whispered, with a faint Parisian accent. Indicating the gorgeous dark truffle with a dash of the purple flower on top.

Clarissa smiled and lifted the truffle from the tray with reverence. She admired its beauty before tossing a flirtatious glance at the owner and popping the chocolate into her mouth.

She closed her eyes, letting the chocolate melt across her tongue. Clarissa savored the exquisite offering for several moments before opening her eyes and gazing straight into the owner's eager eyes.

"Heavenly," she purred, loud enough for the new customers to hear, and winked at the owner. Causing the French woman to blush and press her hand to her heart with gratitude.

Stella growled under her breath, "Wonderful. Not only have you made a scene, we're the toast of the café."

The youngest sister smiled and offered the plate to Jenna. As much as Jenna wanted to taste the silky sweets, when she saw the look on Stella's face, she knew better than to take one at this particular moment.

"We're not leaving the apartment again for three months *minimum*," Stella added.

"Shouldn't we get back to the matter at hand?" Jenna asked. "Fitzgerald and Helen have been waiting for almost two hours."

"Of course," Clarissa replied, relinquishing her provocateur position and switching to an air of professionalism. "Helen may be a competitive young woman, motivated by the chase but she will get frustrated soon enough."

"If you had stayed focused," Stella began, only to be silenced by Jenna's raised hand.

"Enough," Jenna insisted. Startling Stella and Clarissa.

"I may have to put up with the two of you tormenting each other for millennia, but Fitzgerald and Helen do not. We have waited centuries for the right alchemy to appear in a mentor and an apprentice. And I, for one, am not going to let it slip through our fingers. So put a lid on your petty jealousies and get to work!"

Her sisters blinked in stunned silence, staring at Jenna's flushed face. No one knew how to respond to her outburst.

Jenna reached across, snatched up a dark cinnamon truffle, and popped it in her mouth.

"Ready?" she demanded, mouth full of chocolate.

"Yes," Clarissa and Stella replied, nodding. They exchanged a perplexed glance as Jenna marched toward the door.

Hand on the door handle, Jenna turned back and glared at her sisters. Still frozen in shock, they stared back. Jenna heaved an exasperated sigh. "Now," she insisted.

Sparked into action, Clarissa gathered her chocolates in a napkin. Stella pulled out several dollars and left them on the table. They scurried to join Jenna at the door.

Not a moment too soon, Jenna thought to herself, setting a brisk pace for her sisters to follow. *If we're lucky, we haven't lost our last chance to prevent disaster.*

CHAPTER FIVE

This is a disaster, Helen thought, reaching her limit.

She waited two hours with only the exchange of a long silence and a passage from Twelfth Night to show for her time. By this point, she had usually secured at least a bedmate or a three-course dinner.

All she had here was the faint notion that she had earned this gentleman's respect. Or at least his curiosity. Then there was the odd sensation that he saw straight through her … like he had known her for years.

That was the feeling that made Helen bolt.

She pushed her chair back and stood. "Thank you for your time," Helen said. "But I think there has been a mistake."

"Wait," Logan countered, standing.

"I believe we were meant to meet one another, even though —" he said, then paused. She sensed he was considering his next move before completing his sentence. "You did not have an appointment today."

Her eyebrows went up. Logan knew she had come here under false pretenses, without offering as much as a story or a reason. And yet, he had waited. For two hours. Not only that, he wanted her to stay.

What could he possibly want? Helen wondered.

She wasn't worried. She didn't fear for her safety. She was curious.

Helen couldn't help it. She had played this game so many times and not once had someone figured out she was pretending. Logan had figured it out *and* chose not to judge her. That was the clincher.

She had never been around this bend in the road. Her body tingled with excitement. Like she had passed a turn and saw a breathtaking view for the first time. She could not look away.

Helen sat back down, and Logan followed suit. It struck her that he hadn't needed two hours to figure out her ruse. He had known she was lying from the moment she arrived. Or pretty soon after. Yet he wanted her to stay.

Had she been approaching her game all wrong? Was Logan an ally rather than an opponent? She wondered.

Helen was a little thrown by the thought. She had taken care of herself for so long, she didn't have the wiring to process that someone might be on her side.

Let's not get ahead of ourselves, her rational side cautioned. *He just asked you to stay. He didn't offer a trust fund and a penthouse by Central Park.*

"What do you propose we do?" she lobbed the ball back into his court. A cautious step. She was willing to play, but didn't want to appear eager.

Her move brought a slight smile to Logan's face. Followed by a wave of fondness that hit her straight in the chest. Helen knew her chess moves had won Logan's admiration. He genuinely liked her.

And whether he knew it or not, that won her heart.

Helen was so used to moving on that she rarely allowed anyone to like her. Affection was a luxury she couldn't afford. Affection led to attachment. Attachment led to promises. And in Helen's experience, people rarely kept promises. They used them as collateral to get something.

But this man, regardless of his age and position, liked her. He didn't expect anything. Sure, he wanted her to stay to figure out what was happening in this strange and magical room. But he didn't actually *want* anything from her.

Half the reason Helen played with people was because she had been a pawn in so many games by the time she was five years old, she gave up trusting others. She had tried for the first five years. She really did. And all she remembered was getting hurt. Over and over. After that, she decided either she owned her life or other people would own it for her. So she took charge. And since Helen had a sense of humor, she made it a game.

"I propose we get to know one another," Logan offered. "At this point, all I know is your name. And why you claim to be here. So what if you told me what really brought you here?"

"The truth?" she asked, startled. Helen cursed herself for letting him catch her off guard.

Logan smiled. "Preferably."

"Right," she said. Then hesitated. That's not typically how she played. Not that she was a liar. She didn't make up stories to hurt or scam anyone. That was against her rules. She used the game to hone her intuition. And have fun.

But here she was, facing a gentleman who had been around the block more than a few times and took life pretty seriously. They couldn't be more different.

Then it struck her. "Wait," she said, looking at Logan with intense curiosity. "You said you thought we were meant to meet each other."

"Yes," he said.

"But you weren't expecting me," she replied.

"Precisely," Logan added, watching her with his eagle eyes.

"So the fact that I decided to come up here on a whim was meant to happen?" she asked.

"You dodged my question," Logan replied.

"So did you," Helen parried.

Logan eyed her for a moment. She knew he was assessing the next step. Helen admired his poker face. He didn't give her any visual cues. She only sensed what he was weighing. And she'd played enough poker to trust her gut.

"You answer first. Then I will reply in kind," Logan offered.

It was Helen's turn to smile. "Fair enough," she said. "I was on my way to a party when I noticed your building. I saw your name on the sign, Logan & Associates, and something tweaked for me."

"Tweaked?" Logan inquired.

Helen knew all too well how people responded to her whimsical approach to life. And Logan looked more straight-laced than most. Yet she couldn't help feeling like he already knew her.

So Helen took a risk.

"When I saw your name," she paused, nervous to say the next words out loud. "I got a chill up my spine."

Logan didn't react. He stayed completely still. Helen realized she was waiting for some kind of sign. A signal that he either approved or disapproved. Believed her or thought she was crazy.

"Go on," he said.

A touch of Helen's bravado popped back up. Her trusty shield when she wasn't sure what she had gotten herself into. "I use that as a cue. To investigate something."

If he was going to hold back his cards, so was she. Helen had risked enough. She wasn't offering any more until he stepped up.

"Was it my name or the building?" he asked.

"What do you mean?" she responded, thinking for a second he was making fun of her. But Logan's expression was serious.

"When you got the chill," he continued. "Was it because you saw my name and it *tweaked* or did you see the building and the image was familiar?"

Helen wasn't sure what to make of his question. She had to pause to think about how the chill worked. In a flash, she saw his name. Not the building. Or the sign. Her intuition lit up when she saw the "Logan" in Logan & Associates.

"Your name," she replied.

Logan sat back, as though struck by a realization. He stared at Helen. And she stared back. The chill rippled up her spine.

Helen had the sensation that she had already been in this exact moment. Every aspect was familiar. Logan's reclined body position. His furrowed brow. The precise position of the ledger on his desk. And the fact that he just tilted his head while looking at her. As though he sensed what was happening.

All of it unfurled like a movie she had watched before. Had she dreamt it? Or had she seen Logan in a restaurant? Could her mind be weaving a past encounter into current circumstances? In an attempt to explain what was happening?

Helen knew that wasn't true. There was more to this than she could see.

Everything about this evening and her encounter with Logan had been just a hair's breadth away from bizarre. As much as Helen enjoyed unique encounters, this verged on unnerving.

"Your turn," she said. Her body had tensed like it was on high alert. Logan leaned forward. His face was kind. He must have sensed her apprehension and wanted to reassure her.

"You're describing sign posts," Logan began, in a calming tone. "Guiding you down a road you've never travelled."

"Guiding me?" Helen asked.

"Yes," Logan replied. "The sign post, in this case my name, is designed to get your attention. And the chill reminds you of its importance."

"You make it sound like I'm following a map," Helen joked.

"Yes," Logan said, his expression gentle but serious. She got the sense he was waiting for her to figure out an answer. Something that was on the edge of her consciousness.

"But I'm acting on instinct," Helen continued, then stopped. "Wait. You said the chill *reminds* me?"

"Yes," Logan responded. "You get the chill because your body recognizes that you've seen these scenes before. Like a moment ago, when you flashed on my office."

Helen's smile faded, startled by his revelation. "How did you — ?"

"Years of practice," Logan explained. "Your body relaxed at the same time your gaze looked like you were a million miles away. Within seconds, your pupils dilated, your body tensed, and you had a heightened sense of your immediate surroundings."

Helen sat up, wondering who Logan was. He was able to

read her far too easily. *How could he tell what she was feeling? And who notices another person's pupils?*

"You can't tell me you've never wondered why you get these signals," Logan ventured, as though reading her thoughts. If he was gambling, he was a pro. He knew her weakness.

But Helen wasn't letting her curiosity lead the way this time. "I stopped asking why a long time ago," Helen retorted. "I just follow."

"The sign posts," Logan prompted.

"Stop saying that!" Helen was aggravated. "You make it sound like I'm reading someone else's map."

"Aren't you?" Logan asked, calmly.

"No. They're my instincts. My responses," Helen insisted, feeling defensive.

Hadn't she always wanted to have a conversation like this? Now that she was having it, she felt irritated by his insinuations.

"Isn't it possible that someone marked those signs for you?" he asked. "So you would know you were on the right path?"

"What? Like fate?" she asked.

When he didn't respond, Helen laughed. "You're good," she grinned, shaking her head. "Usually I catch on way before a joke gets to the punch line. I have to hand it to you."

This must be Logan's way of paying her back for wasting his time. She had made up the interview so he was giving her a taste of her own medicine. Helen wished there really was a job so she could work for him.

"Rest assured," Logan replied quite seriously, "we've been brought together for a reason."

"What?" Helen jibed. "To teach each other a lesson?"

"Of sorts," Logan responded, leaning on his desk. "More like a test."

"Right," Helen said, shooting him an amused look. "For a job that doesn't exist."

"Oh, the job exists," Logan replied. "Just not the one you applied for."

"So let me get this straight," Helen said. "I was led up here by a series of signs to be evaluated for a job that I didn't know existed."

"Not exactly," Logan replied. Helen relaxed a little.

"This wasn't just about you," he added. "They were testing both of us."

"They?" Helen asked, her sense of foreboding returned. "What do you mean — *they*?" She could sense something coming around the corner. Something she couldn't quite grasp.

"The Fates," Logan gambled. "They brought us together to see how we would react."

Logan waited. He had laid his cards on the table. Helen knew he was waiting to see how she responded. Except she couldn't think straight. She'd been thrown into a tumultuous whirlwind of feeling and memory.

Helen was transported back to a flash of a moment. When she was five years old and insisting she had seen three magical sisters arrive in her hometown. Three elegant women unlike any she had ever seen. Women who held the power to change a person's life in the blink of an eye.

She shivered. Her mind struggled. And the memories flickered.

Helen's head hurt. That incident had been imagined. She'd

made it up … or so she'd been told. She couldn't remember why she would do such a thing. But that story had caused a lot of trouble in her life. She figured most children told tales, but hers struck a nerve.

At such a tender age, Helen still felt vulnerable to the vagaries of adult decisions. She was an orphan, and though her adoptive parents insisted otherwise, she couldn't help but feel like they would send her back for the slightest infraction. And this tale had upset the adults around her on a scale she did not comprehend.

But Helen did understand abandonment. She wasn't about to risk it twice. So she tucked the story away in her childhood of heartbreak and misplaced faith. That was the year Helen stopped being earnest or trying to make a difference. And instead, decided she was best served by looking after herself.

Helen snapped back to the present. Staring at Logan, she stood, abruptly. "This has been very entertaining," she said, in as even a tone as she could muster. "But it's time for me to go."

She walked to the door without a moment's hesitation. Until she heard Logan's voice call after her.

"Helen, wait." She stopped with her hand on the doorknob.

Logan was standing. Gazing at her with serious eyes. "I promise this is not a joke. I may not know the details, but I assure you that The Fates brought us together for a reason. They must believe we are vital to their cause."

"Cause?" Helen asked. Not taking her hand off the doorknob.

"Yes," Logan replied. "The world as we know it is in grave danger."

Helen stared. Hesitating for a moment. Allowing herself to

wonder what strange reality this company must belong to.

She shook it off. And pulled open the door. "Maybe your world is, Logan. But mine is just fine."

And she disappeared from his office.

CHAPTER SIX

David stopped and stood in the middle of the train station. A large, bruiser of a man cursed and almost ran into the black-haired, lean thirty-three year old but swerved in time. Grumbling and throwing back a fierce look, hoping David would grab the bait.

But David didn't respond to such childish tactics. If he started a fight, he made sure the event would be interesting. Not some pathetic brawl with blood and fists in a public building in Amsterdam. He watched as the man plodded into the throngs of people.

Normally, David loved the pulse of the crowd in a major station. He could feel the heart of every person, likely because they were panicked and packed so close to one another. The emotion reverberated through him. He knew with one small push, he could set them all off in mass hysteria.

But something had spoiled it today.

He stayed still, letting the waves of people wash around him. Closed his eyes and focused. He felt the shift. Something important had occurred but the after-shock had not yet reached his reality.

David smiled. The Fates had been chasing him around the

globe, attempting to foil his plans to gather more power. They were worried if he acquired enough raw potential that he might give the sisters a run for their money.

They had no idea how he was doing it. Or who was helping him. Because as adept as the sisters were, they didn't think like he did. They didn't move like he did. He studied the lower forces and simply rode the coattails of the slithering ones to find a crack in this reality or a way through that one.

As much as the sisters loved to think they could improvise and were pulling the strings of the little human puppets with ease and flow, they still played by the rules. And if David was a master at anything, it was flaunting the laws of the universe.

He opened his eyes. Studying the waves of energy around the masses. So easy for him to see and, yet, mysterious to so many. As a mortal, it was wondrous that he had been gifted with his ability but David did not waste time asking *why*. He found it useless. Inquiries that did not promise results had no meaning.

He was much more interested in the question — *how*? That query held all the power. Opening doors throughout the galaxy and showing who was of value. And who was not.

So when he felt a shift in the grid of power, like two forces that were separate entities joined, he wanted to know *how* this would affect his enterprise. Even more because he could tell that in the joining their power had been amplified.

David resumed walking through the crowd. Making his way toward his destination in the business district. Not the one where bankers and stock brokers handled their daily interactions. David had a very different district in mind. One closer to the docks with much more valuable merchandise.

As he stepped through the station doors onto the frenzied sidewalk, a flustered driver rushed up to him full of apologies.

"Mr. Troy," the driver said, trying to avert what he assumed would be a disaster, "I am so sorry. I —"

The young driver paled when he saw David's expression. He had been warned about the triggers of this wealthy and mysterious client. And excuses was one of them.

"Allow me to get the door for you," he diverted, opening the back door of the Mercedes.

David waited a moment before stepping into the car. Few people appreciated the power of a pause. But David knew it was precisely the tool that gave others enough time to make up their own worst-case scenarios.

"What is your name?" David asked, with enough inflection to suggest imminent disaster.

"Samuel. Or Sam," the driver blurted. Cursing himself for his ability to get on the worst side of the nastiest people within seconds.

David savored one more tension-filled moment before getting into the back of the car. "Good to know," he said, throwing a dark look at Sam before the door closed.

He smiled as the driver, *Sam*, scurried around the vehicle. Trying to make up for the abysmal first impression. These were the moments David cherished most. The little power plays that ruined a person's day through their own dark thoughts and assumptions.

His colleagues felt such exchanges were beneath them. Insisting that the little players were inconsequential. But David loved chess. He especially loved the power wielded through the pawns. How easily they fell and yet how satisfying as he watched them go.

Sam hurried into the driver's seat and revved the engine. David smiled at the chaos, enjoying the angry gestures as his driver forced his way out of the parking lot, scattering pedestrians and scaring a cyclist.

David knew why he savored toying with pawns. Unlike his compatriots, he had come from their land. He was born a pawn. Yet he had maneuvered his way to his lofty position. David understood how many had fallen to raise him to his current position. He had honed his skills on them.

So he still found a visceral pleasure in playing with the life of any person … no matter his social position. The sensation kept him young. And ever aware that another pawn could sweep in and knock down the King.

David stared darkly at Sam, catching the young man's eye in the rearview mirror. Spooking Sam sufficiently, David smiled and returned his eyes to his itinerary. Satisfied the driver was no threat.

• • •

Sam waited for Troy to walk down the darkened side street before he screeched away.

Pushing his foot to the floor, he drove as fast as he could, given the lack of light and the high potential for drunks in this neighborhood. He had been planning to get the hell out of Amsterdam for months. But this latest encounter with bad luck just upped his timeline.

Sam took a sharp turn left and a quick turn right to make sure the black sedan in his rear view mirror wasn't following him. After several minutes, he relaxed.

As he drove down Aushlausen, Sam wondered how he could be so good at pissing off the worst people. No matter where he worked in this city, bad luck followed. He sped through a yellow light and laughed ruefully. And here he was, running again.

He never even wanted to be a driver. But after causing a bar fight in a nasty end of town by tripping on his feet and sending one gang member into a rival gang member, he was tossed out the door without a paycheck or a reference.

Sam was grateful that he had escaped with his balls intact. But that's how every turn in his life had gone since arriving in this cursed city. He screeched around another corner and swerved to avoid a pair of giggling cyclists who were clearly lost and headed for their own brand of trouble.

Normally, Sam would stop and warn them. Maybe even escort them in the right direction. But tonight, he needed to look after his own sorry ass. He had a bad feeling about Troy. Even if the guy didn't immediately cause trouble for Sam, he knew it was only a matter of time.

The fact that Troy had asked for a name then studied his face like he would remember it twenty years from now, creeped Sam out. Enough to send him flying toward the limo service headquarters to hand in his notice.

Sam ploughed through a series of yellow lights then slammed on the breaks for one last red. In a strange stroke of good luck, he had caught sight of a police car. And skidded to a stop instead of gunning through the light, as he had planned.

Before moving to Amsterdam, Sam never once used the words luck, cursed, or sign. But after the last two months of hell on earth, he took this final parting gift as a sign he was meant to leave. The Fates, or whatever controlled weird things like synchronicity, had given him a rare blessing. One that appeared as soon as Sam set his mind on leaving. So leave he would. That night.

Eyes still on the cop, Sam crawled forward after the light changed. Then parked in front of the AMZ Limousine head office. He grabbed his badge off the visor and his jacket off the front seat. Cleaning out the car before he could second-guess his decision.

He stopped, abruptly avoiding collision with a bunch of punks that ploughed past. Taking up the entire sidewalk like they didn't give anyone else a moment's thought. Or maybe they just didn't give a damn. Sam guessed it was probably the latter.

He leaned against the car. Taking one last moment to observe the city of debauchery. The chaos underneath strict Dutch attitudes. Seedy activities amid picturesque colorful buildings. Sam didn't enjoy the contradiction. The city made his stomach turn. He didn't know why anybody thought it was cool or even interesting.

Who cares that you can get high or laid at any moment of the day? Practically every other city except Salt Lake offered that service. Hell. He was pretty sure Salt Lake City offered it, too, if you just knew where to go.

Yup, Sam thought to himself, recognizing the signs that he was jaded. He pushed off the car and headed into the main office. *It was definitely time to leave.*

He handed in his badge and signed the final paperwork, all while being berated in Dutch by the shift manager. Sam ignored him and nodded courteously as the manager tossed his belongings over the counter.

He didn't care about the abuse. He just needed to go. Before Troy decided that Sam was a higher priority than whatever nefarious meetings he had at the docks. Normally, Sam wouldn't figure he registered high enough on the "fuck up his life" meter.

But the way Troy stared at him gave Sam the sense that Troy liked causing people pain no matter their status on the social ladder. That look was fueling his exit beyond any duty to his boss.

Sam walked fast down the sidewalk, focused on his departure plan. His pace stood out against the languid drunks and flirty university students. So he stuck to the shadows and kept an eye on any sharp movements in his vicinity.

He hated being paranoid. Another reason he wanted to leave. And the top reason he had given up pot within a week of moving to Amsterdam. His first week had been fun, if you count being in a green haze of delirious confusion for seven days as fun. Not knowing where he was half the time and sleeping in parks while the rain soaked his clothes.

When the paranoia spells kicked in — believing strange creatures were stalking him and wondering why some girls looked different than their reflections in bar mirrors — he gave up the marijuana pronto. No one needed that kind of torture when they were supposed to be feeling mellow and all at-one with the world.

Sam cast a quick glance over each shoulder before he ducked

inside the back door of his apartment building. He took the stairs at a run, sprinting to the third floor and into his apartment before anyone could take him by surprise. He locked the door and took a breath. He hadn't felt this alive — or scared — in a long time.

After a fast survey of his scruffy bachelor pad, he felt confident that he was alone. The worst part about paranoia wasn't the lack of control. Sam sighed and grabbed his dark green duffel bag out of the closet, and threw it on his second-hand couch. It was that the sensation made him feel like his old man.

The look in his dad's eyes — caught in the grip of a belief that other people owned his life. There was no possibility of feeling safe. Sam hated that look. The complete abandonment of power. And an unwillingness to do anything except come up with another theory to terrorize himself and his kid.

Sam unzipped the bag with a fast and angry pull. He grabbed pants off the floor. Yanked open drawers. And banged closet doors. Tossing clothes at the couch. Piling his few possessions into one spot.

Once he emptied the main holding areas, he shoved the clothes into the bag. Taking out his frustration on the well-worn luggage. Pummeling the items like they were the reason nothing had turned out right in a long string of cities.

He paused. Wondering if he was making it all up. If the pot use had triggered something in his brain. Sending him on some predestined genetic path that would spit him out the other end just as messed up as his war veteran father. Not that most people, Sam included, considered the Gulf War a real war.

But the fear and the chemical weapons had wreaked havoc

on his dad. Leaving him a shadow of the man who left to serve his country. Sending him back with bad guys rattling around in his head and a fear of anything that smacked of authority.

Sam felt a pang of sympathy. Then packed it away faster than he was emptying his apartment. He yanked open the drawers in the kitchen. Grabbing the handful of utensils he had lugged all across Europe. Wrapping them in a dishtowel and shoving them into the bottom of the bag.

He knew from experience that sympathy did nothing but fuel the worst in people like his dad. He had spent too many years defending him only to watch the man get worse. Wasting their small savings on stupid quacks and detectives to prove his crazy-ass theories.

Sam zipped his bag with the sharp pull of finality. Swinging the load onto his shoulder and giving his abode one last look. He was sad that his European adventure was over. Not that he had enjoyed the last stretch. But he had hoped to find a home that put a large, cold ocean between him and his family.

Now, it looked like he was headed right back to where he started. New York.

CHAPTER SEVEN

Helen exited the door of the elegant glass skyrise. Stepping onto the street, she felt the cool evening air. She closed her eyes and breathed in the rush of city life. Cars whirring past. Pedestrians hurrying down the sidewalk. The buzz of horns and music and shouts, blending together in a constant stream of sound.

Her body relaxed. The familiar urgency calmed her. She understood its rhythm. Unlike the strange, tense quiet of Logan & Associates. Helen had never felt so grateful for the pushy, got-to-get-somewhere energy of Manhattan.

She opened her eyes. Her world had not turned upside down. The sights were familiar. Helen watched a cluster of elegant men and women, dressed in designer clothes and strolling in shoes not made for walking. They laughed and nodded, enjoying the good life.

On a different night, she might have felt a touch of envy at their easy lives. Their sense of entitlement and lack of care. She knew they were headed to an exclusive eatery where they would spend hundreds of dollars without batting an eye. But tonight, she smiled, finding comfort in their laissez-faire attitude.

The past few hours of her evening were melting away. She

breathed deeply and focused on the pulse of Manhattan. The pull of nocturnal activities. The city was always alive but the night was when things got really interesting.

Time to forget the last game and start a new one, Helen thought. She resisted glancing back at the lobby. Squelching the impulse of curiosity that wondered if Logan followed her down to the street.

Helen realized that for someone who was constantly in motion, she was standing by this building for a surprisingly long time. Didn't she rush out of Logan's office? Hadn't she debated whether the stairs would be faster than the elevator? Yet here she stood. Not an inch further away than the front door.

For the second time, she resisted turning to see if Logan was behind her. Why did she like that serious man? What kind of connection did they have? And what the heck did any of this matter if she had made up her mind to leave?

Enough! Helen thought. *I don't know what kind of strange pull this place has, or if it only works on me, but I am not going back up there. Time to move on.*

She strode forward, determined to lose herself in a decent bar. Released from the spell of the building, the first few steps felt odd, like she had returned from space and was adjusting to gravity.

Once she travelled a block, Helen settled into her familiar, flirtatious stride. She sighed. Finding comfort in the feeling of motion. She loved being in the streets. Soaking in the sensory pleasures, from window displays to art to people.

Every sight, smell, and sound fed her soul. She was returning to her self. Now, she just needed a little dating roulette

in a promising location and she would forget all about Logan &
Associates.

Time to make my own fate, she thought, amused. *Preferably
with a tall, dark stranger who wants to dazzle me with his wit
and wallet*. Helen grinned.

As she took her next step, the heel of her shoe snagged in a
grate. Sending her lunging forward down to her knees. Her nose
landing perilously close to the pavement. Shaken, Helen got back
up, brushing the dirt from her black trousers.

She looked around to see if someone had pushed her. Not
that she was paranoid. Helen just wasn't klutzy. Strange as it may
sound, she never tripped or fell or bumped her elbows. She had a
natural sense of rhythm and awareness. So catching her shoe in a
grate was jarring.

But there was no one near her. All she saw was a typical grate
in a typical sidewalk. Even the people passing by didn't notice.
She checked her heel. Thankfully, it was still attached. Helen
adjusted the shoe on her foot. Then started walking.

One careful step, then another. She was a little less assured.
Like the trip to the sidewalk had thrown off her gait. *So I fell*,
Helen thought. *It happened to people all the time*. Maybe she
wasn't fully back after her encounter with Logan. Her mind
wandered in the direction of the quiet, antique-filled office at the
top of the sky rise.

No! She declared. *I'm going somewhere fun. Enough of
Logan.* Helen shook off their conversation. She focused on
moving forward. But she couldn't help stepping awkwardly, like
she was placing her feet deliberately.

After several minutes, she relaxed. Her gaze scanned for

a suitable bar, while also taking in the ample selection of hot men out for the evening. Lawyers just off work, dressed in their business suits. Hipsters straying uptown for the latest trend. Charming actors seeking a quiet spot to drink whiskey.

She felt the electric pulse of the night picking up and let it move through her body. This is what she needed. The thrill of the moment. The visceral feeling of a crowded bar. Rooting her back in reality.

Whether or not they admitted it, everyone out tonight was on the hunt. Seeking connection. Craving touch. Helen understood the need well. She just chose to play the game openly.

She never understood why people pretended they didn't need human intimacy. Everyone was wired for affection. No matter if you trussed it up with a fancy dinner or just grabbed the first stranger from a raunchy bar. The need was the same.

At that moment, Helen noticed an attractive cluster of lawyers disappear into a classy, yet casual bar. She wasn't drawn to lawyers. She rarely went home with one. But she knew the predictable nature of Manhattan. And where one group of hot, young professionals led, others followed.

Then she saw the name, *The Winding Tree*. It made her smile and wonder why a bunch of business types were going to a bar with a mystical name. But she stopped judging books by their covers a long time ago. Odds were most of those up-and-coming lawyers were desperate to be artists, carpenters, or car mechanics. They just hadn't worked up the nerve to be what they truly wanted. The potent contradiction made the bar even more appealing.

Helen glanced at the traffic, then sprinted across Madison Avenue. She jumped onto the sidewalk in the nick of time, as a car whooshed past. A cab had sped up as she approached the curb. Almost like it was gunning for her.

Rattled, Helen stared after the vehicle. Wondering what the heck was going on. Cabs usually slowed for her. Especially in her bright, pink trench coat. Half the time they winked or even smiled — unheard of among cabbies. She seemed to have a way with them. Some kind of natural affinity.

So to have one try to run her over? On purpose? She couldn't wrap her mind around the fact. And stood, staring at the cars as she gathered her wits.

Helen's game was thrown off for the second time. She wasn't enjoying this bizarre shift of reality. And she couldn't shake the feeling that someone was messing with her. Or worse. That by meeting Logan, she had irrevocably changed how she interacted with the world.

"Are you lost?" a voice asked.

And Helen turned to see the tall drink of water she'd been hoping to find. Kind, yet slightly guarded, brown eyes gazed down on her. His physique reminded her of a swimmer, lean yet muscular. Hidden discreetly behind a dark blue dress shirt and black pants.

"No," she replied. "Just … surprised." She smiled and enjoyed the connection already weaving its electrical charge between them. "Any chance you were headed to The Winding Tree?"

"I am now," he answered. Then held out his hand and said, "Mark."

Helen shook his hand warmly. "Helen."

And with that simple exchange, they walked in silence to

The Winding Tree. The short block to the doorway filled with attraction and building tension.

Helen wondered whether they should go at all.

But she craved the energy of the eclectic mix of people. Helen went to bars as much to watch and enjoy, as to bring home a playmate. She never felt as alive as when she was surrounded by an intricate web of people.

Mark stepped forward to open the door before she could reach for the handle. She enjoyed the gesture. Knowing it was harmless. And getting the sense that this one enjoyed acts of chivalry. She nodded her thanks and strode inside.

The dim light soothed her frazzled nerves. Helen hadn't realized how on-guard she was from the Logan encounter until she walked into familiar territory. The low beat of music and the steady hum of conversation gave her space to release all that had happened and step back into her life.

After a quick survey of the crowd, Helen moved down the bar and sat on a stool. She smiled at Mark and indicated the seat beside her. Within moments, he was at her side, ordering two neat whiskeys.

As they clinked glasses, Helen openly admired her companion. Why waste time? She found him attractive and never understood playing coy. But she was in a bar full of potential. So, as she sipped her drink, she let her gaze drift over the faces in the crowd.

A chill ran up her spine as she noticed that the décor was eerily similar to Logan's office. Dark and antiquated. The chairs and tables carved from oak. Even a corner where the fireplace was framed by two shelves filled with hardcover books. Helen's body tensed and her feeling of escaping Logan's world evaporated.

"Everything okay?" Mark asked.

Helen's attention returned to her striking companion. "Of course," she replied, attempting nonchalance yet knowing she missed. "Why wouldn't it be?"

"You went a little pale," Mark said. "Like you'd seen a ghost." Helen realized what he meant. He thought she'd seen an ex-lover.

She smiled. "None that I'm interested in talking to."

"I'm glad," he smiled back.

Helen wondered whether she should fold her hand and leave with Mark. She loved to play longer. Not assume that her best bet was the first one. But this place had thrown her off.

Still, she couldn't resist taking another sip of her whiskey and checking her options. As she gazed across the crowd, she spotted several possibilities. A blonde painter. He was muscular and wore tattered jeans ripped by actual work, not an underpaid factory worker. He nodded at her with pure desire in his eyes.

Helen smiled, returning the sentiment, before moving her gaze onto a lithe accountant. Dressed more fashionably than she expected with a high-end pair of glasses. Clearly he crunched numbers for his day job but there was a mysterious quality to him that she couldn't resist. Like he was wearing a disguise.

He turned and locked eyes with her. That's when her chill turned into a lightening bolt, ripping down her spine. The shock caused her to clutch her glass. Helen felt the pull of his attraction, like a magnet she had no choice to resist. Pulling her. Willing her toward him. Like he owned her body.

His eyes flashed with not only desire but possession. He had laid claim to her. Her body wanted to respond and her mind couldn't stop it. Far off, as though in another room, she heard Mark calling to her. His voice distant, even though he was right beside her.

The mysterious accountant was making his way through the crowd. Striding toward her like a master claiming his slave. She had never encountered such fear and desire mixed together. Helen was used to being the hunter not the hunted. Even then, her style was playful. Not destructive.

Her mind screamed for her to run. The closer the mystery man got, the more she understood he was not human. She had no rational explanation for it. But she knew.

Deep in the pit of her stomach, Helen realized she had crossed a line and there was no going back. She had stepped into Logan's world and now she was pursued by a being bent on consuming her.

In fact, her senses picked up on a few others who had detected her in their midst. She couldn't see them yet. But she could feel their intent. Some wanted to compete with the mystery man. Some wanted to watch. And some were ready to run and report to whomever they served that a new creature had arrived. One that was human, yet offered —

What? Helen wondered. *What exactly do I offer? What are they attracted to?* She'd never questioned her attraction. She knew exactly what she offered in her world.

But this was a new reality and she had no idea how it worked.

There was only one option. She had to get back to Logan and demand that he fix it. Make him put her life back to the way it was.

But first, she had to get the hell out of here.

Helen focused all of her will with a fierceness she had never summoned. Tearing her gaze away, she could feel the spell break. Her body had freedom to move. And she planned to make the most of it.

"Helen?" she heard again. This time as clear as the man sitting next to her.

She hopped off her bar stool and planted a pure, delicious kiss on Mark's mouth. Grateful for his kindness. And his humanity. He stared at her, stunned.

"Another time," she whispered in his ear.

Then moved as fast as her legs would carry her out of the bar.

CHAPTER EIGHT

David sat in the dark smoky room, waiting for the suppliers to arrive. He didn't partake in the cigars that his partners enjoyed. He preferred to keep his hands free and his senses heightened. Especially when he was dealing with new purveyors.

Yet his mind wasn't on the latest shipment. He was distracted by the young driver. *Sam.* David wasn't sure why the driver had his attention. There was something about him. Something sharp and intuitive. Unlike most others his age, who assumed too much and made foolish judgment calls.

He was taken enough with this young man that David wanted to call the limousine company to request him again. If only to feel the rush of fear when Sam realized who he was picking up.

David sensed his fascination went deeper than a cheap thrill. He felt a string of fate tying them together. He wondered whether he should snap that string and give the sisters a shock to the system. Sending a lightning bolt back through their twisted little wires.

He refused to let them manage his life the way they pulled and toyed with others. David made that clear years ago. His fury grew, as he thought of those meddling witches, far darker than

Shakespeare had envisioned. They had ruled things far too long and needed to be taken down a peg. Or five.

David's rage flared. Reaching a peak until he felt a powerful urge to wipe out the entire room for the pleasure of release. But he controlled himself. Glaring at the man he needed to access the European networks. He knew he could do this on his own, but he required their introduction. Then they would be redundant.

If David learned anything as he grew older, it was that sometimes you traded immediate pleasure for the long term goal. He loathed the company of others and knew his talents were far superior to these princes of pretension. But he had to remember where he was headed. Being patient did not, however, mean he had to accept their way of doing business.

"I'll wait five more minutes. Then I find another source," David stated.

The host jumped and looked uncomfortably at David's European partners. The other gentlemen did not seem unnerved by this declaration of departure. The oldest in the group held his hand up slightly, in a gesture of assurance that all was well.

"Calm yourself, David," the oldest gentleman replied, "these types always run late."

"That's fine for you, Pyotr," David said. "But I have a plane to catch."

"You did not mention that earlier," Siegfried countered.

"Plans change," David said, knowing the lack of explanation would aggravate the German.

"Why do we put up with this ridiculous American grandstanding?" Senegal asked. Infuriated the others were kowtowing to this ridiculous young man.

David smiled. Senegal's honesty was admirable but it came with a price of power. He came to this meeting to test the partners as much as the talent they awaited. He needed to know their allegiances, their weaknesses, and what they had to offer.

Though he enjoyed toying with people and taking what he could, he also knew there was only so much work he was willing to do. Collaborating with others was, quite simply, a necessary evil. If he wanted to pull the strings, he needed puppets.

"They put up with it," David answered, "because I am their gateway to North America. If you had not burned your last bridge to the consortium, you would not be in this position."

"I was not the one who lit him on fire," Senegal glared at Pyotr.

The older gentleman shrugged. "I don't control my cousins. They have a short fuse and, occasionally, it costs me business. Rest assured, dear Senegal, the culprit no longer has any use for oxygen. He rests with the insects at the bottom of a dark pit."

Senegal fumed. Furious that he was in this position due to everyone's mistakes but his own. Even his parents had frivolously spent his inheritance and forced him to partner with drug lords and weapons dealers. He was, quite simply, better than this.

Pyotr pulled a draft of smoke from his Cuban cigar and watched the instigator. He enjoyed working with subtle troublemakers like David. Mostly because they exposed the cracks in a settling foundation before the building was expected to bear any weight. Pyotr admired that skillset.

He was raised with subtler talents. Not to show your cards or fully trust a partner. And never take it personally when the little rungs on the ladder break. They can always be replaced.

Like a simple piece of wood, they were easy to find.

Pyotr tapped the end of his cigar in the ivory ashtray. Watching the slight smile at the edges of David's mouth as Senegal and Siegfried argued about how to handle the unacceptable circumstances of the purveyors being late. They were wasting valuable time and putting this fragile alliance at risk.

He, on the other hand, was debating whether this was an opportunity to partner exclusively with David. Despite the young man's age, he showed instinct and wisdom beyond his years. Pyotr had recently lost his number two in an unfortunate disagreement over the distribution of wealth. Perhaps he had a new candidate.

Pyotr sensed David would expect an equal share in their endeavors. But if that came with free and ample access to the markets in North America, he was willing to consider the concession. At some point, Pyotr would need a skilled set of hands to run the operations for his larger empire. David had the skills. The question was would he have the loyalty.

David had strong ambitions. A trait Pyotr admired, within reason. Pyotr had done his research. And now, he had a sense of the person in front of him. As solid a sense as you had with a shapeshifter. This young man morphed to each situation as effortlessly as a spirit passed through walls. A skill that had been lost in the staid and traditional ways of the European empire.

Pyotr pulled another draft of smoke and pondered, not for the first time, how the mass exodus of shapeshifters matched perfectly to the European famines during the 17th and 18th centuries. As a man who did not believe in coincidence, he knew the Fates had hidden that little synchronicity behind the waves of death and destruction. Pyotr smiled ruefully at their masterful ways.

His people never noticed the trick until it was too late to grab the shifters they needed to keep their empire alive and well. For shifters were a crucial part of evolution and keeping pace with the times. Their loss was one of the gravest nails in the European empire's coffin.

"My dear David," he began, opening a doorway for negotiation. "Perhaps we should leave this little den of incompetence and strike our own alliance."

"I was under the impression that you arranged this meeting," David replied. "You're willing to walk away over a triviality?"

"I do not consider timing a trifle," Pyotr said. "Do you?"

"I consider precision a rare and precious commodity," David responded.

Pyotr leaned in so only David would hear what he said next. "I would expect no less from a shifter."

David raised an eyebrow. He knew the old man had been assessing him for several minutes. He did not expect such an accurate conclusion. Few in Europe knew how to recognize a shifter anymore. Let alone admire their value.

"That is but one of my many talents," David said.

He presumed the old man had done his research. David had done his own. The only reason he bothered with this meeting was Pyotr's deep resources and reputation for empire building. The man had not lasted three hundred years without a masterful understanding of human nature and a talent for changing with the times.

David successfully ran an underground empire in the Americas but he knew he needed an ally. If he wanted to take his power plays to the next level, he needed a pedigree. He considered himself a demi-god but he would never reach the pantheon unless he partnered with someone like Pyotr. Someone who had the respect of the heavy-hitters and could open those doors for David.

As much as David did not believe in the ancient hierarchies, he could not deny that they still held sway in the Empire. Even if that Empire was crumbling. The ones who came from the ancient bloodlines received the power without having to earn it.

David's power had come, ironically, through the blessings of fate. Yes, he gave the foolhardy sisters that much credit. He had been given a plate full of abilities capable of changing worlds — for better or for worse.

He had learned at a young age that no one looked out for you. No one cared whether you lived or died. Not even the gods. So if he had been handed the talent to crumble empires, he was not going to bow and scrape. He would forge his own empire. And make them bow and scrape for once in their charmed existence.

David smiled. As the kings and queens of Europe had realized that they needed the money and flexible thinking of the Americans in the early 20th century, now the gods and ancient ones had come to the conclusion that they needed the more recently evolved attributes of the hackers, shapeshifters, and belladonnas.

He sipped his sparkling water. Eyeing Pyotr over the rim, more as an opportunity to make the old man wonder whether he would entertain his offer. He could not seem too eager. Nor did he want to accept his first invitation to the ball.

David may have grown up as the mythological equivalent to Cinderella, an orphan with no claim to a throne, but he knew this was only the first of many invitations. Reputation had surely preceded him and after one prince stepped up, there would be others.

But Pytor Petrovich was more than just a prince. He was the last descendant of a bloodline that went back as far as the ancient Centaurs. His ancestors had mastered the baser nature of the beast, or so the story goes, and took control of creatures that understood the deep powers of the ancient ways.

Ever since that day, he had the gods eating out of his hand.

David could not ask for a more revered and respected partner. If he played his cards right, Pyotr might ask him to take over the entire Empire one day. For among David's gifts was the ability to see multiple strategic moves ahead. And when he was dealing with such linear thinkers as the Europeans, the game was barely a challenge. The tricky part with Pyotr would be gaining his trust.

"I believe the time has come," said David, "for us to leave these amateurs behind."

Pyotr smiled, putting down his cigar. "I agree. I wish our initial meeting had been more impressive. But when you rely on others to make arrangements," he nodded toward Siegfried, still arguing with Senegal. "You cannot always guarantee the results."

"I must disagree, Pyotr. If you cannot guarantee results, the entire enterprise is at risk. Do not mistake the fluidity of my approach for an acceptance of incompetence. Before we go further, you must understand that I do not allow failure."

"Even when they are the children of an old friend?" Pyotr asked, glancing at the two men arguing in the corner.

"Especially then," David replied. "For such individuals assume they can get away with flaunting your affection. And if they do it once, they learn they can do it again." Pytor acknowledged his point with a tilt of his head.

David offered a gesture of deference in return, as was customary in European dealings. "Though given my age, I cannot say I have often been in that situation."

Pyotr liked this young man. He could already tell David had much to offer. Not the least of which was an unscrupulous approach to the people working for him. A trait Pyotr did not intend to take on, much as he appreciated the quality in David. That was why he had a second in command.

The older man signaled his driver to ready the car. Within seconds, his assistant appeared with Pyotr's coat. "How would you counsel me to respond?"

David eyed the two men. Distracted by their argument. Each attempting to blame the other for failing. Fighting over Pyotr's approval like two resentful brothers. Not aware that the interloper had stolen the prize from under their noses. Or perhaps that was why they fought so angrily. They sensed the loss.

David gazed from the men, up the walls, and around the well-sealed room. He adjusted details of his instinctive assessment of the room, created the moment he entered. He saw this space was highly secure and devoid of security cameras. Clearly he had passed a certain level of trust just being allowed inside.

There was no record of the events transpiring within these four walls. He reached back and placed his hand against the wall. Instantly bonding with the feel of the materials. Letting the blood in his veins bring information to his brain about the substance used to seal this space. Steel and concrete. And no secret wires. Only the obvious ones feeding electricity to the lights in the ceiling.

David was conscious of Pyotr watching his display. He placed his hand on the wall to confirm his assumptions but, even more, he did it to show off for the old man. Like a princess flipping her hair or revealing a little ankle, he did not feel cheapened by showing off what nature had given him. On the contrary, he felt empowered.

His little dance impressed Pyotr beyond any research or resume. The old man had waited his whole life to watch a shifter in action. David could feel it. He resisted a smile. Knowing he had Pyotr hooked.

David slowly took his hand off the wall. Stood up. And pulled on his jacket. Noticing Pyotr's scarf had slid to the ground. David swooped up the scarf and stepped close to his new ally, in one graceful move. He leaned in, whispering, as he handed Pyotr the scarf.

"I will walk out with you," David began, prompting a nod from Pyotr to his assistant. The three of them walked to the entrance. "Just as we are about to depart," David said, "I hold the door graciously, waiting for you and your assistant to exit."

Pyotr walked out, curious about this sequence of events. Followed by his assistant. With Pyotr in earshot, David continued, "I turn to face the incompetent children just as they notice we are leaving."

David made eye contact with the astounded Siegfried and Senegal. Each struggled to understand what was happening. This was outside the realm of protocol. There had been no announcement of a change of plans.

"Then I incite a flame from the lingering cigar in the ashtray." The embers of the cigar grew bright red. Heating to a temperature that was unnatural, beyond the simple combination of flame and tobacco leaves. The fire softened the ivory ashtray, as David poured his rage into the object like invisible gasoline. Separating the molecules in the elephant bone, causing the tray to melt. The burning cigar dropped onto the oil-infused teak table.

Within seconds the table was a bonfire. Drawing all eyes to the primal spectacle of flames. A dramatic but contained event, until David reached into his coat pocket and withdrew a compact explosive. Throwing it onto the fire.

David slammed the heavy security door closed, smiling at Pyotr and the stunned assistant. The sheer force of the explosion rocked the walls and shook the door on its hinges.

He watched as the old man and his assistant braced themselves to keep from falling. Despite the protective metal around the chamber, the explosion rippled shockwaves through the concrete flooring. Unnerving the others. David, on the other hand, was calmer than ever.

Pyotr's assistant checked that the old man was not shaken. Pyotr raised his eyebrows, and appreciated the silence that followed such a violent act. The old man felt a fleeting nostalgia for the Great War. Then gazed with satisfaction at his protégé.

"My dear boy," Pyotr placed a gloved hand on David's shoulder. "I can see this will proceed even better than I imagined."

David smiled. And followed the ancient patriarch out to his car.

CHAPTER NINE

Helen arrived at Logan's building and rushed up to the front doors. She pulled hard, expecting them to open. They resisted. She tried the glass door again, rattling the handle. But to no avail. She was locked out.

She glanced over her shoulder, unsure whether the mysterious accountant followed her. She didn't see him leave the bar. Given that she assumed he wasn't human, she had no idea whose rules she was playing by. Or what to expect.

Helen checked her phone for the time. 9PM. *Dammit,* she thought. *I'm screwed.* Until she remembered walking past a security desk the last time she strolled into the building.

Right! The security guard. Hope fluttered in her chest again. She still had a chance to get her life back. She moved to the pane of glass beside his desk. *Yeah. Easy if he were ever actually at his post.*

As though he heard her, the hulking young guard made his way back to his seat. Helen waved, knowing she was in full view. But the guard sat at his desk as though she wasn't there. No eye contact. No acknowledgement. Helen waved more insistently. Nothing. Finally, she resorted to banging on the glass. Not even a blink.

Was she invisible? She stopped the thought. She didn't even want to know what was happening. She just wanted to be normal again. And she needed Logan to achieve that.

Just as Helen prepared to pound on the glass with both fists, something caught her attention. From the corner of her eye, she sensed movement close by. Probably within a few strides. She turned her head.

And saw the mysterious accountant standing, watching her.

She didn't feel the same spell she had sensed in the bar. Maybe his ability was stronger in close quarters. Or he was able to compound the desire of everyone in a room. Regardless, she knew he was waiting for the right moment. And she wasn't about to give it to him.

Helen was about to yell at the top of her lungs when she heard the *click* of a door unlocking. She turned to see the guard waving her inside. She didn't waste a second. Helen yanked open the door and hurried to the guard's desk. She glanced back at the accountant, but he was gone. As though he had never been there.

"May I help you?" the guard asked, snapping Helen back to her original errand.

"Yes," she smiled with relief. Though she couldn't help looking again to make sure her stalker wasn't there.

"I have an appointment with Logan Sr. of Logan & Associates," Helen lied, turning on her charm now that she was safely inside.

"No, you don't," the guard stated.

"I know I'm not on your roster," she smiled. "But call him. He'll confirm."

The guard sat down. Not acknowledging her request. He simply looked away and continued reading his book.

"Okay," Helen said, puzzled. She'd never met a security guard she couldn't charm. "Well, I'm going up."

The guard didn't say a word as she left his desk to walk toward the elevators. She figured she was home free. Until she pressed the up button and nothing happened. *Crap*, she thought. *If the elevators are pass-operated, how had she sailed up them the first time?*

She glanced back at the guard. But he had disappeared.

"What the hell?" she said out loud. She pushed the elevator button again. But still no response.

"Fine," Helen said, looking around to see if there was a security camera. Unable to find one. "I'll climb every damn stair if that's what it's going to take." She was talking to the air, convinced she was being watched.

She tried every door in the lobby. To the stairs. To an office. To the bathroom. All locked. She was stuck in this glass-framed lobby with the water sculpture and the climbing ivy.

Helen finally lost it. Her only option was to make her demands to the air. And if someone showed up to throw her out, at least she could talk to him.

"Fine," she relented. "You win! The Fates are real. I saw them. Is that what you want to hear?"

Helen was flustered. Years of frustration and denial welled up as she said the words. She hadn't expected so much emotion to accompany her declaration. But there it was. She felt confused and vindicated and upset, all at once.

"I saw them when I was five years old," Helen admitted. "I was outside, playing in my front yard when they appeared. Out of thin air. Three older women, unlike any I had ever seen, standing in the middle of the road. Each one dressed differently. One elegant. One wild. One conservative."

As she spoke, she realized she *had* seen them. The three sisters of Fate. She could picture them as clearly as the day they arrived in her small town. Helen had been so drawn to them, she dropped the balls she was attempting to juggle and walked in their direction.

In that exact moment, the elegant one turned and raised her hand to tell Helen to stop. With a kind smile, she shook her head slightly. And Helen had stopped. Counter to how she typically responded to an adult's commands.

None of her tale was invented, as the grown-ups around her insisted. Even through her present flood of emotion, Helen knew those adults were motivated by their fear. They worried she would get a reputation as a dreamer.

And now, years later, she wondered whether they were afraid because they believed her.

"Do you need me to go on?" Helen asked. She was out of moves but she wasn't above shouting the whole story now that she knew it was true.

She heard a *ding*. The elevator arrived on the ground floor. She turned to see the doors open. Logan stood inside.

"That won't be necessary," he replied.

Logan refrained from chastising her as he stepped off the elevator. No one yells the sisters' name without consequences. The least of which was a spontaneous visit. But he could not risk upsetting Helen. They were on delicate territory.

Her world had turned upside down in a matter of hours. She had come to ask him to fix it. To put her life back as it was. But he could not. Logan knew — and he saw the reality dawning on Helen's face — that there was no going back.

The truth had been unearthed and there was no burying it again. So though her loud confession made him uncomfortable, Logan held his tongue.

Helen took a step in his direction. "The really strange thing," she continued, as though he'd been with her all along, "was that I knew who they were. No one told me. But I knew. Like I had seen them before. Though I couldn't tell you where."

Logan listened attentively, giving no reaction.

She lowered her voice. As though convinced someone else was listening. She was still gun shy about reactions to her tale. "As a child, I knew the Fates ruled the universe. I could feel their influence."

Logan simply raised an eyebrow. "Really?"

"Yes," she confessed, as it all rushed back to her. The flood of memory. The repressed reality. The beliefs she had packed away to keep herself safe.

"Sometimes, I knew what they were going to do before it happened," she said. "I could see it coming. Like it was happening in slow motion. Or sometimes, it was a picture a split second before the event."

Logan wasn't sure how to respond. Lots of people saw visions. In his experience, this was not unusual. The part that concerned him was when they tended to believe it was some sort of superpower and used it accordingly. Or made a common case of premonition into more than it really was.

He maintained an interested expression, as he used his years of experience to gauge whether Helen was telling the truth or weaving a story. She was a skilled storyteller. It was clearly one of her gifts. After all, she had lied her way into his office in the first place. He needed to be sure she was telling the truth now. Especially with so much at stake.

"I wasn't so surprised by the sudden appearance," Helen said, as though she sensed he didn't believe her. "I was a kid that believed in creatures appearing out of thin air. That part didn't startle me."

Helen wavered, as though overwhelmed by the memory. Logan gently took her elbow. And guided Helen in the direction of two cushioned, white chairs in the far corner of the lobby.

She smiled, appreciatively, and sat down. Logan made eye contact with the security guard to assure him all was well, then sat.

"What did startle me," Helen continued, "was how they watched two people heading in opposite directions then turned them around with their minds. Like they had invisible strings attached. They could just pull a little here and a little there. And the two people *changed direction*."

She stopped this time. Logan waited. But she seemed to be expecting some kind of response.

"So what happened?" he asked.

"They walked straight toward each other. In the opposite direction of where they had been going," she said, like it was the most miraculous thing. "And kissed."

Logan smiled. Realizing his reaction had been blown out of proportion. Helen may have seen the Fates, but the rest was the result of a vivid imagination. "That doesn't sound so unusual."

"Maybe not where you're from," Helen replied. "But I grew

up in Maryland. Halethrope, to be exact."

Logan stared at her. Halethrope, Maryland. He did a rough calculation of Helen's age. His brain railing against the possible conclusion. *This was impossible.*

Helen leaned forward. She lowered her voice. "Seeing two strangers turn, then kiss is strange enough. Watching it happen in a town where kissing in public for more than a second is illegal, is off-the-charts bizarre."

She waited for some reaction. But Logan just stared like he had seen a ghost. Finally Helen grew concerned, and tried to lighten the mood.

"I've actually seen people arrested for kissing in public. No joke. Hard to believe that's *my* hometown."

She smiled, waiting for Logan to laugh. Most people did. But he just turned an even paler shade of white.

"Are you okay?" Helen asked.

She knew the story was out there but, when he didn't answer her, she realized that something about her tale struck a nerve. Logan wasn't in the lobby anymore. He had disappeared to a far off place, in another time. One that threatened to bring tears to his eyes.

"Logan? Sir?" Helen prompted.

He blinked several times, then took a deep breath. Logan looked up at Helen. His eyes focused and he realized where he was. When he saw her concerned expression, he nodded. Assuring her that he was back.

Then stated simply, "That young man in your story was me."

CHAPTER TEN

Logan was in shock but he knew Helen was telling the truth. Somehow, twenty-two years ago, in the small town of Halethrope, Helen had witnessed Logan head toward a woman he barely knew to kiss her. The result of which was a maelstrom of drama he never intended to unleash.

But that didn't matter now. He had proof for what he had secretly suspected for years. His spontaneous action was caused by a force greater than his will. A force that sent him with the intention of setting off a powerful chain of events.

The Fates. He had witnessed them playing with other people's lives for years. But he had forgotten about that kiss. That moment of pure joy in the middle of an otherwise dutiful life. A life filled with treachery and danger, mind you, but one where he always played the role asked of him.

And now, after all these years, to find out the kiss was not real. The very thought brought him to his knees.

Helen was staring at him. "What do you mean that was you?" she asked.

But he could not respond. He wanted Helen to leave. To be gone. So he could be alone with his shame. Not at the kiss. That he would never apologize for, though the woman he kissed was engaged to another.

No, he wanted Helen gone so he could go upstairs and tear his office apart. Smash the life he had carefully built. Abandon the service of the Fates. And swear his allegiance to the Furies. No more living prudently. No more being the good man, the dutiful man.

He would unleash every feeling, held back for decades, and finally *live*. Throw caution to the wind. Allow himself to be free. Fitzgerald Logan realized that he wanted, quite simply, to *be like* Helen.

He stared at this young woman who had spent the last three decades living careless and unfettered. Only years of training kept him from revealing the depths of his resentment. The weight of his regret.

Logan suddenly wanted her gone. Out of his sight. No longer a reminder of the one perfect moment in his life. A moment he held in his heart as a candle of true and passionate love in a dark and pain-filled world. And with her revelation, the candle was blown out.

Logan's rational side knew if he ordered Helen to leave, he would be lost forever. He would tumble down the dark tunnel of paranoia. Untethered and without redemption.

Who cares? whispered his fury. *Haven't you been good long enough? Let it all go! Leave the sisters to clean up the mess this time. You have sacrificed your happiness on the altar of duty long enough. Let your son be the responsible one. Free yourself of this burden and find her!*

"Logan! Talk to me!" Helen insisted.

Logan studied Helen. Taking in her youth. Wanting to hold on to his self-pity and resentment. Wishing that he could pin the blame on her and justify his departure. Except he somehow knew that Helen's life had not been easy. She played it as loose and uncommitted as possible but she had not, for a moment, felt free.

That flash of insight saved his life.

He took a deep breath. As though he had been released from a torturous prison. Remembering the sage advice that appearances are always deceiving. Our minds believe everyone else hasit better. That somehow, the person next to you possesses treasure that you want, need, deserve … it was all a lie.

Logan made his choices. And he was responsible for them. Free will had not prompted that moment. But no matter who released the spark, the fire was theirs. The Fates brought them together, but did not create the deep connection. For all of their power, not even the Fates can force love.

And just like that, the candle was lit again.

"The moment you witnessed," Logan began, much to Helen's relief, "was the sweetest moment of my life. The Fates set it in motion. And I am grateful. I fell in love that day. Though the story does not have a happy ending, nothing in all my years has ever come close to those precious seconds."

"But how can you — " Helen stopped herself. She didn't want to hurt him.

"Believe that when I was manipulated?" Logan finished her statement.

"Yes," she said. He could see she was awaiting his answer. That his response meant more to her than his personal story.

"You know how it feels to manipulate another person's feelings," he added.

"Yes," she repeated, softly. Relieved that his words held no judgment.

"What you must understand," he advised, "is that you can manipulate many feelings. Adoration. Desire. Sympathy. Anger. Even hate. But one emotion you can never force is true love."

Helen blushed. She assumed that the people who adored and chased after her, loved her. Now, she could see they were only obsessed. They might have even believed it was love. But it was not.

She had never felt the transcendent emotion — love — that was so apparent on Logan's face. His whole body lit up with its power. Twenty-two years later.

Logan smiled. "You confirmed something I wondered since that day. Whether the Fates had a hand in bringing Jessica to me. And, truth be told, I don't care." As he took a deep breath, Helen swore she saw a weight drop from his shoulders.

"I have watched the Fates in action for more years than you have been alive, Helen. There is not a single life on this planet that they have not changed for their broader purpose. I cannot say that purpose is perfect or even enlightened. But I have to believe, for my own sanity, that it's a much bigger plan than you and I could ever imagine. Let alone understand."

He paused. "Foolishly, I assumed I was exempt from their games and strategies. Perhaps because part of my bloodline is immortal."

"Immortal," Helen repeated. Despite the fact they were discussing the Fates, she hadn't imagined the man in front of her was not human.

"Only part-immortal," Logan said, not missing a beat.

"Still, I imagined the rules would be different. But my human nature must allow them to manipulate me the same way they would you or your brother."

"My what?" Helen asked, confused.

"Your brother, David," Logan reiterated, taking a moment to register her confusion. Then he realized that Helen's bewilderment was not because he knew about David. But because *she* did not.

"I don't have a brother," Helen said, assuming Logan's recent shock had muddled his memory. "You're mixing me up with someone else."

Logan could have taken that as an easy out. He could have decided, just once in his life, to alter the truth. Nod and drop it. His inadvertent disclosure would be covered under the human protection clause. Or what, in his line of work they called, "What humans don't know makes everyone's job easier."

But Logan was far too honest. Maybe it was Helen's influence. Or maybe, after today, something in him wanted the Fates to have to clean up *his* mess for once. Even if there were consequences.

"Yes. You do," he said.

"No. I don't," she returned, just as adamant.

Logan held her gaze and waited. She had put up a wall of stubbornness. So he gave her a moment to sit in silence while he weighed his next words. He had touched a tender place. When it came to family, Helen was more vulnerable than most. Regardless of her lighthearted demeanor.

"Would you agree," he began, "that you just unearthed a memory that deeply altered my life? One that you were not aware would pierce me to the heart. Yet you felt compelled to share it?"

Helen did not respond. She was furious that he had pierced her armor, without so much as a warning shot. So she pulled inside and speculated the possible reasons Logan insisted she had a brother.

"Yes," she said. "So you lied to me to give me a taste of my own medicine?"

"On the contrary," Logan replied. "I chose to tell you the truth when you gave me a very clean escape. I could have dropped the topic altogether without your having ever been the wiser."

Helen could not explain it but she felt cornered. *Could this whole thing have been a set-up? Was he connected to the creepy accountant from the bar? Was his whole, kind mentor act a ruse to trap young women and hand them off to crazed stalkers?*

Even Helen had to admit, she was going a little far. But who made up stories about fictional siblings? Then it hit her. *No more bizarre than a memory of three magical sisters she had assumed was a childhood fantasy.*

"Why tell me now?" she replied. And realized this story about a fictional brother was making her surprisingly upset.

Logan trusted his instincts. In this case, he could see Helen had just landed on a truth. Why get angry about a brother she does not have? Her reaction spoke to a deeper secret.

"Because your brother is connected to why you are here."

Helen shifted back. Suspicious again. "I thought you didn't know why I was here." Her gaze flitted to the front door. Wondering if she should leave. "That all you knew was we were being tested."

"You're right. Until you came back and shared your story," Logan said. "Having been in the business of assisting the Fates for over fifty years, I have remarkable instincts and even stronger powers of deduction."

"What have you deduced?" she asked. Still keeping an eye on the door. But she knew Logan was telling the truth. She could feel it. Whatever fear gripped her mind, her heart was connected to this man.

"That in our short time together," Logan observed, "we have each revealed life-long secrets to one another."

Helen realized that she felt closer to Logan than anyone she had known for years. Her resistance softened.

"I told you about my love for Jessica. A truth I never revealed to another human being. Not my wife. Or my son. A stranger I met three hours ago." Logan looked at Helen with gratitude for the burden she lifted from his heart.

"And I told you about seeing the Fates," Helen replied. "A truth no one has heard since I was five because I knew the consequences. But you believed me."

"Even more miraculous," Logan added, "we had no idea our admissions would alter the other's world. We shared it openly and innocently, only to watch the tectonic plates of reality shift before our very eyes."

"Your kiss…" Helen observed.

"And your brother," Logan stated.

Helen was stunned. She had a brother. *How was that possible? Why had no one told her? And why was she finding out now?*

"What does it mean?" she asked, "Besides the fact that the Fates have a mean sense of humor."

She was revisiting her star-struck five year old impression of the sisters. The Fates had jumped to number two on her top ten list of universal forces to avoid. Death took number one. Pretty hard to dethrone the Angel of the Abyss.

"I have been mulling that very question," Logan said. "And the most obvious answer is that we are testing each other."

"We already covered that," Helen replied.

"Not quite," Logan corrected, waiting to see if she would grasp the subtlety of what he proposed.

"Wait," she said. "You think those sisterly witches put us together just to see what would happen?"

Logan smiled at her explanation. "Simply put. Yes."

"But they couldn't have known we would share what we did," she declared. "That's a hell of a long shot."

"Ah, but they know each of us intimately," Logan said. "They've worked with me for decades. And I would bet they've kept an eye on you since you were five. The rest would be simple algorithms and intuitive guessing. They may not have known how long it would take. But they knew they would get the alchemical reaction at some point."

"Come on," Helen objected. "There's no way. I ran out of your office! Even they couldn't have known I would return. Unless —"

Helen was mortified. *Did the Fates send the mysterious stalker? Would they be malicious enough to chase her back to Logan?* She began to wonder just how beneficent a force these sisters were.

"Unless what?" he asked. Helen realized Logan was not privy to the details of why she had returned.

She hesitated. But she needed to know. "Unless they forced

me to come back."

Helen never considered what it felt like to be manipulated by the Fates. She felt deep compassion for Logan.

He smiled, reassuring her. "If they were testing us, they would not stack the deck. They want to see how we respond without their interference."

Helen did not feel relieved. If what Logan said was true, it meant the Fates didn't control everyone. So her creepy stalker operated under his own free will. And there were darker forces at play.

She repressed a shiver. Then recalled something Logan said. "Wait," she puzzled. "You think they've been watching me since I was five?"

"Yes," Logan replied.

"But why?" Helen asked, "I only saw them once. They never appeared again."

Logan paused. Helen had already been through a lot for one day. And, if she took the job that he wanted her to consider, the days were only going to get tougher. She deserved one last night to enjoy life.

Helen felt the weight of his silence. And now he was gazing at her with kind eyes. The look people give you when they're about to say that your grandmother died or your dog got hit by a car.

"Tell me," she demanded, wanting the truth yet bracing for it. Helen felt the pressure building. Somehow, she knew this revelation was going to be another earthquake in her life.

"They had to keep an eye on you," Logan said.

"Had to?" she asked.

She felt the foreshock. Any sane person would run for cover. But not Helen. She realized a long time ago there was no running from a disaster that wanted to find you. May as well meet it head on.

"They had to be sure you wouldn't turn out like your brother," he said, letting his words sink in.

"And even more important…" he began, then paused.

"To determine if you could stop him."

CHAPTER ELEVEN

S am exited the frantic buzz of the JFK airport. He stood outside amid the fumes of a long line of taxicabs. Bag swung over his shoulder, he reflected on the crazy buzz of activity.

Home. Or where he was from, anyway. Sam still wasn't sure where home was. When he left, he carried the hope he would find home far away from this place. He had never pictured coming back.

And yet, Sam found himself smiling. Not a huge smile. But enough of one to be a surprise. He missed the bright yellow cabs. The forthright people. The direct eye contact when you asked a question. No messing around. No bullshit protocol or weird European customs that were charming at first, then downright infuriating at the end.

Nope. He was back in straightforward, noisy, energetic New York. *With nowhere to stay*, announced his skeptical side. *Shit*, Sam thought. He was in such a rush to get out of Amsterdam that he forgot to set up somewhere to crash for the first few nights.

You could call your old man, whispered the pessimistic, you-are-destined-to-become-him-anyway voice. *Not even if Sam was beat up and about to be thrown into the Hudson River*, his stubborn side countered.

Sam raised a hand high to signal a cab. He made the gesture more for himself than the cabbies. Knowing full well he would have to wait until the folks in front of him got their cabs first. But he missed hailing cabs. And needed to feel the power of being back.

A bright yellow car pulled up and popped its trunk. Sam threw his duffel bag in and slammed the trunk. Yanked open the door and jumped in before he decided he couldn't afford a car ride into the city.

"Where to?" the cabbie asked.

"Grand Central," Sam replied. Not knowing why, except that it would land him in the heart of the city. He would get a strong cup of coffee and make a plan. Plus, he wanted to sound like he knew where he was going. Even though he had no idea.

He splurged on the cab because if he wanted to know what was going on in New York, cabbies were the best bet. If Sam wanted work as soon as possible, these guys would know.

They also knew if anything weird had gone down in the last forty-eight hours. And with the shadow of Troy still haunting him as he bolted from Amsterdam, Sam needed to know if he was heading into troubled waters.

"So what's new?" Sam asked. Already knowing his vague question would annoy the cabbie. The older black man with the dusting of white in his hair shot a look at Sam.

"New with what?" the cabbie retorted.

"Jobs," Sam replied. He was rusty with New York etiquette. Also known as cut to the chase. "I'm looking for work. Got any tips?"

"What do I look like, the newspaper?" the cabbie replied.

Sam persisted. "My last job was as a driver. But I've done a bunch of things." The cabbie ignored him. Glaring at the traffic like it existed only to piss him off.

Great, Sam thought. *I get the one cabbie in New York more interested in silence than a tip.* The Honda two cars up swerved into their lane. Nearly swiping the cab and a Mercedes in one move. The cabbie honked hard.

"Goddamn tourists," the cabbie grumbled. Giving Sam the hint he needed. He read the cabbie's identification plate, catching his name – Bob. And pounced on the chance to prove he deserved this guy's help.

"Look, Bob, I'm from here," Sam explained, "I need a job to get on my feet. I don't want handouts or an easy ticket. Just enough cash to feed myself and pay for a roof tonight."

The cabbie eyed Sam. Sizing him up. Checking if he was actually a kid that needed to eat instead of some brat coming back from summer vacation in Europe. He was too old to help a kid that didn't want to pound the pavement.

"Where you from?" Bob asked.

"Queens," Sam replied, "41st Street. Not far from Steinway and Astoria."

"You been away long?" Bob asked. Closer to helping, but not convinced.

"Long enough," Sam offered. He wasn't interested in spilling his past to a stranger for one contact.

"Right," Bob replied. "You good with wires?"

"Electricity?" Sam asked.

"That's what I asked," Bob said.

"I know the basics," Sam replied. "But I'm better with a

hammer. I've done construction jobs."

"Got your own boots?" Bob asked, swerving into the right lane and laying on the horn. He watched Sam in the rearview mirror. As though to say, don't even try lying.

"Yup. Just have to pick them up." Sam wasn't technically lying. He had boots. But he sure as hell didn't want to get them from his dad's garage. He would figure out how to buy a new pair, then scuff them up to look like he'd been on a construction job more recently than two years ago.

"Hmph," Bob mumbled. Not convinced he wanted to help the kid, but at least this one wasn't looking for handouts. Not like his grandson. Always expecting someone to bring him life on a platter. This generation drove him nuts.

"I'll give you the number of a guy. Frank. He runs a lot of construction jobs and always needs an extra pair of hands. As long as you're legal." Bob eyed Sam.

"Yes, sir," Sam used his respectful military speak. He had a hunch this old man had served and had no patience. Least of all for young men with life at their feet. "Born and raised here. Just need a hand to get started."

Bob grunted as they entered the sharp darkness of the Queens tunnel. Focusing all sound around them into a blur of whirring. The eerie fluorescent bulbs that lit the stretch under the water gave Sam the creeps.

Something about this tunnel made him nervous. Whether it was knowing he was under a huge body of water that could crush the tunnel any second or that he felt like he had entered another dimension, Sam held his breath. The whole experience was unnatural.

"Where are your people, then?" Bob asked. Not because he cared. But he wasn't about to help this kid if he wouldn't even pick up a phone.

"Gone," Sam shot back. He wasn't discussing his old man with anybody. Even if it cost him a job. The belligerent cabbie could keep his damn number.

"Fair enough," Bob replied. Curious what made the kid's back go up, but not nosy enough to ask. People had a right to their privacy. He held firm to that.

Sam stared out the window. Forced to breathe, as the tunnel went on and on like a bad drug trip. He didn't need reminders of his old man or Amsterdam. And the stupid tunnel was messing with his head.

For some reason, Sam couldn't shake the feeling that Troy was coming to New York. He had no proof. Not even any reason to believe the creepy client had plans to leave Europe. But Sam had grown up with an unpredictable addict. If that gave you any singular skill in the world, it was knowing when trouble was headed your way. And Sam felt the dark fog of danger nearby.

He was tumbling into the cavern of paranoia. Staring at each car beside his cab with growing suspicion, when the blast of sunlight came. Straight between the eyes. The sharp relief hit all his senses at once. Sam exhaled, released from the strange spell.

And he was back in the world.

Sam soaked in the honking, pushy streets of midtown. He never felt more grateful to be in gridlock in his life. As long as he was above ground, far aware from the eerie underworld of the tunnel, he could handle whatever came his way.

He didn't even care about the cabbie. Sam was on the

other side now. He felt the rush of possibility that came when he returned to Manhattan. No matter how many places he travelled, New York was the only place he felt anything was possible. Not in some corny, American dream kind of way. More like, the whole city ran on power sourced from creative ideas.

Sam smiled as he watched the cool kids strutting the latest look down the sidewalk. The tourists staggering around, staring up and looking lost. The busy office workers dodging the visitors like obstacles on a slalom course.

He took comfort in the crazy crowds and the ever-changing scene. Even if Troy made it to New York, there was no place Sam felt safer. Other folks found the city scary. Sam believed if there was any spot in the world where a person could hide in plain sight, it was Manhattan.

The cabbie drove closer to 42nd Street. Sam knew his window was closing to ask the big question. This was his real reason for taking a cab. Jobs were necessary but Sam could find those without breaking a sweat. This question was trickier. And required subtlety. He watched the meter tick as they closed in on their destination. Sam had to give it a shot. Even if he pissed the old man off.

"Bob," Sam began, getting the sharp look in the rear view mirror. "I haven't lived here in a couple of years. Any neighbor-hoods I should avoid?"

"All of 'em," Bob shot back. Dead pan. But somehow Sam knew he was joking.

"Look man, I'm serious," Sam had only a few more blocks. He didn't know how to ask what he was asking. How do you tell a world-weary cabbie there are dark forces running rampant and one might be headed his way?

"I don't want to end up in some building where a serial killer's been dropping the neighbors one by one," Sam opted for dramatic. He didn't have time for tact with Grand Central Station looming straight ahead.

"You think they're gonna bother with you?" Bob asked.

"You never know," Sam retorted. "Maybe there's a killer with a thing for Queens kids making a comeback."

"Yeah. That's real likely," Bob said, rolling his eyes. Sam stayed silent in the hopes that Bob would realize he was serious about finding a safe end of town.

Bob honked his way through the traffic. This was as close as he was going to get to the station. So he put the car in park and turned on his hazards. Setting off a spree of honks around them as drivers protested the obstacle in heavy traffic.

But Bob ignored them. He turned around and looked Sam right in the eyes. "Look, I don't put much stock in people's opinions. And I sure as hell don't listen to gossip."

Sam got a sinking feeling. Like Bob was done with this conversation and about to lecture him on growing a pair if he planned to live in Manhattan.

"But there's one person I always listen to," Bob continued, "and that's my sister, Susan. She may frustrate other people with her mumbo jumbo, but every time she's warned me about a place, she's been right."

"Okay," Sam replied, and fell silent. Bob wasn't lecturing or messing with him. He was dead serious.

"You go wherever you want, kid," Bob said, "but stay away from the Meatpacking District and anything within a couple blocks. It's all fancy now. Fussy shops and special bakeries. Folks think if you dress a place up, all the history goes away. Don't be fooled. Susan says it's filled with evil."

Bob locked Sam in a gaze like a steel trap. Daring him to poke fun. Sam didn't flinch. Not a smile. Or even a blink. He was listening with every cell in his body.

Satisfied, Bob nodded. "You want to be safe in this town. You give that place a wide berth. Don't go knockin' on those doors for nobody."

Sam understood. He reached into his pocket and pulled out enough bills to include a huge tip. And handed them to Bob. Nodding in silent gratitude.

There wasn't enough money in his wallet to thank this man who might have saved his life. But Sam would give him whatever he had.

CHAPTER TWELVE

Logan sat back and gave Helen a moment.

He knew the questions would come. But first, she needed to process that the brother she had never known was not a gift. He was a threat. Harsh truth arriving so quickly on the heels of the revelation had to be crushing.

Helen stared at Logan. Since she entered this world, she had been tripped, stalked, rattled and enraged. Now, her entire past was thrown into question. She had a brother. But not just any brother. One that is a danger to the most powerful forces in the universe. How the hell was she supposed to process *that*?

What began as a playful lark, pulling the wool over some mysterious executive's eyes, had landed Helen right in the heart of a war. She had no evidence for a war. But by Logan's tone and the look on his face, she could see they were headed for one.

Helen wasn't a coward. She was the first to run toward a challenge. Loving the dare. The rush. But this was a very different scenario. This was life and death. And she was no warrior.

She stood up. Took a deep breath. And looked Logan straight in the eyes.

"And if I'm not interested?" Helen asked.

Logan stood and locked his gaze on hers. "You would walk away. After everything I have told you," he stated. Not accusing. Not blaming. But disappointed.

Helen couldn't remember the last time she had cared about disappointing someone. She was probably five or six years old. By the time she reached seven, she no longer gave a damn about the opinions of others and was well on her way to living life purely for pleasure.

"This isn't my fight," she replied, folding her arms. But she couldn't hold his gaze. She already cared. And Helen really needed *not* to care right now.

"That's where you are wrong," Logan returned. "If you think you can escape this, you can't. It is only a matter of time before your brother discovers your identity. And he will either seek you out or destroy you."

Helen knew Logan meant it and was genuinely concerned. But it pissed her off all the same.

"If he hasn't found me before, why would he find me now? Is someone going to leak my file to him?" she accused, addressing the imaginary cameras again. Just because she couldn't see them didn't mean they weren't there.

"No," Logan responded, leaving out whether there was a file. "But your brother is an exceptionally talented man. The moment connections are made — like between you and me — he seems to have a sixth sense that picks them up. Like he sees the power on a grid. Any surge registers for him."

"But he has no way of knowing an anonymous power surge was me." Helen tried shrugging it off.

"You don't know your brother," Logan replied. Talking

about him made Logan uncomfortable. As though he was tempting the very circumstances.

"No. I don't," Helen said. She looked at Logan with sad but determined eyes, realizing that she would miss him. "And given everything you've said, I think it's best if I never do."

She hesitated. Helen didn't want to leave. But she was no match for the forces of Logan's world. The best thing for everyone's safety, including hers, was to leave.

She smiled sadly and placed her hand on his arm, hesitating for a moment. "Best of luck, Logan," she said.

Helen walked toward the doors. Then stopped. Giving Logan a moment of hope. Until he realized she was staring at the glimmers of daylight, confused. Their conversation had felt like an hour. Maybe two. But the whole night had passed.

Time worked differently in this building. Logan could even manipulate the clock when required. But he and Helen had experienced the kind of natural magic that confuses the senses and contradicts the rules of time. When two people connected on a powerful mission, they stepped into the kind of time warp reserved for long-lost lovers and soul mates. Hours magically disappeared when you were swept up in the mysteries of love. Or brought together to save the world.

Helen shook her head, determined not to ask what had happened. She kept walking straight out the doors.

Logan stood alone in the lobby. Feeling more isolated than he had in many years. *What was he going to do now?*

Go after her, a voice said. Logan's brow furrowed. Ignoring whatever conscience was goading him to act like a twenty year old chasing after a date. He was a senior advisor. A respectable mentor. He didn't chase candidates.

This isn't about a date, you old fool. This is about the fate of the world. Logan realized the voice sounded familiar. Along with the faint scent of cinnamon and sandalwood.

He whirled around to see Clarissa leaning against the wall. She grinned and her eyes glinted with mischief. But her tone was dead serious. Logan had no patience for her paradoxical ways tonight.

He turned his back to the youngest Fate. "Helen knows that and she walked out. *Twice.* I can't force her, Clarissa," he said.

"She doesn't understand how important she is," Clarissa replied, pushing off the wall to stand right behind Logan.

"Of course she does. I spelled it out," Logan countered.

"No," Clarissa spoke softly in his ear. "You told Helen we need her to stop her brother. You said nothing about our fate lying in her hands."

This gave Logan pause. So he was right.

"Have you met Helen?" he asked sardonically. "She doesn't want the responsibility. And I don't want someone on my team who won't pull her weight. Especially when the chips are down."

"You didn't even give her a chance," Clarissa said.

"What are you talking about?" Logan shot back, infuriated she implied he hadn't done his job thoroughly. "I gave Helen plenty of chances."

Clarissa whirled in front of Logan. Staring into his eyes with an intensity that would have knocked a mortal back fifty feet. "Go tell her that you need her."

Logan held his ground. But he could feel the love and fury of Clarissa's heart coursing through his veins. Her determination made Logan wonder if she was manipulating him. But he realized he didn't care. She was right. He needed to swallow his pride and go after Helen.

He had no idea what to say. All he knew was that none of his excuses mattered. He needed Helen. The Fates needed her. And whatever it took to convince her to join his team, he would do it.

Logan strode toward the doors with more purpose than he had felt in decades. Clarissa smiled as she watched Logan rush outside. "That's my boy," she said. And promptly disappeared.

Logan remembered Helen veering to the left as she exited. He didn't have much more to go on. He hadn't chased someone in years. His instincts were rusty and he was out of shape.

Enough! He chastised himself. *Just find her.*

Logan noticed the startled security guard staring at him. *The poor man probably thinks the world is ending*, Logan thought. *And he would be right*. Peering through a scattering of early morning risers, he searched for Helen's hot pink trench coat.

He spotted the coat immediately. Logan grumbled as he launched into the crowd, "I'm going to have to teach that girl how to blend."

Logan's height gave him an advantage with a long stride and an imposing manner that naturally made people move out of his way. He was grateful. Helen was young and energetic and moved quickly, and Logan was not used to navigating the streets by foot. Even as a young man, he did not chase. Except in that one instance that Helen witnessed at the age of five. He was struck by being back in a similar scenario, this time with the witness of his one gesture of recklessness.

What was this young woman going to do to his life? Logan

could not help but wonder. Helen had already changed it forever. And now he was planning to invite her in to the inner sanctum of his team? A team that held a tenuous balance in their hands?

May the gods give me strength, he prayed, as he strode faster and followed Helen across a busy intersection.

Logan closed the gap between them, watching her weave deftly through the crowd. He could not help but realize he felt alive. Invigorated. That somehow working so many years in the stratosphere of the top floor had kept him numb.

He was filled with a new appreciation for Helen. Sensing that her spontaneous ways were going to be both a gift and a curse. Regardless, he needed her. And though she may not understand it yet, she needed him.

Logan was only a few steps from Helen. He did not want to scare her. But he couldn't risk calling out her name. As he stepped closer, he reached out to touch her bright pink shoulder.

Helen whipped around. Eyes sharp and hands ready, she was poised to take on the creep from the bar.

Logan took a step back and held his hands up. "It's just me," he offered.

"Logan?" she blurted. Relieved, but startled to see him. He looked out of place down on the street. She couldn't say why. "What are you doing?"

Something caught her eye behind him. She spotted what looked like two huge, plain-clothed cops. Maybe they were bodyguards. Either way, they were following Logan.

She whispered, "Are they yours?"

Logan glanced back, nodded acknowledgement to the bodyguards, and turned back to Helen. "Indeed they are."

Helen breathed a sigh of relief. Then noticed the poor guys trying to assess the growing number of threats posed by the city waking up.

She guided Logan toward the buildings. Safely putting brick at their backs, and giving his bodyguards a chance to spot any threats. Helen had no intention of giving in to Logan's request, but she felt protective of him all the same.

"I am not going to change my mind," Helen stated. "I appreciate your effort. But its best for everyone if I just go away."

"I don't think you understand —" Logan began.

"Yes, I do," Helen interrupted. "I have a powerful brother. A guy dangerous enough to scare someone as seasoned as you and as powerful as the Fates. I can't stop him. I don't even *know* him. So the best possible scenario is for me to find somewhere to hide. He won't hurt me and he won't use me against you."

Logan was impressed at her understanding given how little information he had actually shared. Helen cocked an eyebrow at him. "Does that about sum it up?"

"You left out just one minor detail," Logan responded.

"What would that be?" Helen asked.

"You may not have met him but you know your brother instinctively," he said. "You share his blood. And, likely, many of his talents."

Logan gave them both a moment to allow the truth to sink in.

"That makes you the only person who can save your world. And mine."

CHAPTER THIRTEEN

Helen stared at Logan. She wanted to laugh. Like he had told her a bad joke and people with cameras were going to pop out and tell her she was about to be the latest YouTube sensation.

But she knew he wasn't kidding. Helen was being given a choice that wasn't really a choice.

Either door she chose — to run or fight — she had a damn good chance of dying. And she didn't like admitting she could die. She preferred taunting death with notions of not caring whether she had one or a hundred more days.

And now she made a difference not only to one world, but two. If that's what Logan was saying. Her head began to hurt. Helen wasn't used to mattering to anyone, let alone everyone.

"You get that I am not messiah material," Helen said.

"No one expects that of you. Least of all me," Logan replied.

"Well, thanks for the vote of confidence," Helen retorted, somehow offended and relieved simultaneously.

"What I meant," Logan clarified, "was no one expects you to do it alone."

"Logan, in case you hadn't noticed," Helen gestured to her lack of company, "I am not exactly a team player."

Logan smiled. "Excellent. Neither is anyone on your team."

"There's an actual team?" Helen asked. Then caught herself when she noticed Logan's smile.

Damn her curiosity! She was supposed to stay focused on survival but all it had taken was a few intriguing remarks from Logan and she was hooked. *Well, hell*, she thought. *If she was being asked to save the world, she may as well have a good time.*

"Let's go for a walk and discuss it," Logan said. He nodded to the bodyguards to follow.

Logan led Helen in the direction of Central Park. The guards wouldn't like his choice of venue but he needed to walk somewhere that had distance from security cameras and potential listening devices.

His instincts told him that David had not discovered their connection. Yet. Most likely he was distracted with the European deal. Logan had a window of opportunity to bring Helen up to speed before her brother sensed any threat. A window he needed to use judiciously.

As they crossed Central Park West, Logan could not help but notice the attention drawn by Helen's beauty and her bright pink coat. She had spent a lifetime trading on that beauty to open doors and distract men. He wondered if she knew he was about to ask her to put that fundamental skillset away. If not give it up altogether.

Logan progressed into the park. Allowing the bodyguards to check the surroundings before relaxing into a casual stroll with Helen by his side. He did not want to broadcast the contents of their conversation.

He already felt the easy rapport of a mentor and a young

apprentice, despite the challenges of getting her to agree to join him. He was grateful she had accepted the initial invitation. Whether she would stay on longer term would have to be a conversation he worried about at a later date.

"So this team …" Helen prompted, not content to wait for Logan.

"Yes," he replied. "Most of them are loners like you."

"Hey," Helen interrupted. Logan raised an eyebrow. "Fine. I travel alone," Helen admitted. "But I don't like the implication."

"You're assuming there was one," Logan said. "I happen to like loners. They observe well. They aren't beholden to societal rules. They think for themselves."

"They shoot strangers from the top of isolated buildings," Helen added, glancing at the tall buildings lining the park. She was grateful they were moving deeper into the trees.

"Yes," Logan admitted. "The dangers of isolation are losing your connection to the world. And falling into the dark pit of blame and paranoia."

They fell silent for a moment. Each observing the stray passersby.

"Is that what my brother is like?" Helen asked, in a lowered voice. She was nervous to speak the words but her gut told her the sooner she understood her sibling, the better.

Logan looked toward clusters of old trees. Appreciating their patient, elegant beauty while the human world rushed and pushed. He heard her question. And felt her impatience for an answer.

He chose to give Helen a moment with the vulnerability of her inquiry. She would find out many hard truths about her brother. Under her curiosity, he could feel her anger. He wasn't sure Helen was present to the complexity of her feelings.

The gift of her brother had been stolen from her in the same moment it was discovered. She would ride through a variety of emotions. He looked at her with restrained compassion. Not wanting to put her on edge with a prescient understanding of her journey.

"No," Logan replied. "Your brother is not paranoid. Or vengeful. Or even alienated. On the contrary, he is a high-functioning psychopath. He has impulsivity issues and a strong proclivity for violence. But he is also brilliant, talented, and magnetic."

"Right. A real prince," Helen said. Keeping her gaze directed ahead, not wanting to catch Logan's eye.

She did not live in the past. Or begrudge the many mistakes her parents made. But growing up an orphan left her with an ache in her heart that always longed for home. Finding a brother she didn't know existed was the closest she had come to getting that longing fulfilled. *So much for any family reunion,* she thought.

"Interesting that you chose that title — prince," Logan replied. "Your brother has risen quickly in the esteem of the highest rulers of the criminal underworld. Largely due to his belief that he is the heir. He recently partnered with the man many would consider the Emperor of the European crime consortium."

"But we didn't come from royal stock," Helen said, puzzled.

She stopped, folded her arms, and leveled a gaze at Logan that dared him to hit her with another secret. Any other day, she would have been up for the ride, but she'd had about enough twists on this rollercoaster.

Logan shook his head. Helen breathed a sigh of relief and resumed walking as Logan explained.

"Neither of you has royal blood," he said. Helen nodded. Then something tweaked. "How do you know?"

"Gene analysis," Logan replied.

"What?" Helen declared, staring at Logan. She knew it. Just as she dropped her guard — SLAM! — another sharp turn sent her head spinning. "What do you mean *gene analysis*? You only get that from DNA."

"The Fates secured a strand of your hair years ago," Logan explained. "When David began acting out, they needed to get a picture of what your tendencies might be. They felt the analysis was best for the safety of everyone. Yourself included."

"No wonder I'm so messed up," she grumbled. "I always figured it was being adopted. Meanwhile, I had strangers snatching my hair and analyzing the likelihood I might blow up the planet." Helen shot him a dirty look. "That wouldn't make a kid weird at all."

Logan kept a disinterested expression.

He enjoyed Helen's candor and wanted to reveal his affection with a smile. But the timing was insensitive. She was handling the shock of this reality shift with admirable equanimity, yet he knew that each revelation sent her reeling through another wave of adjustment.

"Wait," Helen realized. "The Fates must know who my — our —parents are."

"On the contrary," Logan replied, as though he had anticipated her inquiry. He wished he could offer Helen comfort in certainty. Such revelations were, however, not his purview.

"The Fates know many things. But there are unions and mysterious circumstances that escape even their meticulous plans and watchful eyes. The Fates cannot control everything. They are servants to the greater forces just like you and me. They have a lot more power, but they are not omnipotent."

"They can't just time-travel back to check the records?" Helen asked.

Logan fell silent as they strolled past a frazzled mother, cradling a crying baby, desperately trying to comfort her. The mom had thrown a trench coat over her pajamas, yet still managed to look fashionable.

Logan cast a quick look to the bodyguards, who took measures to keep Helen and Logan safe. Helen watched, amused, until she realized Logan would never make unnecessary moves. She stepped closer to him and wondered just who that mother might be in his world.

After they placed a stretch of distance between them, Logan answered her question. "That would be like my asking you to walk into the New York Library and find the birth record for a Jane Doe without the year or place. There are millions of records leading down one rabbit hole after another. The Fates could spend years chasing after where you might have come from rather than using the evidence in front of them."

"What evidence?" Helen asked. Her heart might have notions about a family, but that ship had sailed. She needed to wrap her mind around the fact that her bloodline, whatever it was, had spat out a resentful, formidable brother who saw her as a threat.

Logan led them toward the path by the reservoir. He admired

the glint of the rising sun on the water. The light at this time of day was breathtaking. He was grateful Helen had forced him away from his dark and depressing office. He didn't enjoy the world enough.

Helen had no interest in their surroundings. She needed to know the immediate threat and how best to neutralize it. Like a switch had been flipped. She had always been a woman who acted quickly.

Logan waited to let a pair of runners go past. Helen's focus did not flinch. She stared at him awaiting an answer. He pondered whether to dissuade her from that proclivity. Or task one of the other team members to watch her back.

He weighed how to share some of the unique abilities her brother had honed. Logan did not want her to feel compared to a sibling she had never met. Over the years, he had watched enough recruits to know that sibling competition was as hard-wired as eye color and height.

"Evidence like your brother's preternatural ability to know what people want," Logan answered, "and using it to manipulate them."

Helen's face paled slightly. Logan realized his example had hit on the primary talent the two siblings shared. Helen just used her ability for more pleasurable pursuits with less devastating results. Or so he hoped.

"That's not so unusual," Helen said, trying to make light of the similarity. "I see that in the bars every night."

"True," Logan admitted. As much as he admired Helen's levity, he could not joke about this. "But have you watched someone follow a target across three continents with the sole intention of exploiting his weakness to take over his resources and convince his people they had been betrayed?"

"No," Helen said. She looked away, needing a moment. She did not believe she was anything like David, but the similarity in their talent was eerie. And a little too close for comfort.

"I understand," said Logan, as though answering Helen's silent concern, "that you have done your share of manipulation. Playing a game that entertains you or gives you something you might not acquire directly. That talent brought you into my office. Without your courage and spontaneity, I would never have met you. Even if your original intention was to gain some sort of prize."

Logan shot her a piercing look. Helen knew he was secretly impressed. She smiled. Only the slightest blush appeared on her cheeks.

"But do not think for a second that I consider you like your brother," Logan continued, watching her with eagle eyes. "If I did, we would not be having this conversation. You would be in handcuffs in a secure cell being interrogated."

"Thanks for the comforting thought," she retorted.

"I like you, Helen," Logan replied. "More than I have liked a recruit in many years. But I do not mishandle dangerous talents. Why do you think the Fates watched you for so many years? They knew you had crossover talents with your brother. They misread the signs with him. If they did the same with you, they might have been outmatched."

Helen stopped, grabbed Logan's sleeve and pulled him close to the reservoir fence. Glancing around, she waited for an overly affectionate teenage couple with leaves in their hair to pass by.

"Are you saying," she inquired in a hushed tone, "that if my brother and I had worked together, we might have taken on the Fates?"

Helen had never been one for superstition or, up until this morning, believed in any kind of magical synchronistic forces. But she didn't know what to believe anymore.

"I am saying," Logan began, choosing his words carefully, "that the sisters could not take that risk."

Helen understood that as a yes. Whether Logan wanted to say it or not. And she was beginning to understand why he might not. She realized all of her assumptions about power were wrong. Helen might understand how to wield power in her world but in Logan's, she was far less equipped.

For the first time in her life, she was grateful for a guide. She glanced over Logan's shoulder at the burly bodyguards. And doubly grateful for the protection.

They had called in reinforcements to watch the outer perimeters. Helen was impressed. There were more uptight, swarthy guards staking out the park than if the president had gone jogging at midnight.

Helen looked at Logan. She had a question she needed to ask. But she wasn't sure if it was wise to say the words. She knew Logan could feel her inquiry. And was waiting. *Screw it*, Helen decided. She needed to know.

"What's to keep David from coming after me, for that exact same reason?" Helen asked.

Logan locked his steely gaze on hers. And did not flinch.

"Nothing at all," he replied.

CHAPTER FOURTEEN

J enna sat, curled up on the antique couch. She stared out the window of their penthouse apartment. Lost in thoughts of another world and another time. Many assumed Clarissa was the daydreamer. But they were wrong.

Jenna was the one who always wanted to be somewhere else. She watched the birds on the tower across from their building. Longing for their wings. Their freedom. Their lack of commitment to anything but their next meal and finding a spot to nest.

Jenna could only imagine what it must be like to lead a life with no responsibilities except your next destination. She sighed. Smiling sadly at the notion of a life she longed for but would never have.

She turned to the ornate living room. Filled with chaise lounges from the 1920s, brocade lamps, and hand-woven rugs from some ancient dynasty. Jenna admired the beauty, yet she couldn't help feeling suffocated.

Her sisters argued in the kitchen. Still at each other about yesterday's events in the pastry shop. Jenna had long forgotten the affair but her sisters weren't wired like she was. They held onto information and argued over tiny details forever.

The longer she listened, the more she was convinced the

arguments allowed her sisters to feel like they had a life. If you yelled about something with an urgency that masqueraded as passion, clearly you must be alive. But Jenna would claim the opposite.

Jenna gazed out the window. If they were *really* living, they wouldn't have to rage at every little thing. All that energy wouldn't be wasted on talking, it would go into *doing*. Pursuing the next great adventure. Jumping off waterfalls. Exploring mysterious jungle trails.

She watched the window cleaners hanging from the nearby skyscraper, dangling in their little contraption. She was awed by their trust in slender ropes and measly metal. Jenna had no idea if she had the courage to do what those window washers were doing. Let alone adventure in far off countries without a map.

But she didn't care. Her heart longed to feel. Her feet itched to run. She wanted anything other than being the caged bird of the gods, singing only for their pleasure. *They didn't even need her*, Jenna lamented and folded her arms. The only purpose she served was to keep Stella and Clarissa from killing each other.

She may as well disappear off the planet. And force those two to work it out on their own for once. Clarissa and Stella could manage perfectly well without her. All they needed was an extra servant to keep their laundry clean and the fridge stocked.

Jenna rolled her eyes as her sisters raised their voices louder, as though they could feel her resistance. *They probably wouldn't even notice she was gone*, she thought. Then gasped, as the truth of her thought sunk in.

She listened for their voices to stop. Waiting to see if her sisters had heard. They didn't always pick up on her thoughts.

Even though they were capable. They had to be paying attention.

The arguing continued. Not missing a beat.

Jenna unfolded her legs. And placed her feet on the floor. *Could she do this? Should she? How far could she get?*

She'd never even let herself think these kinds of thoughts. But, on this day, she was filled with the exhilarating notion that she could actually get away with it.

Jenna glanced around the room. Checking if there were enough resources at her fingertips so she wouldn't have to risk going past the kitchen or as far as her bedroom. She needed money, shoes, and a decent jacket. The rest could be made up as she went.

Her body felt electrified and she stood up. Her legs shook. *Was she ready? Could she get out the door in time? What if …* *Enough!* Jenna had to stop the doubts. She had a window of time and it was closing rapidly.

As much as her sisters could argue all night, they also had a tendency to ask her to weigh in at some point. Usually once they had so frustrated each other that they needed another opinion. Or one of them wanted someone — anyone — to say she was right.

Jenna marveled at how the two of them could manage the lives of billions yet still find the energy to argue about ridiculous minutiae. They were so connected to their work, they could pull it off without thinking. The less thinking the better, really. Intuition was a faster and more refined method than thought.

Which, Jenna scolded herself, *was precisely what she was doing right now. Overthinking.* And the reason why she hadn't taken a single step toward the door.

She stared at the beautiful white door with the multiple locks. That was her destination and, along the way, she needed to grab money and a coat. Somehow, she needed to get through that door without her sisters hearing her or the servants appearing to ask what she was doing.

Jenna fixated on the door. She needed to move her feet. But they were frozen. She had finally screwed up enough courage to get to this place. To will herself to run. And here she was, struck with fear without having even left the apartment.

A bead of sweat appeared on her brow. She had no idea what was happening. *How could she be this close and not be able to take the step?* But Jenna knew why.

She was the baby bird at the edge of the nest that knew it had wings and had watched other birds fly. But until you take that leap, you have no idea whether you have it in you. Would your wings work? Would it all make sense? Did that matter?

Of course she was terrified, her mind chimed in. Arguing for Jenna to be sensible. She had built a life here with her sisters. She had a posh position that everyone envied. She had gods at her beck and call. She didn't want for a thing.

And that was just it, Jenna's heart countered. She didn't want for anything … yet she didn't want any of this. She hadn't chosen it. Or maybe she had. But she didn't want it anymore. And once you know the truth, you cannot un-know it.

Jenna had worked in the Fate and Destiny business for far too long to doubt that insight. People spent lifetimes denying the truth, pretending their loved ones didn't mistreat them, or weren't addicted to something — alcohol, sex, work, gambling, shopping, criticism, despair — that was devastating their lives. Ignoring the signs over and over.

Until one day, a light came on and they saw what was happening.

Once they saw the truth … once they looked it straight in the eye and did not flinch, they could never un-see it.

Here she was at that precipice. She had wondered for hundreds of years how anyone could stand so long at that edge and not leap. When the edge begged them to choose life. They would hesitate and hang on, in some horrible seventh ring of hell, just because someone had convinced them it was home.

Now she understood the depth of panic. The surge of fears coming up. Battering her with reasons not to leave. Hitting her with wave after wave of doubt. They were overriding her heart's clarity with the frenetic panic of her mind.

Just when she was in the thick of battle, scared it would overwhelm her and send her fleeing back to her safe little window perch, a deep sense of calm arrived. Like the proverbial eye of the storm. The quiet settled into her body. Giving her just enough space to feel the peace in her heart. And beckon her to the door.

Jenna curled her toes against the priceless Turkish rug. Feeling the warp of the wool and digging in to the reality of what she was about to do. She moved the toes of one foot, then the other. Matching the motion on each side. First the right, then the left.

Her toes said goodbye and prepared for the leap, all in one small motion. The gentle curling steadied her nerves. She looked at the side table by the door. Spotting a small pile of cash. As though the treasure had been left there especially for her.

Clarissa left piles of money all over the apartment.

Clarissa thought so little of the substance that she picked it up when needed, then left it behind in whatever spot felt right.

But in this life-changing moment, Jenna imagined the pile of bills had been placed there with purpose. The sign she needed that this was written in the stars. She had no idea why, but maybe, just maybe she was supposed to take this leap.

Jenna's right foot moved forward. She gasped. Then covered her mouth. Listening for her sisters. Their voices had lowered, which meant she did not have a lot of time before they stopped talking to each other and brought her into their current drama.

But Jenna didn't care. She was so exhilarated that she kept her hand over her mouth to cover her giggling. She had done it! One step! Jenna calmed herself to focus on moving her left foot. She kept her gaze on the door. And boom! Her left foot moved forward.

Just like that, the spell was broken. Her feet moved. She took one step, then another. In seconds, she was within reach of the money. Had she been more practiced at spontaneity, like Clarissa, she would have done a twirl. An elegant dance move to mirror the joy she felt inside.

But she was shy and unsteady about her rebellion. So Jenna swooped her hand over the cash and stuffed it into her pocket. Dropping a few coins on the carpet with a cascade of thuds.

She froze. Expecting someone to come running in, pointing an accusing finger. Jenna held her breath. But no one arrived. Not a soul knew what she was up to. Or that soul wasn't coming forward.

Jenna reached for the first lock. Slid the latch out of its hold. And lowered the chain without a sound. One down, four to go.

She turned the second deadbolt. Listening for the satisfying *click* when the lock released its hold on the door.

Her hand shook as she reached for the third lock. A simple key waiting to be turned. The key was in the lock because they left the apartment so infrequently that leaving the key was easier than spending hours searching for it.

As Jenna wrapped her fingers around the last lock, she felt eyes on her. Or, more accurately, on her fingers. She stopped. Pulling together a story in her head that was plausible enough to put her in this delicate position.

Her fingers still stubbornly clutching the key, she turned. Her eyes did not land on anyone. Confused, Jenna glanced around. She saw no one. Then she instinctively looked down.

The family feline, Peaches, stared at her with accusing green eyes. Waiting for Jenna's next move. Delighted to have caught her in this forbidden act.

Jenna had no idea why Clarissa had named the damn cat, Peaches. The arrogant little thing was all black with a small patch of white on his chest, like he was born to be a butler. Knowing Clarissa, the entertainment of calling a black cat with a snotty attitude, Peaches, was enough to keep her laughing for millenia.

Jenna nodded at him. Acknowledging his presence but not wanting to engage in conversation lest the noise bring her sisters into the room. Jenna rarely spoke to the cat. She always felt he was judging her with his little green eyes. Acting like he was more important than the sisters who ordered the universe.

Typically, he sat curled up with Stella. No wonder since they were a perfect match. Occasionally, he deigned to follow Clarissa because she snuck him fish and treats, contrary to Stella's orders.

But Jenna and Peaches had a silent understanding. They avoided one another.

Until now.

Peaches sat staring. Jenna felt like he was daring her to make a move. They didn't waste this kind of attention on each other. Their dislike was mutual. So for Peaches to sit and stare? He knew.

On the day he mysteriously showed up on their doorstep, Jenna wondered whether Peaches was a spy. A means through which the gods and goddesses could keep tabs on them. Technically, they had to abide by the divine rules of not interfering in the Fates' work. But the gods, especially Zeus, could never help but meddle. They seemed to think it was their right. Or maybe they got bored.

Her sisters insisted Peaches was merely a stray. That Jenna was being paranoid. Now she knew her instincts were right. She wished she could show them. Prove her wisdom. But she wasn't willing to trade being right for freedom.

Jenna had a choice. Head back to her perch, pretending that none of this had happened. Or take advantage of the ten seconds she had between Peaches launching into a caterwaul and her sisters running into the foyer.

She took a deep breath. This was her moment. Jenna narrowed her eyes at Peaches. Then turned the key. *Click*.

Peaches stared at her for a second. Stunned she did it. Then his surprise was replaced by satisfaction. Jenna swore the smug feline smiled. Then he wound up and let out a wail worthy of the Sirens of Cape Pelorum.

Jenna turned to the door. She yanked the heavy door toward

her, feeling the whoosh of air surge into the apartment.

Before she could think, Jenna ran into the hallway. She couldn't stop. Not even for the elevator. She bolted toward the fire exit and yanked the door open. Careening down the stairs like a woman fleeing from prison.

As the door slammed shut behind her, the siren sound of Peaches disappeared. And Jenna had only one thought in her mind.

Run. Run like hell.

CHAPTER FIFTEEN

Helen decided to walk home. She'd been up all night with Logan but didn't feel tired. She needed to process everything they had discussed. Logan didn't want to let her out of his sight. But Helen convinced him that she wouldn't be ready until she had some time alone.

She rarely walked for long stretches. Helen usually grabbed the subway or a cab. When she did walk, it was to work something out. Then she wandered for hours.

And for some strange reason she couldn't explain, she wanted to see her apartment one more time. Helen knew it wasn't what most people would call home. Her place was minimally furnished and had only a few plants, but it was hers.

So if she was entering some kind of seclusion with Logan, then she wanted to see her apartment one last time. Helen laughed. *Wouldn't a therapist have a field day with that.* She couldn't think of a single human being to visit before disappearing for weeks but she needed to see a one-bedroom apartment?

She smiled. Helen stopped caring about other people's judgments a long time ago. They never reflected what she needed. So why should she listen to them? If she was laying her life on the line for this crazy mission, she was damn well going to do what she wanted before taking the plunge.

Helen strolled along Fifth Avenue. On any other day, the window displays of gorgeous dresses, sparkling jewels, and seven-layer cakes would light her up with pleasure. They whispered to her of decadentjoy and carefree indulgence. That the touch of a rich fabric can bring you into the moment as surely as a full-bodied kiss from a lover.

She glanced away from the elegant stores. Helen hoped she would be able to hold onto her whimsical spirit. She believed in the power of small moments to anchor you in life. But she wasn't sure who she was now, let alone who she might be after … After what exactly?

Coming face-to-face with her brother. Her mysterious brother who made powerful immortals nervous. Helen walked faster. Her instincts told her that David was biding his time. He might work with allies for now. There was no way he would be satisfied as number two for long.

How the hell was she supposed to take on a brother she didn't know or understand? *Oh, you understand him plenty,* her judgmental side answered. *You've wielded the same dictatorial power over a person's heart. You may not have held a continent in your palm. But you've acted on the same instincts.*

Helen stumbled. Knowing she had done exactly that. She caught herself with a hand on a building. She took a sharp intake of air. As she steadied her nerves, she noticed the security guard from Saks eyeing her. Probably wondering if she was going to throw up in front of his store. Even in the midst of an existential crisis, security guards had no damn sympathy.

She took it as a sign that moving would help her find her center. Helen pushed away from the cold stone. And forced herself forward. Feeling his eyes follow her along the sidewalk. Not in the way she liked, either.

Helen would have thrown him a haughty look, but she knew he was doing his job. And she didn't actually care that much. Her mind was too busy taking a blindingly fast inventory of people she had toyed with since being in Manhattan. She had played with them from a place of fun, but she couldn't be sure she hadn't hurt them all the same.

Maybe that was the difference between her and David. Intention. *Yes!* She felt a split second of relief. Until she remembered the road to hell. But Helen knew she had discovered something — that her aim had always been playful. And while she may have caused some bumps and scratches, she hadn't wiped people out or crushed their spirits.

Helen wove her way through the clusters of tourists already gathered around the Rockefeller Center. She gathered her wits, knowing not a single visitor would be looking where he was going. They were caught up in the spectacle, the photos, the mundane miracle that they were seeing something in person that they had only ever watched on television.

As she encountered friends and families giggling over pictures, Helen thought about the disappearing act she was about to pull. She didn't have many close friends. Heck, she barely stayed at the same job for a year. But she needed to be sure no one would come looking for her.

Her heart twinged as she watched a mother pull in her cluster of children to get a photo. As convenient as it was that

Helen wouldn't need to chase a ton of people to give them a concocted story about leaving town, she secretly wished there was *someone* who would miss her. But that wasn't the life she lived.

Helen's adoptive dad died when she was too young to remember much about him. Her adoptive mom had lived a decade longer until Helen was sixteen. At which point, she was old enough to fend for herself. She finished high school then ditched Maryland on graduation day.

Since then, Helen moved on. She tried a series of small towns until she realized she was a bit too laissez-faire about relationships to last long in a tight-knit community. People got a bit miffed when you dated every available bachelor within a span of a few months.

That's when she landed in Manhattan. And she had been home ever since. New York never disappointed. Plentiful restaurants, ample job openings, and more dating opportunities than a gal could clink a glass over.

Helen temped at multiple offices. She enjoyed the variety and her agency got rave reviews as long as she wasn't in long-term gigs. When they were short, Helen dazzled. When they were long, she got bored and caused trouble.

She needed to call and leave her agency a message. Logan told her no loose ends. In an age when people were used to up-to-the-minute status updates, Helen needed to be sure she didn't cause any panic. As much as she believed no one would miss her, there were people who cared enough to wonder if she'd been abducted.

Helen strolled faster. Getting her wind back and no longer

feeling nauseous, she tried to think of a positive spin on her life getting turned upside-down. *This could be healthy*, she posited, *like a spring cleaning. Out with the old, in with the new. Maybe she needed one of those. Start fresh in the same city.*

Except Helen knew this was less like a spring cleaning and more like a wildfire. Burning up every assumption she had about her past. Still, she needed something to make her feel better about the intense heat chasing her out of her existence. She was on the verge of suffocating.

She didn't like this feeling of a piece of news swooping into her reality and changing the game. But Helen had a feeling her brother did that wherever he went.

As Helen crossed 45th Street, she heard a cacophony of honks. Either some celebrity was in town getting married or another cabbie had blocked traffic near Grand Central Station. She had money on the latter. She smiled and breathed a little deeper.

Helen drew solace from the urban flow. The artists enjoying a morning cappuccino and dreaming up the next project. Assistants rushing back from the same café carrying drinks with an urgency that suggested the sky was falling. And the ever-present tourists who wandered about staring up rather than ahead, struck by the majesty of a world that had not existed for them until now.

As she crossed 42nd Street, Helen knew she had a long walk before getting home, but she slowed her pace anyway. She was approaching her favorite spot. She didn't care that her colleagues at the agency thought it was cliché. Helen adored the New York Library.

Whenever she had a crappy day, she headed straight for the lions. When she felt like she didn't fit anywhere or was especially lonely, she could count on the lions to make her feel at home. She secretly wondered whether she lived a past life as a gladiator or a queen who kept them as guardians in her bedroom.

Helen wanted to shoo the tourists away but the lions never appeared diminished by people climbing all over their backs. They held their heads high and calmly surveyed the territory in front of the regal edifice. These lions had more dignity than anyone she had met in her life. Except maybe Logan.

She felt compelled to pay her respects. As crazy as it sounded, she thought they might miss her a little — that's how often she came to see them. Not that she had that many bad days. But she wasn't one to let a whole lot of folks in. And the lions knew how to keep a secret. If any day counted as a day for the secret books, this was it.

As she approached, Helen saw a couple of scruffy looking street kids. She spotted them a mile away. And kept a close eye on their location, figuring they were pickpockets ready to take advantage of distracted tourists. They looked innocent enough, but she could tell the girl had been on the streets most of her life.

Helen knew there was a strange underbelly of New York filled with kids. They didn't go by their real names, even to each other. That's how scared and scarred they were by what they escaped. No one chose the street unless the alternative option was about as close to hell as you can imagine.

Although Helen was an orphan, she scored big time with her adoptive parents. Despite losing one of them at six and the other at sixteen, she had been loved. She may not have felt understood, but she always felt safe. Helen knew she was lucky, despite the recent surprise of her brother.

She couldn't blame her wayward approach to life on her adoptive parents. Helen put that one on the shoulders of the cowards who gave her up. That was harsh, she knew. But she figured there was some connection between her crazy phobia of intimacy and her brother's desire to blow up the world.

Somehow her thoughts about crazy families made her want to approach the scruffy teen urchins and give them cash. She never handed out free money, especially to kids who looked like they pinched things to survive, but she was having a tender moment.

"I wouldn't go near them," a voice said, as she climbed the steps beside Fortitude, the northern lion. Helen turned to narrow her gaze at a fresh-faced guy leaning against her lion, holding a huge baguette sandwich. She had been so curious about the street kids, she didn't see him.

"Why not?" she countered. Not wanting some guy hitting on her right now, no matter how cute he was. And this one had just the right combination of scruff on his face, slightly curly hair, and a tousled look like he had stepped off a train. Or a plane. Helen began wondering where he had been and where he was going before she caught herself and shut it down.

He leaned in conspiratorially. Pointing to the wiry guy who watched over the young redhead with a fierceness that reminded Helen of a wild animal. "For one thing, that one goes by Rat," he began, clearly fascinated by the eclectic pair. "And if you get within two feet of the girl, he goes all SWAT on your ass."

Helen couldn't help but laugh. Spooking the two street

urchins and causing them to bolt. So much for her act of charity. Looks like she'd have to channel that urge into protecting the world instead of giving a couple of bucks to Rat and Redhead.

Sandwich guy stuck out his hand. "I'm Sam." He waited with his hand hanging mid-air and a curious, but definitely interested, look in his eyes.

Helen decided it couldn't hurt. She wasn't going to ever see this guy again. *Why shouldn't she have one last moment of fun before going underground?* She clasped his hand, held it for a long pause then pulled him closer. Sending chills down his arm.

"Helen," she replied. "And just because you made me laugh, doesn't mean I'm going to sleep with you."

Sam choked. Coughing from surprise, as Helen released his hand and enjoyed a light-hearted laugh. She leaned against Fortitude next to him. Giving her lion a loving tap before focusing on the guy she had sent into spasms.

"You okay?" she asked. Drawing strength from Fortitude while her body relaxed after the much-needed laughter.

"Yeah," Sam replied, catching his breath. "I forgot how direct New York women are."

Helen grinned. "Why waste time? Now you know where you stand."

"Right. Not that I was angling to get in your pants."

"No?" Helen gazed over at him. Not believing a word.

"Okay, maybe it crossed my mind," Sam admitted, "But I sure as hell wouldn't try for a home run two minutes after meeting you."

"Shame," Helen said, grabbing his sandwich and taking a huge bite. Then handing it back. "I might have played ball."

Sam laughed. The longer he was back, the more he loved it. European women might flirt, but it rarely led anywhere. New York women flirted and meant it. "No, you wouldn't have. You were gone the moment you saw those kids."

"And you were watching me for how long?" Helen asked.

"Only a few minutes," Sam admitted. "You're hard to miss."

He figured there was nothing to lose. Helen had already declared she wasn't going to sleep with him. He could tell that she had no interest in being distracted by a guy. She had heavier things on her mind. No matter how much she laughed it off.

"Why, thank you," Helen replied. Though she often heard this kind of line, somehow from Sam, the compliment felt genuine.

They fell into a friendly silence. Side-by-side, leaning on Fortitude. Sam took another bite of his sandwich. Then offered it to Helen without even looking. She smiled and tore off another bite. She hadn't realized how hungry she was before she took the first teasing bite. Now she was famished. And grateful that he didn't mind sharing his breakfast.

She couldn't explain it but she felt more at ease with Sam in five minutes than she did with most friends after a year. Helen didn't know if it was his casual approach or his shared affinity for this particular spot. He also didn't force the conversation. Something she appreciated, especially today.

Of course, she thought. *Of all the days, she had to meet a guy who felt right.* She could actually imagine hanging out with Sam *and* having incredible sex with him. Two qualities that, in her experience, never conspired in one man.

Helen wanted to curse those three sisters who ran the

universe. She was sure they must be having one hell of a laugh right now.

Helen didn't think she was wired for a serious relationship. But Sam was the first hint of a guy she might have considered for the role. If she actually wanted that. Not that she did.

Oh my god, Helen thought. *A few short hours ago, she was discussing the fate of the world and here she was developing a crush like a freshman. This was ridiculous. She had a bag to pack. And a life to abandon.*

Helen pushed off Fortitude. She would have stayed longer but clearly her low blood sugar was playing with her head. She didn't believe in immediate connections of the love persuasion. She believed in one-night stands and sexual chemistry.

"Well, Sam. It's been fun. Thanks for sharing your sandwich," she said.

"Anytime," Sam replied. He wanted her to stay longer but he knew a brush-off when he heard one.

Helen walked down a couple of steps. Feeling Sam's eyes on her. Usually she had some witty parting remark. Not this time. She couldn't make light of the fact that, for once, she actually wanted to stay.

"You know," she heard Sam call behind her, "It's bad luck to say hello to Fortitude and not pay your respects to Patience."

Helen loved that he knew both of the lions' names. *Why had he shown up on this morning? Why hadn't he appeared days or even weeks ago?* She understood now why people thought the Fates were cruel.

She shot him a beautiful smile. "You're absolutely right. How rude of me."

Helen crossed the steps, feeling Sam's gaze on her the whole time. She placed a gentle touch on Patience, then whispered a greeting and a goodbye. Just in case. Though her heart broke at the thought of never seeing them again.

She stood directly across from Sam. Feeling their connection, despite the wide expanse of stairs. Helen gazed at him. Admiring his lithe, muscular body leaning against her favorite feline.

"Goodbye, Sam," Helen said. Her voice was soft, yet it carried the distance to his ears. She descended the stairs before he could reply.

Sam watched her melt into the crowd as though she had never appeared on his horizon. But she had.

"Goodbye, Helen," Sam replied.

Knowing she couldn't hear him. But needing to say it all the same.

CHAPTER SIXTEEN

Jenna couldn't believe she made it past the doorman. She knew she needed to keep moving but she hovered by the doorway, stuck in a moment of panic. She had never ventured anywhere without her sisters. She wasn't used to making decisions alone.

Which way should she go? What was the plan? She didn't have a plan. And for an instant, she felt the terror and the total thrill of that notion. The rush of personal power electrified her body like a lightning bolt.

Wait! Jenna panicked. *Was that her? Or was Zeus crashing onto the scene, thunderbolt in hand?* She looked around, ready to make a run for it. But all she saw were nannies pushing strollers, assistants juggling cell phones and dry cleaning, and a wealthy woman stepping into a limousine.

Jenna stared after the car as it pulled away. *That was it. She needed to get out of town as fast as possible.* But when Jenna watched the limousine sitting in traffic, she realized a car was not going to work.

She knew people relied on a strange system of trains that ran underground. Frankly, the notion scared her. *High-speed transportation underneath the streets? That could not be safe.* Yet, as she caught sight of people far off in the distance disappearing down a staircase, she knew the underground train was her best bet. Her sisters wouldn't expect her to take such a risk.

Before she jumped into the crowd, Jenna donned an appearance that would blend yet embody the excitement of her leap to freedom. She transformed herself into an up-and-coming thirty year old. Ready to take on the world.

With that thought, Jenna merged into the flow. She headed north, toward the staircase heading under the street. As she got the rhythm of the people, she felt the rush of their energy. The pure power of having a destination.

This was what it was like to have free will, Jenna thought. *How amazing!* She wanted to stare at every person to get a feel for the choices they were making in this very moment. Of course, they only got to steer the car. The Fates set the roads and the traffic. *But still! How exhilarating!*

She had always been completely flummoxed by the notion of free will. Especially because it flew in the face of everything the sisters did. And yet, the gods insisted that free will was an essential component of the universe. That humans wouldn't learn anything without it.

If the gods had only let the Fates experience free will, they would have saved the sisters a lot of headaches and confusion. *Maybe that was exactly why they didn't let them feel this,* she thought. Otherwise, they might have wondered why it had never been offered to them. And then the whole train would go off the rails.

Just like it was doing now. Jenna couldn't help but feel

sinfully bad and deliciously good all at the same time. She had never disobeyed her parents, the gods, her sisters, not a single soul. And here she was flaunting the biggest rule of all! Thou shalt not abandon a post bequeathed by the gods.

Jenna focused on moving. She wouldn't let her nerves get the best of her. She could not risk her brave act only to get spooked and run home. This was a delicate moment. If she didn't concentrate on the thrill of being free, she would bolt back to the cage.

She watched the woman in front of her. Gorgeous and riveting in a red, form-fitting dress. The way she sashayed her way to wherever she was going. Like an advertisement for lust and love all in one package. Her heels were taller than anything Jenna ever imagined a person could walk in. And her hair flowed like a wave of rich auburn, nacre velvet.

Jenna was entranced. As was every man in the vicinity. When the woman swiveled to enter a restaurant, every head turned with her. Male, female, canine. No matter. They all wanted to see where this goddess was going.

That thought snapped Jenna's head down. And quickened her step. She couldn't risk looking back to see whether that was, indeed, a goddess. Jenna walked briskly away from the red seductress. Hoping that the adoration from everyone else would cover Jenna and give her time to duck down the stairs to the 77th Street subway station.

As she descended the stairs into darkness, she felt panic rising. She commanded her feet. *Keep going.* Jenna had no idea why she felt so urgent about her escape. Why her heart needed to experience life away from her sisters and her duties. But she was compelled to follow her instinct.

Deep underground, the fluorescent lighting had her blinded and confused. Jenna staggered toward a ticket machine, not knowing which train she would board. She was overwhelmed and felt the urge to run home rising in her chest.

Jenna focused on the machine. She just needed to figure out how to get a ticket. Staring at the machine, she had no idea how to start. She could see graphics indicating money. Jenna pulled cash from her pocket. But she was puzzled by what to do to exchange one strange piece of paper for another.

Besides the rarity of leaving the apartment, the Fates had multiple servants who handled the day-to-day tasks. Ostensibly, so the Fates could focus on their work. Now Jenna wondered whether thearrangement also rendered them helpless.

As Jenna stood, puzzling over the ticket machine, she felt grateful for Clarissa's endless fascination with human behavior. Jenna wouldn't have known an underground train existed. But her younger sister chatted constantly about humans and their quirky inventions like money, airplanes, and telephones.

She felt a pang, missing her sister. Wondering what she might be doing. Or if Clarissa would be panicked that Jenna had disappeared. Jenna realized she hadn't changed only her life by leaving; she altered the lives of her sisters. *What would happen to them now that they were separated?*

Jenna caught herself. *She would not obsess over taking care of her sisters! For once in her life, she was putting herself first.* That started right here with a train ticket. If only she could figure out the bizarre dispensary.

Her heartbeat increased. Thumping faster and faster as

her panic went up. She knew she was relatively safe down here. Those looking for her would assume she'd use her immortal gifts to travel. But Jenna knew better. Gods and goddesses could easily track her in the stratosphere. They would have a harder time finding her hidden among the electrical pulses of billions of humans.

She knew, however, it wouldn't be long before her sisters would be searching. They would have a harder time doing their work without her. But, truth be told, they had never tested this scenario. So Jenna didn't know what would happen to their fate-weaving talents. She did know her sisters would be anxious to find her before Zeus got wind of the debacle.

Jenna's heartbeat calmed. Her flight had strengthened her courage. *So what if she pissed Zeus off? If she were captured, where would they punish her? In Hades?* That place was shuttered decades ago when the humans started throwing around nuclear bombs and wiping out entire species. The gods had a hard time intimidating mortals given the horrors that humans were coming up with in this modern landscape.

She needed to move forward. Jenna looked around. Maybe someone could help her. Jenna watched as men and women pushed their way through the turnstiles. Talking on their phones. Rushing with coffee. Staring down at little glowing screens in their palms. Every one of them wrapped up in a world that did not involve Jenna.

Despite her need for help, Jenna smiled. Not one of them saw her. Not a soul wanted to interfere with her life. She was free to do as she pleased. She wanted to do a little dance but she wasn't ready to risk that kind of attention.

Yet her feet would not be restrained. They needed to express joy! She perched up on her toes and lowered down. Then did it again. And again. Such a miniscule movement and it filled her heart with such bliss!

"Are you a dancer?" a voice asked.

Jenna whipped around. Stumbling back a step into the ticket machine. *Someone was watching.* Her heart raced.

She stared at the attractive young woman. Dressed like a man. Butch, as the young ones say. Jenna disliked that term. She found it insulting and derogatory to women who simply carried warrior energy.

Jenna could see that's what this woman was, some kind of warrior. Dressed in grey jeans and a brown leather jacket that fit well, allowed for movement, and could hide a weapon. Jenna wasn't sure whether to trust her. But this was the first person who had attempted a connection, let alone eye contact.

"Um, no," Jenna replied. "They," she said indicating her feet, "have a mind of their own."

"Right," the warrior woman replied. Though Jenna could see she had no idea what Jenna was talking about. Jenna got the impression this woman's body didn't move an inch without clear instruction.

The woman stepped up to the machine beside Jenna's and retrieved her ticket in seconds. She noticed Jenna watching her. She was about to tell the strange ballerina to stop staring, except she saw Jenna's confused expression and the bill in her hand.

"Having trouble with the machine?" the woman asked.

"Yes, actually." Jenna knew she should be cautious. But she would never get on a train if she didn't accept some assistance.

"I'm Jenna," she offered.

"Felicity," the woman replied. She must have noticed Jenna's surprise when the name didn't match her attitude. "Yeah, I know. Save it."

Jenna smiled. Felicity's directness allowed her to relax. Though she could tell there was more to this woman than met the eye, Jenna could tell she had a good heart. A conflicted heart, but a kind one. So she took a risk.

"I've never ridden the train before," Jenna said, feeling foolish but relieved at the admission.

"You mean the subway," Felicity corrected.

"Right. The subway." Jenna responded, then indicated the machine. "How do I —"

Felicity stepped next to Jenna and pressed the glowing screen. Jenna watched, but was distracted by Felicity's closeness. Her energy pulsed with a strength Jenna had not felt since being near Pallas Athena. Yet she had the physical magnetism of Lilith. *Who was this woman?* Jenna wondered.

"Where do you want to go?" Felicity asked.

"Oh …" Jenna stumbled, staring back at the screen.

She had no idea. *Out* — was all she could think. She searched for a map so she could come up with a name. Any name. She felt Felicity's scrutiny. Jenna knew she must look like a lost child.

She heard another wave of feet clamoring down the stairs and something clicked. She didn't have time to care what Felicity thought. She needed to get going. Jenna realized she better get used to looking foolish. Because she didn't know how things worked in the human world.

"I don't know," she said. "I want to get out of the city."

Felicity watched her. She knew Jenna was telling the truth. She also knew Jenna was in trouble and desperate to get away as fast as possible. Felicity sighed. *How was it she always attracted the damsels in distress? Hell. It didn't have to be a damsel. Anyone in distress.*

But there was something special about Jenna. Felicity wanted to protect her and run away with her at the same time. She had never met a woman who struck her as so vulnerable and strong at once. Never mind that she was breathtakingly beautiful.

"How far do you need to get?" Felicity asked, forcing herself to stay focused. She didn't have time to be distracted by dark-haired beauties at subway stations. She had a meeting with an old boss that did not take kindly to anyone being late.

"As far as possible," Jenna replied. Relieved that Felicity wasn't asking for details.

"Do you need help?" Felicity offered, kicking herself as soon as she said it. She didn't have time to help. Yet her attraction to Jenna was more powerful than the threat of her boss being angry. And that was saying something.

Jenna was struck speechless. She wasn't used to people offering assistance. That was her role. "I should be okay once I am on the train," Jenna replied.

"You don't look okay," Felicity observed. "Who are you running from?"

"No one," Jenna answered too quickly. Unable to keep from glancing at the staircase, the turnstiles, any entrance where someone could capture her.

"Clearly," Felicity said. She made up her mind.

Felicity turned to the machine that was flashing, waiting

for a decision. She punched in the fare. Jenna watched as the machine made strange crunching noises, then spat out her change and two tickets.

"Come on," Felicity said, resisting taking Jenna's hand. She walked toward the turnstiles. Jenna rushed to keep up with Felicity's powerful stride.

At the turnstile, Felicity passed the ticket back to Jenna. As their hands touched, a pulse of electricity swept through their bodies. Startling them both. They stared at one another. Felicity finally pulled her gaze away, showing Jenna how to get through the electronic gate.

"Like this," Felicity said, swiped the ticket, and pushed her way through the turnstile. "Now you."

Jenna clutched the paper. She took a breath then swiped the ticket. She watched the light turn green, pushed her way through, and shoved the turnstile so hard that she stumbled out the other side.

Felicity smiled, holding back a laugh. Jenna felt like an idiot. But as she steadied herself, the foolishness turned to relief, and she burst out laughing.

"I did it," Jenna exclaimed. A few people glanced her way, then kept moving. Jenna felt a protective instinct to shrink and hide. When she realized the victory was all hers and no one else cared, she felt liberated.

Felicity shook her head, then headed in the direction of the northbound trains. Jenna followed, through the corridor and down the stairs. She stopped beside the tracks. Jenna couldn't believe she was within minutes of getting on a subway out of New York.

And then what? Her doubt asked. *You have no idea where you are going or what you are doing. You're just a helpless runaway.*

Maybe. But I am free, Jenna's strength countered. She wasn't sure what that meant. But in the exhilaration of making her own decisions, she felt powerful. She had no idea what she was doing but she knew she was doing it by choice. From her free will.

A chill went up her spine. Jenna wanted to hug every human being on the platform. She understood what the mortals had that immortals didn't. Spontaneous choice. She knew from watching that choice was messy and complicated and often painful, but it was the path to true freedom.

She smiled at Felicity. A smile so warm and inviting, she could feel Felicity's desire to hold her. Or was it more? Was Felicity looking at her lips? The electricity between them was unmistakable. Jenna could feel the reciprocal desire to kiss her. She was so caught by the attraction that she didn't notice the train approaching.

The rush of people toward the track broke the spell. Jenna turned to see the headlight get brighter and brighter. She felt the thrill and terror of freedom. This was it. She was leaving her predictable life. As wind preceded the subway through the tunnel, Jenna closed her eyes and allowed herself a moment of release. The rush of air swept over her body. Blowing away the past.

The subway stopped. The people pushed forward. Jarring Jenna out of her tranquil moment and back into panic. She glanced around. *Where was Felicity?* The disappearance of her warrior left Jenna feeling frightened and exposed.

Had Felicity led her to the very train that would get her caught? Was she even helping her? Jenna suddenly wondered if her sisters were right. They always told her that she was far too trusting. Jenna was in a throng of strangers getting on a subway to who knows where. And the person who sent her in this direction was —

"Right here," Jenna heard beside her. The subway doors shot open. And a surge of people emptied from the car, pushing through the center of the waiting crowd.

Felicity hooked her arm around Jenna's waist. The flood of people jostled Jenna but Felicity stood strong. Jenna felt comforted and unsettled by the closeness. Felicity not only looked like a warrior, she must train like one. Her stance was solid and unwavering.

"Your turn," Felicity said, shepherding Jenna into the subway. Jenna hesitated as her foot crossed the gap between the platform and the car.

For Jenna, the threshold made the moment real. Whether she was passing through a door or transporting through time and space. The moment of crossing was powerful.

She held her breath as she made the leap. Felicity stepped behind her. Jenna turned to watch the doors close, her heart leapt with conflicting emotions. Excitement, terror, and sadness — all at once.

Jenna stared out the window at the platform disappearing. She hoped she knew what she was doing. Either way, she had crossed over.

There was no going back now.

CHAPTER SEVENTEEN

H elen made it back to her apartment. Though it had only been a day since she'd been home, she could have sworn a week had passed. She looked at her home with sadness and a bit of regret that she hadn't shown it more care.

Her bag was packed with only the essentials, as Logan had instructed. Whatever that meant. *She had no idea what she would be doing. So how could she know what to pack?* She had stared at her closet for so long, she finally gave up and packed as though she were travelling for a long weekend.

Helen sat on her window ledge and took a moment to watch her noisy and colorful Greenwich Village neighbors. She watched as a gay couple flirted and kissed each other all down the block. The young couple across the street pretended to fight but Helen knew it was foreplay. They acted out this drama every week.

As she enjoyed her final episode of what she called *Greenwich TV*, all she could think about was Sam. *What was wrong with her?* Helen wondered. She only met him a couple of hours ago. She couldn't remember the last time she had a crush on someone. Probably in Grade Three.

And she had a world to save now! She didn't have time for languid looks and cute boys who shared their sandwiches. As much as she argued with her mind, it insisted on seeing Sam in every gesture, hug, and kiss.

Helen turned away from the window. But her body wasn't giving in so easily. As she thought about their meeting at the lions, a chill rippled up her spine. She realized that the moment she saw Sam, she recognized everything. Like she had seen it before. Every detail was familiar from his smile right down to the sneakers on his feet.

None of it made sense. Why was meeting Sam so important? On today of all days? Sure, she could think it was romantic. But she was a practical girl and she didn't want to start believing in fairy tales and destined lovers just yet. Even if she had discovered that the Fates were real and Logan had initiated her into another world.

Helen whipped around, expecting the door to her apartment to fly open revealing three sisters. Nope. Just her closed door. She was overtired and getting jumpy. She needed to say her goodbyes, grab a coffee, and get back uptown before she convinced herself this whole thing was a weird dream.

Her apartment looked so bare. As a rule, Helen always went to her date's apartment. So she never worried about decoration. The thought never bothered her until now.

Maybe because she was leaving her nest for an indefinite amount of time.

She felt bad about the lack of attention. Like the sad little plant in her living room. The one that was supposed to cheer the place up but, in her place, showed how little time she spent here.

Helen picked up the last plant, ready to add it to the others that she had put with a note outside her neighbor's door. She didn't have a lot in her place, but what she did have she loved. And she wanted her plants to thrive without her.

She stood in the middle of her living room. Knowing the time had come to say goodbye. She made her calls. Left a note for the landlady. It was time to go.

But she was frozen to the spot. She had a sinking feeling that the moment she stepped out that door, her life was never going to be the same. She might never see this apartment again. More than that, she had no idea what was waiting. Or what was expected of her.

Normally, that thought excited Helen. But this was different.

She wanted to stay one more night. Sleep on her couch. Hear all the normal sounds of people getting up and making coffee and heading out to work in the morning. All the sounds that might have driven her nuts any other day but now seemed nothing short of miraculous.

Holy crap. One encounter with a semi-immortal and a cute boy who gave her chills and she was a wistful romantic.

Even as she chided herself, Helen had tears in her eyes. For the first time in a very long time, she was willing to risk everything for the world she adored so deeply. Right down to her tiny, bachelor apartment.

Helen took one last look and smiled. "Goodbye," she whispered aloud.

"But we haven't had a chance to get acquainted," a voice replied.

Helen turned to see her front door was wide open. A well-dressed, strangely familiar man with dark hair and vibrant blue eyes stood on her threshold. The sinking feeling in her stomach turned to a heavy rock.

She needed to pay closer attention when her intuition gave her a head's up. She may have assumed it would be the Fates, but she should never have doubted that somebody was on his way. Whenever she ignored the warning, she got knocked off guard.

"Who the hell are you? And how did you get my door open?" Helen asked.

The lithe, self-confident man ignored her question and stepped inside. He gazed around with a mixture of amusement and disgust. Then spotted the bag at Helen's feet.

"I would have thought you'd recognize me. Even though we never spent much time together," he said. "I assumed blood would always recognize blood."

"David," she whispered, more to herself than to him.

"Very good," he answered, taking a step toward her. "Someone's been filling you in on your history."

Helen knew he was baiting her. Seeing what she would reveal. And how much she had discovered. She refused to bite.

David sized Helen up in a detached, observant way. Gathering a fast assessment of her height, weight, and age. What her clothes revealed about her income, tendency to risk, and her sexual proclivities. He picked up on the slightest clues, seen and unseen, to determine what he should make of this girl. *His sister.*

Helen half-hoped when she met David that she would feel a bond. That her brother would be more than Logan's severe assessment. She wondered if she would notice a redeeming feature. But now that he was near her, all she felt was his strange mix of cold analysis and a deep appetite for pain.

She forced herself to stand still as David came closer.

Somehow, she sensed how many people he had killed. She couldn't see their faces but she felt them trailing behind him like a distinct odor. Every last one sacrificed to increase his power.

Helen had no idea how she knew these things. Yet she was sure they were true. Her brother had built his strength through a trail of human sacrifice. And now his sights were set on her.

"How did you find me?" Helen asked. If she was facing down a predator, there was no point wasting time.

"That would ruin all the fun," David answered.

Helen could see how her pleasure-seeking had turned dark and twisted in David. Where she toyed with others in a subtle and sensual way, he found pleasure in torment.

Staring at him was like looking in a warped mirror. Her harmless power games turned into something vengeful. She forced herself to breathe as he stood within a foot of her.

She held her ground. Noticing details about David calmed her nerves. When she gave her mind a specific task, her emotions quieted and she could view David through the lens of an anthropologist.

Helen saw that he was similar in height, but they had different coloring. Her dusky blonde hair and hazel eyes contrasted to his dark hair and tanned skin. Yet despite the visual differences, she felt the same blood coursing through their veins.

Logan had told her the truth. Not that she doubted him. Still, she liked to confirm things for herself. This was, beyond a shadow of a doubt, her brother.

"I hear you kill people," she said, not being able to stop herself.

David threw his head back and laughed, caught off guard. Helen held steady. His response made her want to throw up.

"Yes," he replied, thoroughly enjoying her candor, "Yes. I do. Were you hoping to join the family business?"

"What family?" she retorted, offended by his implication.

David smiled. And Helen knew he fired off the question to see if it was a button. She had given him exactly the answer he wanted.

"Quite true," David replied, walking to the window. Glancing at the view. Then looking around the living room. Judging every nook and cranny. Helen wanted to strangle him. She was unnerved by her visceral reaction.

"We weren't raised as family," he said, and turned his cold gaze back to her. "That doesn't mean we don't belong together."

"Yeah, right," she said.

She couldn't help but think of the kind of power they might yield if they partnered up. Logan hadn't confirmed her assumption, but Helen was not going to risk finding out. She eyed the door and calculated whether she could make a break for the stairs.

"You don't think I'm serious," David replied, sitting on the edge of her windowsill.

"I think you're obsessed with *your* needs," Helen said. "So don't pretend you care about me just because we come from the same gene pool."

David quite enjoyed her lack of reverence. He guessed her kneejerk, candid replies were provoked by terror. She wasn't sure what he wanted.

Yet, her courage and finesse were refreshing. Most of his underlings and associates were so careful around him there was no banter in his life. Of course, he insisted on winning but he missed the opportunity to play.

David moved from the windowsill toward Helen. As he approached, her skin began to crawl. Like every nerve in her body screamed to push him away. He circled her, examining her as closely as he had scrutinized her home.

His motion made her dizzy. So Helen locked her eyes on the door and used her other senses to track him.

"We may not know each other, dear sister," David offered. "But I can only imagine talent runs in your bloodstream. The same way it does mine."

Helen held her tongue. She viewed him as a snake slithering close to its prey. She did not want to provoke a sudden response from a predator she did not understand. His words were flattering, but they were like a rattle. Mesmerizing her with their sound.

"So while I may not care about you, per se," he brushed against her shoulder, "I care what you may be capable of."

"I'll pass," Helen replied, before she could stop herself.

David halted directly between Helen and the door. Locking her gaze in his. "If you don't come with me," he inquired, pointedly glancing at her bag, "where will you go?"

Helen knew this was why he had come. She recognized the poker technique. But was David asking because he already knew about Logan, or was he bluffing to get her to reveal her alliances?

"None of your business," she fired back, using a classic little sister reply. She knew it was a risk. Especially given his reputation.

"Just because you waltz back into my life," she continued, "doesn't mean you get to know shit about me." Helen grabbed her bag and swerved around David, ready to bolt. Except he took an easy step backwards and shot his arm up, blocking her way.

"Not so fast, sweet sister," he breathed in a soft, blood-chilling tone. "Tonight, you walk out that door. But only because I *choose* to let you go. I know you haven't honed your talents. Or even figured out what they are. And, today, I have more pressing business."

David enjoyed watching Helen struggle. He knew her intuition was strong, but she didn't trust it yet. His, on the other hand, had been well trained.

"But know that I am watching you," he continued. "I am patient. I will wait until I know you are of most use to me. Then I will come calling. So walk out that door. But don't, for a moment, believe you are free."

David lowered his arm. Smiling at Helen. She moved around him like he was a land mine. David turned to watch her at the precise moment Helen turned to keep him in her sights. They stared one another down and she walked backwards out her door. Saying goodbye to her apartment and her life.

As soon as she was free from his gaze, she broke into a run. Her brother's menacing expression indelibly seared into her mind.

CHAPTER EIGHTEEN

S am lay on his back and stared at the hostel ceiling. He told himself he was just renting a bed. Not that he was a snob. He just wanted to be further along in life than he was at this moment.

If he was honest, Sam thought, *for the first time in his life, he actually cared about impressing a woman. Okay, maybe the first time since grade school.*

After that, Sam discovered his place in the social pecking order and decided there was no point trying to impress girls. They either liked him or they didn't. The rest was game playing.

Yet here he was staring at a rented ceiling when he should be looking for a job. And all he could think about was Helen.

He had tried distracting himself by talking with the students staying at the hostel. Even then, Helen's face kept popping into his mind. *Where was she? Who was she with? How could he find her? What if she had left town?*

There was something about how Helen looked earlier that morning. Like she was leaving on a long trip and didn't want to go. Or at least, she didn't want to say goodbye. She had shown up at the lions with a deep sadness. A feeling he wanted to change.

That was probably the only reason he had the courage to

speak to her. Helen was *that* beautiful. Drop-dead gorgeous, in fact. He usually avoided those women like the plague. They typically came with a boatload of baggage. Either theirs or from others, but exhausting all the same.

Even more of a surprise was Helen's sense of wit. Sam smiled at the thought of her banter. She made him laugh and almost made him blush. Luckily, he had enough encounters in Amsterdam to practice controlling his reaction to flirtatious women. Regardless of how beautiful they were.

A shock rippled through Sam and he sat up, startling one of the tenants sleeping off a late night bender. The sleepy-eyed guy put up two fists.

"Sorry," Sam said and swerved around the prizefighter as he jumped off the bed. The wiry guy mumbled something and dragged his bag closer to the wall.

Sam couldn't shake the feeling that Helen was in trouble. Her fear struck him out of the blue. He had no reason to believe she was in danger. But his whole being felt an intense urge to protect her.

He stood by his bunk, unsure what to do. *You need to get your butt on the street to find a job. And not chase girls who are out of your league.* His practical side had an annoying habit of dousing water on any fire that sparked in Sam's chest. Especially for a girl.

That's when Sam realized every decision he made in Europe, with the exception of getting the hell out of Amsterdam, had been made by his practical side. Resulting in four miserable months. For once in his life, he was not listening to that voice.

Sam looked around at the young students. Flirting, chatting, not doing one damn sensible thing with their day. If being an adult meant listening to his rational mind, he was damn well going to spend today taking a chance on his heart.

Sam grabbed his jacket and pulled it on, shouldering his way out of the crowded hallway. Before his mind and his feet colluded to get him back inside. He had to see Helen. If only to make sure she was okay. Sam knew she was capable of taking care of herself, yet he had a feeling that Helen needed him.

How the hell do you plan to find a girl in a city of eight million people when all you have is her first name? His rational mind jeered.

Sam stepped onto the street. The collection of students smoking near the door gave him a quick glance then went back to their conversation. He stood for a second at the corner, then headed south.

Sam knew if he was going to stand a snowball's chance in hell of finding Helen, he had to count on his instincts. Even if he started in the wrong direction, he was sure a plan would come to him as long as he made a decision. He could always turn around.

Striding down the sidewalk on the upper west side, he reveled in the sounds, the smells, the crowds. This city always felt alive. Like something was brewing on every corner. He loved that most things in New York were out in the open. Nobody tried to hide what he stood for. Unless, he was operating in the shadows.

He froze in his tracks — *Troy.* Surprising a couple travelling too close behind him. They swerved with the reflexes of city dwellers and kept going. Troy was in Manhattan. A chill shot up Sam's spine.

No. No way, his mind countered. *Why would Troy leave the place where he was building business connections? You're being paranoid.*

But Sam knew it was true. He knew it as clearly as he was standing at the corner of Amsterdam and West 100th Street. Sam practically growled when he saw the street name. His mind insisted he was making assumptions based on coincidence. But if there was one thing Sam did not believe in, it was coincidence.

Was Troy connected to Helen? Why would he pop into Sam's head after he felt compelled to find her? he wondered. *It made no sense.*

Sam hoped there wasn't a connection. But he had a strange feeling there was. He forced himself to move. Even more concerned about Helen. If she had anything to do with that guy, she was in serious trouble.

Shouldn't you be thinking about yourself, you idiot? His rational mind countered. *Not walking into the lion's den? You travelled across the Atlantic to avoid that maniac and now you're heading straight for him.*

Sam couldn't deny that his rational side had a very good point. The wise decision would be to turn around, go back to the hostel, and forget he ever met Helen. But his feet kept moving in the direction of the New York Public Library. And his heart beat faster at the thought of helping her.

Sam remembered there was another way to find Helen. He hadn't tried it since he was a kid. All it had done was lead to trouble. But Sam had a talent. One that had landed him in fights with his parents and on the outside of every social group at school. Despite the aggravation, he still believed it was a gift.

Sam had a natural ability for finding people. Especially ones with whom he had an emotional connection. If he closed his eyes and focused — preferably with his feet on real earth, not pavement — he could see someone. And if he could see the immediate surroundings, trees or bricks or people, he could hone in on their location.

Sam discovered the trick when his little sister went missing. Everyone was terrified she had fallen in the river and drowned. He just wanted to block out the sound of his parents screaming at each other. Instantly, he got a clear picture of his sister happy and safe, under their porch, playing with stuffed animals.

He thought it was just a calming vision. When Lilly went missing, his parents went berserk. Everything they ever wanted to blame on each other rushed out in a wave of bitterness.

Lilly hadn't been missing that long. Her disappearance was the trigger they needed to expose their hatred in public and feel completely justified. The whole thing made Sam nauseous. When he covered his eyes and ears in an attempt to block out their reality, another world presented itself.

Sam had to find out if Lilly was under the porch. As he approached the wooden lattice door to the cubbyhole under the stairs, he was scared to open it. He didn't know whether he wanted his vision to be true.

But at eleven years old, he couldn't resist knowing. Curiosity won. He opened the lattice door. And there, smiling up at him, with a surprised and oh-so-innocent look on her face was Lilly. Not drowning. Not lost. Not even five feet from their home.

Sam had yelled for his parents. And when the inevitable questions were asked, Sam couldn't help himself. He blurted out that he had seen a picture of Lilly in his head. Like a vision. His mother pulled him aside and covered his mouth.

She must have been nervous that one of the neighbors or the local police officer would hear her son. But they were all so entranced with Lilly, offering blankets and cookies and hugs, they hadn't noticed Sam and his parents. His mother ordered him never to share such nonsense again. Ever.

He was crushed. He finally had something special. Something all his own. Not only that, but the gift had found his little sister! Sam swore on that day that he would never share anything with his parents. Ever.

Sam continued to practice his ability until high school. One day, Sam was under the bleachers, eyes closed and hands over his ears, and the jock had snuck up on him. Taped Sam's hands to his head, wrapped the duct tape around his mouth, then secured his ankles.

They stuck him outside the front of the school with a sign on his chest that said, "I see dead people." Sam never lived it down. He got the nickname *sick sense* and his gift turned into a curse. He didn't know how word had spread, but it didn't matter. He shut down his intuition.

Now, Sam had a reason to try again. He took a left and walked fast toward Central Park. As much as he didn't want to try this in the park, he knew he needed somewhere with fewer distractions and more natural power. He needed all the help he could get.

He strode along 96th Street. Sam didn't want to run. Even though he didn't anticipate any cruel jocks sneaking up on him, he preferred not to draw unnecessary attention.

Sam was feeling vulnerable enough. *What if he was rusty?*

What if his talent had an expiry date? He had no idea if it could go away as quickly as it had appeared.

Sam shook off the doubts, walking faster to outpace them. If his heart pumped hard, his mind got focused. As the worries cleared, his inner clarity spoke. *Focus on Helen.* The thought of her relaxed his shoulders.

Despite meeting her only once, Sam didn't have to try to recall her face. Every feature, from her mischievous eyes to her dark golden hair and her teasing smile appeared. As he thought of her, their connection grew stronger.

Before he knew it, Sam crossed into Central Park. He set aside the image of Helen so he could get his bearings.

He moved into the park. The lunchtime rush was over but the park had a steady flow of people seeking shade and solace. He knew it would be tricky to find a quiet spot. Maybe if he could find a large tree that he could lean against. If he looked like he was resting, no one would wonder why he had his eyes closed.

Sam walked deep inside so he felt the pulse of nature. The water and trees muffled the sounds of the cars. He was still close enough to the entrance that if he needed to bolt, he would be back on the street in minutes. He didn't care if it sounded paranoid, he needed an escape route.

Sam spotted a huge red oak tree and he knew that was his spot. He approached the old gal with reverence. He felt these trees were the memory keepers. They had been here longer than most people and seen more than any human eyes. Sam imagined they kept all kinds of secrets.

He knew this was one of the things that had made him odd. After all, he grew up in Queens. But he always had a special connection to the earth and, especially, to trees. Sam couldn't help but wonder why he had been born in New York and not Oregon or Colorado.

Sam walked up to the oak. Glancing around to ensure he was safe from human interference, he asked to lean against her trunk. He felt approval and breathed a sigh of relief. Like he had come home. This beautiful red oak was waiting to embrace him like a long lost aunt.

He stepped carefully around her massive roots. Then found a slight dip, large enough for him to stand. He reminded himself that if anyone came at him, there were roots all around. He'd have to pick his feet up to avoid tripping and smashing his head on ancient oak wood.

Sam leaned his back against the tree. A rush of calm came over him. He knew he would be safe while he sought Helen. He couldn't say how, but he knew. And so, Sam closed his eyes.

He felt like he stepped into a room that had been waiting. The connection was at his fingertips. Not angry that he had been away so long, but loving and patient. Sam was in the nurturing flow, like the wisdom of the universe was tangible. Holding him in its embrace. He had never felt so safe.

Sam wanted to stay forever in this place far away from the pain of human existence. But he remembered that he was on a mission.

Sam asked where Helen … he didn't have her last name. So he brought up her image, clear as a photograph, and asked where she was.

Sam felt the wisdom pause. Checking his motive. So he waited. Breathed. Kept focused on Helen's face. And waited.

After what felt simultaneously like a second and an eternity, the darkness in his mind disappeared.

He received a visual of Helen rushing up a set of stairs from a subway station. He couldn't see enough to get a bearing, so Sam asked: *What station?* The image broadened to reveal the sign: 86 Street Station.

Sam caught the red number one on the sign. She was on the Upper West Side. But where was she headed? He waited. Needing to know more. But all he got was a foreboding feeling that she was being followed. He hadn't seen anyone behind her. But maybe the person wasn't physically with her. If he could see where she was. Couldn't someone else?

He kept his eyes shut. Desperate for another visual of Helen. *How could he help her if he didn't know where she was going?* His panic blocked information. So Sam quieted his mind. And asked for insight. *Which street? Which direction?*

Again, Sam felt the wisdom pause. He had never encountered anything like it. Images always entered his mind when he asked. This was different. Like the infinite source was protecting Helen. Not wanting to give him access until it was sure he could be trusted.

Then he got a flash of her on the street. Though he didn't see it, he felt the message, *North.*

Sam's eyes snapped open. She was heading towards him. A rush of energy swept up his body and threatened to bring him to his knees. Sam steadied himself against the tree. Knowing full well he had received an acknowledgement *and* a warning.

He needed to be watchful. For his sake and Helen's. There was evil near. If he led it to Helen, he may as well be the hand that killed her.

Killed her? Evil? His mind questioned the dramatic tone. But here, by the red oak, Sam was able to ignore the doubt. He knew what he felt. He was sure of what he saw. And he needed to tread carefully.

He also knew he needed to reach Helen. *How was he supposed to get to her and avoid revealing her location?* That's when the realization hit him. Whoever was following her didn't need his help. They weren't tracking her power.

Sam shivered. Troy popped into his head for the second time. There was definitely a connection. But Sam wasn't going to waste any more time. If he didn't act now, he was going to miss Helen.

He pushed away from the great oak. First, he offered his silent gratitude. Then, he stepped through the immense roots until he was free of obstacles. Sam hit the ground running. He no longer cared if he drew attention. His window of opportunity was closing.

Sam flew out the park entrance. He had a sense that Helen was heading toward West 90th Street. He didn't have much time. Sam hadn't run so hard or fast in weeks. He was in better shape before he went to Europe. But he had focus on his side now. Focus and determination.

He took a sharp right down West 93rd Street and picked up his pace. As long as Helen saw him, she would stop. Wouldn't she? He felt doubt creep in. *What if she decided he was dangerous?* His legs got heavier. Hesitation dragging down his steps.

Sam shook it off. Refocused on helping her. If she rebuffed his offer, that was her choice. But he would get to her.

He made it to the chaos of Broadway. And took another right. Swerving between pedestrians and sharpening his gaze. Sam knew Helen was wearing her bright pink trench coat. She would be easy to spot.

Even as his lungs burned, he laughed. If Helen was wearing that damn coat, *she* wasn't worried about being tracked. Or she was naïve. Either way, it was a glimmer of hope.

As his legs turned to lead and his lungs couldn't take much more, Sam passed 91st Street. Then forced himself to continue until he could see the sign for 90th Street. He searched the sidewalk — nothing. He slowed and scanned the west sidewalk — nothing. No sign of Helen.

Sam stopped. Out of breath and doubled over, he braced against a building. Sucking in oxygen and berating himself for not acting sooner. He took another blurry scan of the street, but saw nothing. He had missed her.

He hit his fist against the concrete and let his head hang. He could feel regret seeping into his heart. Knowing he would carry this one forever.

"Sam?" a familiar voice asked.

He looked up. Helen stood in front of him. Looking perplexed and carrying a coffee. "What are you doing here?" Helen inquired.

Sam's world took a spin from the shock of seeing her and the lack of oxygen to his brain. He gripped the building with white knuckles, trying not to pass out. Helen placed her hand on his shoulder.

"Focus on me," she advised. "Keep your head up and push all the air out of your lungs." Sam took a few deep breaths. His world came back into focus. Complete with a smiling Helen.

"I was looking for you," he managed to say. "You're in danger."

Helen stared at him. Sam couldn't tell if she thought he was crazy. Or creepy. Or possibly both. But he had done his job. Even if she wrote him off.

"How did you know?" she asked in a low voice.

"I felt it," Sam replied. "I wish I could explain why. Or how. But I can't. All I can tell you is I knew."

Helen gazed at him for what felt like forever. He sensed she was weighing his words. And making some sort of decision. So he waited. Praying she would accept his help. Knowing the next step was up to her.

"Come with me," she said, in a quiet voice. She strode up Broadway. Not looking back.

Sam didn't give it a second thought. He followed.

CHAPTER NINETEEN

C larissa and Stella knew something was wrong when they heard Peaches howl. That cat didn't howl over anything.

Truth be told, Clarissa couldn't remember whether she had ever heard him howl. Except when she named him. She smiled.

"How can you laugh at a time like this?" Stella accused.

"I wasn't laughing," Clarissa retorted. Though she couldn't resist a wicked glance in the direction of Peaches, who turned and flicked a highly annoyed tail back.

Stella stood immobilized when they entered the living room — unable to process that Jenna was gone. Once the fact of her missing sister sunk in, she started pacing. Panicked by what Jenna's disappearance meant for the three of them. *This was bad*, she kept thinking, *this was very, very bad.*

"Stella, please stop pacing," Clarissa appealed to her sister's goodwill. With Jenna gone, they had to figure out how to work together. Their mediator was missing. Putting them in strange territory.

"I will do what I want," Stella barked. Clarissa knew her oldest sister was acting out of worry. That realization gave her hope. She had never bothered to understand one stitch of why Stella did anything. And now, with Jenna missing, Clarissa was growing.

People assumed immortals had no need to grow. In fact, they had a lot to learn. They were always making mistakes. When humans made a mistake, they got into a car accident or caused a fight with their spouse. When gods and goddesses made mistakes, entire civilizations went missing.

The immortals had large egos but they also had the screw ups to match. If they wanted to evolve into better beings, they needed humility to equal their talent. Pallas Athena was a shining example of one who owned her mistakes. She took the name of the goddess she wronged.

Clarissa and Stella had to face the fact that Jenna's departure was their fault. They were always so caught up in their drama, that they ignored their middle sister.

"Maybe she's out getting some air. Could that be?" Stella suggested, trying not to pace. But she was so upset she couldn't keep her body from moving.

Clarissa was startled to hear doubt in Stella's voice. Her sister *never* doubted herself. But when Clarissa truly noticed her older sister, she realized. Stella secretly doubted herself all the time. She just didn't show it. Stella always felt responsible.

Clarissa was struck with a bolt of humility. This event was meant to shift their reality. They had been stuck in their roles so long, they needed a startling incident to shake them up. And the Fate Sisters had not had anything rattle their world in a very long time.

"No, dear Stella," Clarissa replied, "Jenna has not gone out for air." She stepped up to the window that gave a stellar view of Park Avenue with its dazzling lights and stream of elegantly dressed people. "She's run away."

"Run away?" Stella stopped, staring at Clarissa in disbelief. "No! She wouldn't. She couldn't." She waited for her youngest sister to take it back. To admit she had made a tasteless joke. But Clarissa regarded Stella with kindness. The worst possible reaction because that meant what she said was true.

Stella simply could not comprehend abandoning her post. She saw their work as critical, necessary, even urgent. She viewed herself much like a General in the army. Always on call, always needed, always in charge. Her work was her life. Stella saw no other way to be.

Clarissa felt compassion for her sister. But as Clarissa gazed at the humans on the street, heading out for their latest adventure, she understood completely. She recalled seeing Jenna in this exact spot.

Jenna sat here, watching the humans, dreaming of the lives they live! Clarissa realized. *How had she not seen it before? Her dreamy sister, always somewhere else!*

Clarissa was over the moon. She had their first clue! Clarissa had no idea where it would lead. But she *knew* she had the tail end of the thread that would take them to Jenna.

She spun away from the window and hugged Stella. Clarissa held her startled sister for a full three seconds before releasing her. She grinned, knowing her sister thought she had lost her mind.

"Jenna ran away to have an adventure!" Clarissa blurted out, as thrilled as if she had discovered a second sun in the solar system.

Stella stared at Clarissa then replied politely. "How is that a good thing?" With one sister lost to a crazy quest, Stella couldn't risk throwing the other one into the nether-reaches of insanity.

"Don't you see?" Clarissa urged. She was so excited that she did an ecstatic twirl then locked her gaze back on her sister. "Jenna didn't leave *us*, she left because she needed to explore."

"Why does that make it any better?" Stella asked. Still convinced that Clarissa was losing her mind. More than usual.

"Because, silly," Clarissa replied, pulling Stella toward the door, then grabbing their coats from the closet. "Jenna isn't abandoning us or our work. She felt trapped. So she ran."

"I still don't understand how that helps," Stella replied, frustrated and folding her arms. *She would not abandon their posts.*

"I'll explain on the way," Clarissa said, and tossed Stella's coat at her.

Stella caught the coat before it hit her. "No! We are not going out," she blurted, throwing her coat on the floor.

Clarissa stopped, her hand on the doorknob. In all their years of fighting, she had never heard Stella take the tone of an indignant three year old.

"I am not running after her like some indulgent parent. *She* left *us*. She made this mess. Jenna is out there doing Goddess knows what, undoing all our work. And who's going to have to clean it up? Me. Always me. Well, I am not doing it this time!" Stella snapped.

She turned from Clarissa and folded her arms. Stella was so frustrated she could feel tears brimming in her eyes. *She did not cry! She would not cry!* But Stella was tired of everyone else acting impetuous and childish. She refused to pick up after them.

Did they think she — the immaculate and responsible Stella — never wanted to run away? Of course she did! But she quashed the desire. Like a renegade dandelion in a beautiful garden.

She didn't harbor desires and let them grow and grow — until one day they were so strong, they took over. She knew what to do with thoughts that ran counter to everything. You trounce them!

Clarissa approached Stella and placed her hand gently on her arm. She wanted to wrap her sister in a loving embrace but she knew she needed a cautious approach. And so Clarissa offered her sister sympathy.

"I know this doesn't feel fair," Clarissa said. "But we need to find her. We cannot leave her to her own devices. You know as well as I do that Jenna is too trusting."

"Maybe it's about time she learned," Stella said, unmoved. "If she wants adventure, let her have it."

Stella refused to look at Clarissa but she didn't brush off her hand. Clarissa decided that defending Jenna would get her nowhere. But appealing to Stella's duty might work.

"Yes," Clarissa conceded. "Jenna could use a lesson or two in real world consequences. We should leave her out there. See what happens." Clarissa paused for dramatic effect then added, "But we might be risking the safety of humanity."

"She should have thought of that before she disappeared," Stella countered. She wanted to stay indignant but she knew that Clarissa had a point.

"We don't know how this works without Jenna," Clarissa said. "Maybe we can pull the strings but we don't know if we'll have the same effect."

Stella stewed silently. They really had no idea what would happen with only two of them. Stella could already feel their dynamic effect was diminished.

Two was a powerful partnership. But there was a reason why the mightiest goddesses had three faces. Three was by far the more energetic combination. She could not risk what might happen with only two sisters pulling the strings of Fate.

"Well, I wish we could give Jenna room to shoot herself in the foot. But I cannot allow free will to gain the upper hand," Stella decided. "We know what humans are capable of when left to their own devices." She shot Clarissa a firm look.

Clarissa was relieved to see the fire back in Stella's belly. She hadn't realized how much she relied on Stella being the firm one. Her lack of wavering offered the structure that Clarissa and Jenna needed. Without it, she did not have the freedom to be wild and Jenna could not be so dreamy.

She placed her hands on each of Stella's shoulders. "Let's go."

Stella nodded her head. "Ready," she replied.

Clarissa picked up Stella's coat and handed it to her. Stella accepted the coat and slipped it on. For the first time in their tempestuous life, the sisters walked out of the apartment in peace.

"Should we bring the guardians?" Stella asked, as Clarissa locked the door.

"As wise as I think that would be," Clarissa replied, "I don't want to risk them reporting this to Zeus."

She pushed the elevator button willing the machine to appear. Which of course, it did. Happy to serve the two most powerful tenants in the building. They stepped inside their private chariot. Gliding to ground level without stopping on a single floor.

"We could ask for their silence," Stella offered, as they strode through the empty lobby.

"Those boys will always feel beholden to Zeus first and us second," Clarissa grumbled. "I swear they spy on us."

Stella followed Clarissa through the glass doors onto Park Avenue, nodding politely to the aging doorman. "Don't be paranoid, Clarissa. That's my job."

Clarissa stopped in her tracks, put her hands on her hips, and shot a look at her sister. "Stella Agnes Philomena Moirai. Did you just tell a joke?"

Stella restrained a smile and donned the illusion of being a fifty year old lawyer, complete with dark blue Armani suit. She walked up Park Avenue. Then called behind, "We have work to do."

Clarissa rolled her eyes and groaned. She donned an illusion as a younger lawyer dressed in a red Escada power suit. Then chased her sister up the street. Clarissa couldn't help but smile as she smacked Stella. Reminding her sister that Clarissa was by her side, no matter what came their way.

"So what's the plan?" Clarissa asked. The two sisters marched straight up the middle of the sidewalk, parting the waves of people as though they were a powerful ship on the ocean.

Stella walked in silence. She allowed her lightning fast mind free reign to see what might appear.

Her face lit up. "I know someone who can help," Stella said.

"Help without involving the big guns?" Clarissa asked.

"Oh yes," Stella replied, growing more confident with every step. "She has no interest in the establishment."

"Then how do you know her?" Clarissa asked. Then

backpedaled. "I mean ..."

Stella waved it off. She knew how she was perceived. "You assume I only ever hung out with the aristocrats. But to do our work, we always need extra assistance. The lower the profile, the better."

Clarissa was stunned. Stella was pulling out one surprise after another. She hadn't realized how her perceptions kept Stella packed in a tight box.

She was grateful for the breath of fresh air that blew through their lives. Though Clarissa could not help but wonder whether this escapade had been provoked. The timing felt suspicious.

She could not put her finger on it but she knew that Jenna running away so soon after Helen showing up was no coincidence. They were so used to pulling strings, they assumed no one could pull theirs.

What if that was no longer true? What if all it took was luring one away, leaving the other two vulnerable? Who would want to provoke them, challenging their roles for the first time in millennia? Was it a benevolent or malevolent force?

She stored the question away in the back of her mind — somewhere safe. For the moment, she was simply grateful that Jenna's rebellion had thrown open a window in their house.

Clarissa was thrilled to be outside among the living for the second time in days. And now, her stuffy and rule-fixated sister was taking her somewhere mysterious and illicit. *Could life get any better?*

She refrained from skipping. Knowing that her joyful action would send the wrong message to Stella. But she let the ecstasy of adventure course through her veins like adrenalin. Riding the glory as quietly as possible, while fanning her hands out to catch the wind.

Clarissa followed Stella north on Park Avenue. Her sister was in the zone. Focused on her destination; honed in on any threats. She trusted Stella to keep them safe.

They walked several more blocks in silence. Until Stella made a sharp turn into a dark, stone tunnel. Clarissa reminded herself that she had faith in her sister, as they stood in the darkness.

Clarissa thrived on mystery more than most creatures. But she was not a fan of awaiting fate in a dark tunnel. She knew how ironic that must seem. But she preferred adventures that kept moving. Not ones that awaited the crazed killer.

So when a looming figure appeared at the end of the tunnel and blocked out the streetlight, Clarissa gasped. Stella squeezed her sister's arm. Reassuring her.

Clarissa wasn't sure whether to be more or less nervous after her sister's gesture. But she held her breath and restrained from more outbursts. Which was more challenging than she expected as the figure moved toward them.

The large, verging on giant-sized man approached. Then stood assessing them for what Clarissa thought was an eternity. He reached in his pocket and thrust something at Stella. Clarissa refrained from leaping forward to protect her. Their filial connection assured her that Stella was not afraid.

Stella waited until the giant man retreated back out of the tunnel and into the shadows. Then, and only then, did Stella turn her hand over to reveal a white slip of paper.

Clarissa peered over as Stella opened the crumpled paper and read: "Meet me at 127 Bellows Terrace. Bring your sister.

No one else. Don't forget the payment."

Clarissa had so many questions. But she knew this wasn't the time. So she limited herself to one. "When?"

Stella didn't even turn. She slapped her hand into Clarissa's with the paper between their palms — sparking like a fuse. And declared, "Now!"

The two sisters disappeared in a brilliant flash of light.

CHAPTER TWENTY

Logan sat by the phone. Waiting for a signal that Helen had arrived. He knew there was a risk she would not return. He sighed. Logan hated this part of the job.

Sending new recruits on an errand that seems innocent enough but is really a test. The test operated on many levels. First, a positive temptation that might lure her away. Next, a disturbing occurrence that could stop her cold. And finally, the mental fears that might cause her to run. Any one of those hurdles could keep a candidate from returning.

He stood up and paced the windowless, basement room. He had no way to know if she was coming. That wasn't true. He did have ways. He was choosing not to engage them. Logan did not want to sway Helen. Like the proverbial butterfly effect, he knew if he used any method to watch her or track the fluctuations in her mood, he would never know for sure if she joined him from her free will.

He was alone and blind down here in the Bunker, as his staff called it. Purposefully choosing to be isolated until he knew whether she had returned. Now, he was getting restless. He did not get anxious. Lesser men chose that route. But he did need to move when he waited for a decision out of his control.

Logan knew Helen would have to confront her shadows, both light and dark, before she came back. And when the shadow is involved, the outcome is never predictable.

Ring! Ring!

Logan moved toward the desk and grabbed the receiver. "Yes?" Logan answered.

"Sir, we have a bit of a situation. We need you to come upstairs," the security guard said.

"What kind of situation?" Logan replied. "Can't you deal with it?"

"No, sir. I'm afraid we need your authority on this one."

"Fine," Logan grumbled and hung up.

Once he was down in the Bunker, he loathed leaving. This level put him in a specific headspace. Calm and focused.

He took a deep breath, pushed the elevator button, and readied himself for human interaction. The kind with niceties and deceptive language. Logan had learned years ago that humans liked to dance with meaning. And, quite honestly, he found the dance exhausting.

The elevator arrived. Logan stepped in and closed his eyes, travelling the distance to the lobby in darkness. He readied himself for whatever strange event had flummoxed his security staff.

Ding! The elevator doors opened, as did Logan's eyes. Before he moved a muscle, he could see that Helen was waiting in the lobby. His heart leaped with anticipation. She had returned. Just as quickly, his heart settled. She had someone with her.

Logan approached. His eyes locked on Helen and the young man at her side. He vaguely recognized her friend. Something about the set of his eyes and the color of his hair. Even the way the young man held himself, proud but not wanting to be noticed. Still, Logan couldn't put his finger on the familiarity.

As Logan drew closer, he saw that Helen was preparing to use her powers of charm and persuasion. Logan steeled himself.

"Logan!" she began. "I made it."

"Yes," he replied in a cool tone. "And you brought a friend."

"I did," she said, unfazed by his cold manner. She gestured between the two men. "Logan, this is Sam. Sam, Logan."

"Nice to meet you, sir," Sam extended his hand.

Logan put both of his hands behind his back. And stood looking at him. Sam pulled away his hand. He felt uncomfortable, but he did not drop Logan's gaze or look to Helen. Sam waited.

Logan appreciated Sam's steadiness. Especially when being scrutinized. Most young people attempted a verbal tap dance. But Sam was silent and respectful. Then there was the unnerving familiarity.

"Why are you here, Sam?" Logan asked.

"Sam helped me — " Helen began, until Logan's raised hand silenced her. His gaze did not waiver from Sam.

She raised an eyebrow, not appreciating the treatment. But Helen realized, as she watched the two men, that this conversation did not involve her. This was all about Sam. Logan needed to know his motivation. And Helen could not influence the outcome.

The lack of control infuriated her. Yet, she had a feeling she was going to have to get used to it. Not only to work with Logan, but to be part of a team. Even if he wanted her to be a leader, she was going to have to collaborate. Not manipulate or convince.

"I came to protect Helen. And to contribute to your cause,"

Sam replied.

"And what, precisely, do you believe that cause to be?" Logan asked. He might have mocked Sam's chivalry but he knew the young man meant every word. This was no romantic gesture. Sam would lay down his life for Helen.

"To save the world," Sam answered.

Logan laughed. Catching all of them off guard, including the security detail. Helen wondered whether he'd been drinking. The security guard stood up, expecting the old man to collapse. Sam stood his ground.

"Dear boy," Logan said, and leveled a bemused gaze at Sam. "I think you've been reading too many comic books."

"No," Sam replied. "But I did just return from Amsterdam." Sam paused to see if Logan would react. He swore there was a fluctuation in the old man's energy, but not an ounce of reaction on his face.

"Oh?" Logan replied, still regarding Sam with amusement.

"That's where I met David Troy," Sam continued. "I was his driver one night. I knew he was bad news. And I thought it was just me. That Troy was the creepy customer who got off on messing with the people who serve them."

Logan said nothing. But Sam had his attention. "So I got the hell out of town. Came back to New York. And on the same day I got back, I met Helen."

Sam glanced at her. She was staring at him. Half-amazed, half-terrified. He wasn't sure what to make of her reaction. But if he had wondered whether there was a connection between Helen and David Troy, he had his answer.

"What does that have to do with saving the world?" Logan asked.

"From the moment we met, my world shifted," Sam replied. "And not in the way you think." He paused. Sam knew his world had shifted in multiple ways after meeting Helen. But now was not the time to share the whole truth.

"I mean," he continued, "I knew I had to protect her. At first, I didn't know why or from who. But then I understood. I was meant to shield her from the very person I thought was gunning for me. But Troy wasn't after me, whether he knew it or not. He was gunning for Helen — *through* me."

Logan raised an eyebrow. This was unexpected. This young man spoke like he understood the intricacies of —

That's when it struck him. *The resemblance. Dear Gods and Centaurs.*

Logan blanched, and for the second time, the security guard stood up. Helen wondered what spooked the guard. Until she saw how Logan was staring at Sam. Like he had seen a ghost.

"Logan?" she asked. Logan didn't look at her. His gaze stayed fixed on Sam.

"Does the name Hekate mean anything to you?" Logan asked, in a low voice.

Sam hesitated, feeling his throat choke up. He took a moment to steady his emotions. Then replied, "That was my grandmother's name."

"Did you know her well?" Logan continued.

"Not really. She held me as a baby," Sam said, his gaze drifting as he recalled the memory. "I don't even know why I remember. But that was the only time I saw her. After that, my mother refused to let her near the family."

Logan nodded. Sam could see in Logan's face that he knew

much more about his family than Sam.

"Wait. How did you … " Sam began, confused. "Why did you ask about —"

"We can talk about that downstairs," Logan interrupted, walking toward the elevator.

Helen stared at Sam, then at Logan. She hadn't expected this day could get any weirder. She realized life was about to get more surprising than she had ever imagined.

She tapped Sam gently on the shoulder and said, "Let's go." Then followed Logan.

Sam hesitated. He finally walked in their direction because he had sworn to stay by Helen's side. But he was thrown by the old man's question. What had been a clear decision to protect Helen, now made him uneasy. Why had Logan asked about his grandmother? And how was *that* the information that made Logan trust him?

Logan turned to face Sam, pushing the elevator button.

"Your grandmother and I knew each other many lifetimes ago," Logan said, answering Sam's unspoken question. "I knew there was something familiar about you. Not how you look, exactly. But the way you stand. Your voice. And more than anything, how you talk about your gift."

"I didn't say anything about a gift," Sam protested.

Ding! The elevator door opened. Logan pierced Sam with his sharp gaze. "You most certainly did."

CHAPTER TWENTY-ONE

The two sisters appeared on the upper terrace of a rustic apartment complex. Clarissa looked around wondering where in the world they had landed. But she couldn't see any further than two feet. The whole place was surrounded in dense fog.

Clarissa glanced down over the railing. The old building only had a few floors. *Good thing*, she thought. Given the appearance, she had no idea how this rickety place was still standing. She also had no idea where they were. But she guessed that was the point.

Stella knocked on a bright fuchsia door. Clarissa noticed her sister was singularly focused. She wasn't looking around. Or curious about where they were. *She's been here before*, Clarissa thought.

The door swung open. No one stood at the threshold. Stella glanced at Clarissa and changed her illusory appearance to a casual outfit. Elegant pants with a blouse and tailored jacket. Clarissa followed suit, but donned more flamboyant colors.

Stella stepped inside, carefully and without a word. Clarissa hesitated, unnerved. But she could not leave Stella alone.

They walked over toys and shoes and rolls of paper towel.

Picking their way over the mess. Clarissa was a little horrified. "*Where are we?*" she whispered, not wanting to take another step but unwilling to leave.

Stella hushed her with a gesture of her hand. She continued leading Clarissa down the hallway, when a voice called out. "In here, Stella Bella."

"Stella Bella?" Clarissa repeated. And got a smack on the hand in return.

Stella walked further down the labyrinthine hallway, until Clarissa began to wonder whether they entered another dimension. She turned left then right then right again. Until they arrived in a kitchen.

By contrast, the kitchen was absolutely immaculate. Aside from one ashtray, overflowing with clove cigarettes. Through the smoke, a statuesque woman appeared like something out of a spy movie. Gorgeous but imposing.

Clarissa gasped and stepped back. But Stella moved forward, right into the arms of the mysterious old crone. She towered over Stella, pulling her into the tightest hug Stella had ever endured.

Until Clarissa realized she wasn't enduring it at all. Her stern sister was melting into an embrace. Like a lost child finding the arms of her mother. Clarissa felt she was witnessing an intimate moment. She dropped her eyes to the floor. Until the woman released her sister and stepped in Clarissa's direction.

"And this must be the infamous Clarissa," she declared. Holding her arms out, offering a hug. Clarissa wasn't sure whether her infamy was good or bad, but she stepped into the embrace all the same.

Instantly, she knew why Stella melted. Her hug was like

curling up in a safe nest and feeling protected. Like she had come home to a place where no cruelty could touch her. Clarissa felt loved deep in her core. Until this moment, she had never felt such pure acceptance.

When the woman's arms opened, Clarissa felt a little vulnerable and confused. She looked around, reorienting herself to the peculiar yet warm kitchen. The woman guided her to a chair next to Stella.

"We never had a chance to meet," the woman said, as she lifted the whistling kettle from the old wood stove.

Clarissa didn't remember the woman filling the kettle, let alone setting out three mugs and a teapot. She watched, still a bit dazed, as the woman poured water into the pot. The tea steeped instantaneously.

Their gorgeous host prepared each mug with just the right proportions of milk and sugar for each guest. She handed one to Stella, with a wink. Then one to Clarissa. The woman lifted her mug and blew the steam away with a luxurious attention that caused Clarissa to blush.

"By the time you came along," she continued, addressing Clarissa. "The powers that be didn't particularly want me associating with you and your sisters. Claimed I was a bad influence."

The crone grinned with appreciation for her reputation. She clearly wasn't fussed by the opinion of others, let alone the rule-makers. Clarissa liked her immediately. But she could see the loss was painful for Stella. Her sister wiped away a tear. The woman touched her hand in comfort.

"Clarissa," Stella said, when she had regained her composure, "This is my godmother, Lilith."

Clarissa practically spat her tea across the room. She caught herself, resulting in a massive coughing fit. She managed to get her mug on the table. Stella glared at her, upset with her reaction, but Lilith burst into gales of laughter.

"Weren't expecting that?" Lilith chortled. And pulled out a bottle of tequila to add a splash of spice to her tea.

Lilith offered it to Stella who shook her head. Then to Clarissa, who nodded. Lilith smiled. And added a large dollop of liquor to the hot liquid. Clarissa took a drink. The hot tea and fiery alcohol twisted and burned down her throat, yet the combination soothed her nerves.

This day was getting more and more interesting, Clarissa thought. First Jenna bolts for the hills and now Stella reveals her unorthodox, secret godmother. Clarissa thought she had seen everything. But this took the cake.

"Right! How could I forget?" Lilith exclaimed, as though Clarissa had spoken out loud.

She jumped up and pulled out a seven-layer, dark chocolate cake from the fridge. Lilith lowered the cake in front of Stella, smiling with satisfaction. Clarissa had the distinct feeling Lilith had concocted the tower of chocolate in honor of all the birthdays she had missed.

"I made it myself," Lilith declared, as she cut a huge piece for each of them. Clarissa tucked into hers. Practically cooing at the incredible taste of this sweet delicacy. Stella picked up her fork, but let it hang over the dessert.

"Thank you," Stella said, looking with tenderness at her godmother. Lilith nodded, acknowledging the loss that hung between them. "I don't mean to rush our visit, but we need to find Jenna."

"Of course," Lilith replied, wiping chocolate icing from her mouth. "This kind of work cannot be done on an empty stomach, though, Stella. You must take a bite."

Stella complied. Filling her fork with dark chocolate goodness and forcing herself to eat. As far as Clarissa had come in understanding her sister, she did not understand that. The cake was pure divinity wrapped in butter and cocoa.

Clarissa finished her first piece and held up her plate for another. Lilith complied with a delighted smile. Placing one piece on Clarissa's plate then one on her own. Lilith put her fork at its side, promising the cake she would return soon for their rendezvous.

Then Lilith sat up tall and closed her eyes. Clarissa was struck with the goddess's breathtaking radiance. She had to be over twelve millennia old but she glowed like a young woman. Her gorgeous silver hair careened down her back and her silken robe caressed her elegant figure, showing off every luscious curve.

Clarissa had often been flattered for her sensuality and beauty. But she was a pale lantern next to this bonfire. She could only imagine what she might have learned had she been raised with a godmother like Lilith. Which was the precise reason their parents banished her.

She snuck another bite of cake as Lilith lit up with power. Her essence shone brighter than all the lights in Times Square. Clarissa swore Lilith could give Venus a run for her title. This goddess beamed with the natural light of confidence.

Clarissa was so in awe, she forgot to ask whether she was supposed to help. Lilith reached out and clasped each of their hands. The two sisters responded, bowing their heads. They completed the circle.

Stella and Clarissa felt the surge of power rush through their bodies. They knew and controlled high levels of current but this was unlike anything the sisters had experienced. Clarissa focused to keep up with the surge of energy. The simultaneous force of light, sensation, and sound took her breath away.

Clarissa realized — not for the first time that day — that even the Fates must remember they were not the source of power. They were a conduit.

She thought of Jenna. A flicker of worry passed through her, then all doubt emptied from her body. Clarissa felt her limbs fill with the most incredible feeling of peace and faith, combined with a rush of adrenalin.

Clarissa felt the wave of calm flow through her, pass to Stella, move on to Lilith then come round again. Each time the wave circled, the feeling strengthened. Until the three of them were but a ripple in time and space. Clarissa no longer knew where she ended and the others began.

Lilith whispered in their minds, speaking words rhythmically, like a gentle incantation. "Beautiful Jenna, you have slipped from our circle. You believe you must run away to be found. But such was never so. You are one with us. Ever connected. Ever held. Ever loved. Show yourself. Light up our vision like the star we know you to be. Shine for us, Jenna."

Lilith paused for a second. Stella picked up the incantation intuitively. As though the three women had been making music together for years.

"Jenna, my sister," Stella spoke. "Return to the fold where

you belong. We know your heart. We honor your soul. And we long for your safe return. Reveal your wisdom to us, Jenna, so that we can follow you."

Stella swayed with the rhythm of their invocation. Clarissa felt the passing of the tune to her. She was the least familiar with the rhythm of this particular music but she was the improviser in the family. And so, followed the melody without effort.

"My sister, my light," Clarissa incanted. "Show me the way to your heart. Reveal your lessons to me. Light my path. Burn my soul. And be with me again until the end of eternity."

Lilith pressed their hands tighter, lighting up the room with their brilliance. Stella and Clarissa felt the surge burst through them. Until, in the center space, a vivid image of Jenna appeared.

Jenna stood before them. Life-like in three dimensions. Aside from her reduced size and soft glow, her sisters would have thought Jenna was in the room.

Jenna stood on the street. Next to a stairwell that led to a subway station. She looked both exhilarated and terrified. Jenna watched a strong woman in a brown leather jacket flag down a cab.

The car that stopped was not a taxi. But a dark blue, elegant Mercedes. The woman tucked Jenna behind her. She was unnerved by the car and looked around, gauging if they had the chance to run.

The driver stepped out, looming over the car. He stared at the woman in the leather jacket. Commanding her to step aside. The woman glared back, then barked an order at Jenna and shoved her away from the car.

But the driver was too fast. He appeared in front of Jenna in a flash. Grabbed her arm and dragged her toward the vehicle. He knocked the woman out of his way, opened the back door, and threw Jenna inside.

The driver turned to handle the woman in leather. But she stared him down, spat at his feet, and claimed the shotgun position. Slamming the door behind her. The driver hesitated, not sure how to handle this unexpected turn. Then shrugged and opened his door.

As Jenna sat up in the back seat, the hologram shifted to follow her. She was not alone. A dark-haired, mysterious man was waiting — David Troy. She gasped and turned to bolt, only to have the door lock. Jenna tried the handle. But the door did not relent. She was trapped.

The car sped forward, throwing Jenna back against the seat. She pushed far away from David. Then turned to face him. His eerie smile revealed delight. Like the cat who had caught the canary.

The light dissipated and Jenna's image disappeared. The power surge drained and their hands unclasped. Clarissa and Stella folded forward, unused to the immense energy that had lit up then left their bodies in a matter of seconds.

Clarissa and Stella stared at one another in disbelief. Jenna in the hands of David Troy. Their worst nightmare had come true.

Lilith nodded toward their plates and said, "I recommend you both finish your cake." Then took a drink of tea.

For the first time in centuries, Stella and Clarissa were afraid. David Troy had their sister. There was no telling what that man would do. Or what he had planned. But of one thing they were sure, he had been hoping for this moment for a long time.

Waiting for a chance to exact his revenge.
    And now he had it.

CHAPTER TWENTY-TWO

elen stared in awe. She wasn't often taken by surprise so that her mouth hung open. But this was one of those moments.

She and Sam followed Logan into what could only be called a command center. A room roughly the size of a large theatre. Rows upon rows of computers. Large screens for sharing critical information. People having huddled conversations. The closest Helen had ever seen was NASA. And this was much more impressive.

"Welcome to IRIS," Logan said. "I need to check with my Chief Guardians of the four directions. The updates won't take long. Then we'll get started."

She was mesmerized. Taking in the impressive structure as Logan descended the stairs to the main floor. Helen and Sam stayed glued to their spot. Stunned by thousands of screens displaying scenes around the world.

As far as Helen could tell, the room was divided into four quadrants – north, south, east, and west. North had the top tier. East and West shared the middle tier, wrapped along the sides of the room. And South had the main tier.

Each had a Chief Guardian, an imposing figure that towered

over his staff. Analysts tracked events, calling over supervisors when they needed assistance.

Helen wondered whether the analysts paid attention to country borders or if the areas were archaic. *Were they tracking people or regions?* She wondered. *Did they look for events? Anomalies? Did they watch regardless?*

She had so many questions. Her eyes were glued on Logan as he conversed with the Chief Guardian of the South. Aside from the Guardian's impressive height, she knew he was powerful. She could sense his strength. Or maybe she felt his insight.

Then the Chief Guardian of the South turned and stared at her. Helen gasped. She caught a glimpse of enormous wings tucked behind his back. She wasn't sure if the feathers had caught the light or fluttered in the air. She only saw them for a second. But they took her breath away.

Helen checked to see if Sam had noticed. He looked mystified but didn't say anything. His eyes were riveted on the Guardian. Sam had seen something but maybe he dismissed what he saw or couldn't process the information.

Either way, she wasn't ready to broach the subject. She didn't even know what a Guardian was. He wasn't an angel. He felt too earthly. Yet not quite of the earth. Maybe a demi-god? Of the air?

She watched Logan as he climbed from the main tier to the second tier. Finished with the South and moved on to the East. He must have anticipated that she and Sam would need time to process.

As she watched his interaction with the Chief Guardian of the East, Helen realized Logan brought them here for more than reports and acquainting them with IRIS. As with the first Guardian, she noticed a pause in the conversation, then a look in her direction. Logan's organization was being informed of her arrival.

Helen wasn't sure they were impressed. But she didn't hold much stock in the opinions of strangers. Even demi-gods. Then she realized no one looked at Sam. Maybe they assumed if Sam mattered, Logan would tell them in due course.

Except the omission was significant. If Logan wasn't bothering to introduce Sam, he wasn't convinced that Sam was here to stay. She felt a flare of indignation, wanting Logan to trust her instincts.

Until Helen realized that Logan had trusted her. He interviewed Sam on the spot. Instead of telling his guard to throw Sam out the door. And now Sam was here at her side.

Helen was amazed that Sam found her. *Who manages to track a stranger in a city with millions of people?* Never mind his mysterious grandmother, Hekate.

She glanced at Sam, fascinated. Looking at him caused butterflies in her stomach. A sensation that frustrated her. Helen didn't have time for fluttery feelings. Romantic sentiments clouded judgment.

Not that she was thinking about romance with Sam, Helen insisted. Locking her gaze back on Logan. She was focused. Determined. Ready to save the world. But as hard as she stared, she couldn't circumvent the sensations coursing through her body, demanding that she grab Sam and kiss him.

She risked another glance in his direction. And was saved by his awe-struck expression. The fluttery feelings calmed and curiosity took over.

"So what do you think?" she whispered in his direction.

"I can't believe it," Sam replied, staring at the screens. "It's like they have a view on every corner of the world. Is that possible?"

"I think so," Helen replied. She watched Logan conclude his meeting with the Chief Guardian of the West. One more to go.

She had a small window before Logan returned. She wanted to fill Sam in. She sensed Logan would keep those cards close. She felt Sam deserved to know what he was getting into. And, if she were honest, she wanted to give him an advantage. So he would stay.

"How much do you know about the Fates?" she asked.

"You mean the sisters from mythology?" he replied. She could feel his mind whirring. Wondering why she brought up such an obscure reference.

Helen nodded. She kept her gaze on Logan. Watching Logan listening, then explaining Helen's presence, followed by the Guardian sizing her up. She was less bothered by the scrutiny with each repetition.

"Yes," Helen replied. "The three sisters that weave threads that dictate people's lives."

"Right," Sam said. Then stared at the screens depicting people's lives, world events, strange occurrences in dark corners. *No. That's not possible.* He felt Helen's gaze, willing him to understand something she had not yet said.

"Are they messing with people's lives?" he whispered, indicating Logan and his Guardians.

"I think they monitor them," Helen ventured.

"Like the NSA," Sam said, not sure how he felt about the comparison. Except he knew Logan didn't work for the government.

Helen knew Sam wasn't getting it. She didn't know how to spell this out. She wasn't subtle at the best of times. Let alone with unfathomable realities.

"Kind of," she said. "Except they're monitoring for the Fates."

"What? Like a covert operation?" Sam asked. "Is Logan black ops?"

He wondered if Helen might laugh at him, as Logan had upstairs. But her expression was not only serious, it was uneasy. Sam saw she was tracking Logan. As Logan finished his final report with the North, Helen grew impatient.

"No," Helen replied, exasperated. "The Fates. The three sisters that run the world."

Sam shot her a look. "Hilarious. Haze the new guy."

"I'm not hazing you, Sam," Helen said. "I'm trying to tell you something that is hard to explain. Let alone comprehend."

"Okay," Sam said, confused. "If you're serious, spell it out for me."

Helen saw Logan stepping down the last series of stairs. She didn't have much time. Maybe Sam was right. Maybe there was no subtle way to explain this.

"The three Fates," Helen said. "Three immortals who orchestrate events, weaving the direction of the universe. They're real."

Sam stared. He wanted to laugh. But he knew she wasn't kidding. He liked Helen. He trusted her. But this was beyond weird. This made him wonder whether she had bumped her head.

She kept glancing in Logan's direction like this was a secret she shouldn't be sharing. Sam didn't know how to feel. The whole thing was preposterous.

Sam looked around. The cameras. The screens. The views of the Egyptian pyramids to Tiananmen Square to the Midwestern wheat fields to a familiar red oak tree in Central Park. *The oak tree.*

Sam was startled to see his special spot on the monitoring screens. The trigger prompted his mind to leap through a series of events from the past 48 hours. His encounter with David Troy. Coming home. Meeting Helen. Reconnecting with his childhood gift. Meeting Logan. All bizarre and inexplicable. One might even say …

"Fated," he whispered, stunned. Sam stared at Helen. Piece by piece, a puzzle clicked in his mind. "You're not kidding."

"Not even a little," Helen replied. They glanced simultaneously in Logan's direction. He stepped off the final stair, past the South tier, and crossed the floor. He would reach Helen and Sam in a matter of minutes.

"Logan works for them," Helen continued. "I'm guessing this is their operation."

Sam was floored. He wanted to argue. To dispute this outrageous idea. But in his gut, he knew it was true. As crazy as the whole thing sounded, Helen offered him a bridge into her reality.

"Why are you telling me this?" Sam asked.

"You deserved to know," she replied.

"And you're not sure Logan's going to let me stay," Sam added.

Helen nodded. Then turned to check on Logan. He was closing in on the staircase that lead up to where they stood.

"So you've met them," Sam stated. But Helen knew it was a question.

Helen hesitated. She hadn't foreseen this little twist to the conversation. How could she be so stupid? Of course, he would ask if she'd met them. Trouble was, even standing in the big command center, her old promise never to tell a soul reared its head.

Logan climbed the staircase. Soon he would be within earshot. She had to make a choice. She liked him way more than she had any reason to like someone so fast. Heck, she risked bringing him here. *What was the big deal? Why couldn't she force herself to say, "Yes. Yes, I saw them in the flesh and blood. And not only that, they wanted me to see them."*

But her lips stayed sealed.

Sam could see Helen was struggling. He wanted to help but he was holding out hope that the lives of every person on the planet were *not* run by three controlling sisters. He would rather Logan had fed Helen the scenario. Or she had dreamt it up to explain away some very strange events.

Those ideas made him feel better than thinking her story could be true. Maybe this operation orchestrated people's fates. Like a top-secret combination of the CIA, NSA, FBI, and Homeland Security. Given how the world had changed, that wouldn't be so strange.

But not as outrageous as the notion the world was run by three immortal sisters. That was a floodgate of crazy. Opening the door for the existence of gods, for example. Nope. Sam was holding firm to his reality.

He waited for Helen to say something. But for the first time since they'd met, she was at a loss for words.

Logan arrived. He felt the awkward silence. At first, Logan

assumed they'd discussed something they didn't want him to hear. Then he knew the awkwardness was between them. *Interesting*, Logan thought. Then set it aside. He would broach it later.

"Follow me," Logan said.

He led them to a steel door. Pulled a set of keys from his pocket and slid one into the lock. Opening his executive office.

Helen was startled by the contrast between this room and Logan's upstairs office. Compared to the elegant space on the sixty-first floor, this room was minimalist and cold. There were subtle touches — like old-style maps, messages on paper, and no computer. But this looked like a General's headquarters where hard decisions were made and few distractions desired.

She had formed a certain image of Logan. And this precise and efficient commander jarred. She preferred to think of him as a kind uncle who happened to help the most powerful women in the cosmos.

Sam, on the other hand, was impressed. The maps and papers calmed him. Logan's office felt like a hideaway he pictured Churchill using in wartime. The décor spoke of efficiency, clarity, and control. The promise made Sam want to be part of what Logan was doing. He could feel the importance. The gravity.

He was sure now that Helen had been playing some kind of prank. Sam shook his head. He might have known the two of them would pull something. He didn't take Logan for the trickster type but Helen must have talked him into the joke. Maybe this meant he had passed the test.

As Logan sorted through his papers, Sam glanced over at Helen. He wanted to wink so she knew he was onto her. She should expect payback. Sam grinned. But when he saw the confusion on her face, he dropped the plan. There was something about this room that threw her.

She was a carefree soul. Maybe the military atmosphere of this secret office pushed old buttons. Though he guessed that under her make-life-up-as-she-went-along attitude was a desire for order and reason. Much like his own.

Sam made his way over to Helen. He brushed his arm against hers. No matter what had thrown her, he was by her side. Sam was careful to be gentle. He didn't want to spook her. She must have needed a friend more than he realized because she didn't move away. She leaned in.

Electricity shot through his arm. He almost stopped breathing. Her touch was so charged. Sam forced himself to focus on sending her reassurance. He had reached out to help. He needed to keep that in mind, despite his body's reaction.

Logan glanced up, sensing a shift in the room. He saw Helen and Sam nestled up to one another. Logan wondered whether Helen would shift away. Perhaps feeling awkward. Instead she stared at Logan like she wasn't sure who he was. And Sam was providing much-needed comfort.

"Excellent. You two have met," came a female voice behind them.

Logan stood up straight and Helen and Sam whipped around. Helen gasped. When Sam saw her face, he stared at the women. They couldn't be.

"The Fates," Helen whispered to him.

"But there's only two," Sam protested.

Helen didn't have an answer. "They're definitely the Fates," she replied with a concerned tone. "One of them is missing."

Sam stared at two sisters who were far from his image of the Fates. They were not Greek goddesses or Elizabethan witches. Though, if he were to imagine two self-assured sorceresses in elegant modern attire, they would match. Never mind that the power radiating off them felt like an electrical storm in August.

"Clarissa. Stella." Logan said. "To what do I owe the honor?"

"We're out of time," Stella replied. "Troy has declared war."

"How?" Helen asked.

Clarissa stared at Helen with a force that almost made her pass out.

"He abducted Jenna," Clarissa said. "We must prepare for battle."

CHAPTER TWENTY-THREE

ogan knew the sisters were in crisis mode. But Helen was not ready to be on assignment. Especially one this critical. She had no training. No instruction. She didn't even know how IRIS worked.

"Clarissa, may we speak in private?" Logan inquired.

"No," Helen interjected, unable to remove her gaze from the sisters. She couldn't believe they were standing in front of her. Real. Alive. Like she remembered. Except one. "If this concerns me, I want to be part of the conversation."

"This concerns Jenna, first and foremost," Logan said. "We'd be risking both of them by putting Helen in a situation she's not ready for."

"Aren't we in more danger if I don't step up?" Helen asked. She was arguing with Logan but her gaze stayed on the sisters.

Clarissa smiled, knowing Helen must have many questions. As much as she loved a dramatic entrance, Clarissa envisioned a much different reunion with Helen. She wished they had more time.

"She's right," Stella replied before Logan could argue. Stella stepped past a stunned Sam, before placing her hand on Logan's desk.

"Logan," she continued. "I agree with you, philosophically. Helen is not ready. This is absolutely the wrong way to initiate her. But Jenna is in danger. We have no choice."

Stella turned her gaze to Helen. Scrutinizing and imploring her with one look. "Helen understands David better than any of us," she continued. "They have a special connection. One we must trust. Despite the treacherous circumstances."

Logan was thrown by Stella's earnestness. He had never seen her flustered, let alone anxious. "Troy has eluded us time after time," Stella said. "And his power has grown over the past year. The only advantage we have is Helen."

"I'm not much of an advantage," Helen said, believing the sisters deserved the truth. "I don't know David. He may as well be a stranger."

"You forget, dear Helen," Clarissa interjected, "that blood is thicker than water. Those words are more than a quaint saying. The blood you share is like two rivers that flow to the same sea. Though you were not raised together, you understand on a subconscious level every twist, turn, and move your brother makes."

"We're talking about from a distance, right?" Sam interrupted. He was still in shock and hadn't been invited to the discussion. But he was damn well going to speak up to stop them from putting Helen in Troy's path.

"No, Sam," Logan asserted, recognizing an ally. "They're talking tactical. On the street."

"Are you crazy?" Sam asked. Stepping forward, to put himself physically between these insane immortals and Helen.

"Sam, relax," Helen said. She was touched but this was her battle.

"You haven't met this guy, Helen," Sam countered. "There's something dark and twisted about him. He'll hurt you for entertainment."

"I have met him," Helen said.

"What?" Logan and Sam responded.

"When I was packing my apartment," Helen explained. "He showed up out of the blue."

"And you didn't think to mention it?" Sam asked, stepping toward her. Wanting to take her hand. Wishing they had crossed that bridge of familiarity, so he could pull her out of this place and insist that they run. *Now.*

"We've had a lot going on," she replied. "I was planning to tell you when the time was right."

"I believe the time is right," Logan said.

The two sisters did not say a word. They already knew Troy had confronted Helen. Not because they orchestrated the meeting but because they read her reaction the moment they mentioned David.

Helen's adrenalin had spiked to a level that revealed she came face to face with him. Now they saw the sudden encounter was for the best. If Helen was going to take him on, she needed to know what she was up against.

"I was ready to leave," Helen explained, "when he appeared in my doorway. I don't know if he already had Jenna. But he came to figure out who I was and get a sense of my talents. I don't think he was impressed. "

"If we're going to have this conversation," Logan commented, conceding he lost the battle of keeping Helen out of this, "then I recommend we close the door."

Clarissa swept her hand. She enjoyed the startled look on Sam's face as the door slammed closed. Even in the midst of terrible circumstances, she couldn't resist a playful moment. *Without joy, what was the point?* Clarissa pulled out a chair to join the others sitting in front of Logan's desk.

"Even if Helen understands David intuitively," Logan continued, "she has no training for battle. He would assess her weaknesses in the blink of an eye. We'll lose her before we gain the advantage."

Helen blanched. She hadn't heard Logan speak of her death. Hearing him say it in point-blank terms brought the reality home. She wanted to be brave. To be her brazen self. But this was a frightening game.

"You're assuming," Clarissa said, patting Helen's arm, "that we're sending her in without support."

"No. Logan is right," Stella said. "We cannot in good conscience send the girl in without *some* preparation."

"Stella, we talked about this," Clarissa replied in a lowered voice, "We don't have time. Every moment he has Jenna —"

"You're assuming he knows what to do with Jenna," Sam interrupted. He approached a white board behind Logan's desk. Sam picked up a marker and looked to Logan for permission. Logan nodded.

"Of course he knows," Stella asserted, glaring at Logan and Sam. Sam kept his back to Stella. Not wanting to be thrown by her power.

"No," Sam said, honing in on his memory of Troy. Like when he focused on a lost person. Sam recalled every detail from Troy's gaze to his movements to each word he spoke. Or did not speak.

Sam wrote down a corresponding list of David's strengths and weaknesses. Fluid. Instinctive. Creative. Spontaneous. Incisive. As he wrote, Sam was amazed. He had always been great at reading people but this was impressive.

Sam realized opening up to his gift in the park must have given him insight into more than location. As he recalled their encounter, Sam sensed Troy's traits like a kind of signature. Or frequency.

"I don't think he does," Sam began. "Troy's an opportunist. I bet he didn't plan this. Either he lucked into seeing Jenna or someone brought her to him. Either way, he hasn't figured out what to do with her."

"Luck?" Stella seethed, pushing her chair back. Clarissa placed a gentle hand on her shoulder, guiding a fuming Stella to her seat.

"Even if that's true," Clarissa said. "What does it matter? David won't waste time. He'll hurt her. Torture her. Force her to give up all kinds of knowledge. Maybe even drive her mad. Which I promise you, young man, is a fate worse than death."

With both sisters against him, Sam froze. He couldn't refute the onslaught. Logan followed Sam's logic, and picked up a marker as though he were taking the baton in a relay race. Sparring with the Fates didn't fluster Logan.

"If we rush in," Logan said, "We'll be giving David the advantage. In fact..." Logan paused as he underscored a few of David's strengths: spontaneous, flexible, fast thinking. "He is the master of chaotic decisions. If we come in unprepared and improvising, we'll be playing to his strengths. And he will best us in no time."

"Giving him more than Jenna," Helen implied.

"Right," Sam said, shocked he hadn't seen it before. "She's the bait."

"Wait," Stella objected. "You insisted David didn't plan this."

"He didn't," Helen interrupted. "But you can bet the moment he had her, he knew there was bigger action at stake than just one sister."

Helen stood up, full of energy. She rushed to the whiteboard, grabbing her own marker and not waiting for Sam or Logan. She wrote "gambler."

"You're right," Helen said, turning to Clarissa and Stella. "I *do* know my brother. He's a gambler at heart. He would never be satisfied with only one Fate when he could have all three."

The room fell silent. As urgently as the two sisters wanted Jenna back, they could not deny the truth. To launch a rescue without a strategy would play right into David's hands.

Clarissa slammed her hand down on Logan's desk, furious. She held her tongue, knowing the manifesting power — and infinite repercussions — of her words. But she wanted to curse David Troy to the ninth circle of hell next to Count Ugolino and Archbishop Ruggieri.

Stella placed her hand on Clarissa's, understanding her wrath. Under the anger was powerlessness. Stella's heart was breaking. As the oldest, Jenna was her responsibility. After an innocent attempt to seek freedom, Jenna had landed in grave danger.

Stella should have seen this coming. Her job was to see the warning signs. And she had missed them in her own sister. Stella desperately wanted to fix her mistake. So desperately, in fact, that she wanted to ride in on a white horse and rescue Jenna. Balancing the scales for her lack of attention.

Stella understood she would have to risk her sister's wellbeing a little longer.

"What," Stella asked Logan, "would you recommend we do?"

Logan paused. All eyes rested on him. Waiting for an answer. Logan evaluated the whiteboard, weighing David's strengths and weaknesses. He assumed David was counting on them being upset and acting rashly. David could win based on his quick response but his greatest weakness, however, was lack of patience.

"We spend the rest of the night on strategy," Logan began. "We have file after file on Troy. But never before have we had his sister. Helen needs to read up on his exploits, gain insight into his psychology. She may know him intuitively but his history will help her to understand his tactics."

Helen nodded, understanding the consequence of her position. She would have to set aside the nerves in her stomach and the doubts in her mind.

"Sam can assist Helen," Logan added. "If he's going to protect her in the field, he needs more than one encounter with Troy. He must know exactly what he's up against. Then they can brainstorm ideas."

Sam and Helen looked at one another. This was as official as Logan might get. Sam was part of the team. If they weren't going head to head with a man gunning for their destruction, they would be hugging.

"And you're forcing us to sit and wait?" Clarissa fumed.

"Absolutely not," Logan replied. "You, Stella, and I are

going to take the fifty thousand foot view. Even if Troy did not plan this, we need to regroup and consider what his master plan is now."

"You mean what he would use us for," Clarissa clarified.

"Precisely," Logan said.

"Knowing David, he had something in motion," Stella commented. "Finding Jenna advanced a plan he was already fostering. Waiting for the right time to hatch."

"Does he have a grudge against you?" Helen asked, surprising the sisters.

"I wouldn't say that, exactly," Clarissa began.

"Of course he does," Stella protested, shaking her head. "That man couldn't take responsibility for his actions if we gave him the reins and told him to ride off into the sunset."

"What did you do?" Sam asked, curiosity spurring his bravery. Helen smiled, delighted he was finding his feet with the sisters.

"Nothing more than we do with everyone else," Clarissa replied, seeing Stella was too furious to speak. "But the intense ones have a harder time. They tend to take things personally. Whether they want to admit it or not, they chose a more arduous path. Usually their soul is up for the challenge. Unfortunately, they don't remember asking for the advanced course. And in David's case, he blames us."

"For what?" Helen asked. "For being an orphan?"

"Being an orphan, losing his parents, not being an immortal, having to pick up his own dry cleaning," Stella replied, fuming. "You name the event, he blames us. He's never once shown gratitude for the beautiful things in his life. Like his natural talents.

Or the strength he built fending for himself. No. He has to focus on how hard life has been and who's done him wrong."

"Meaning us," Clarissa added.

"There must be something more," Helen probed. "Something more personal."

"More personal than losing your parents?" Sam whispered under his breath.

"Yes," Helen said. "Or more recent." She corrected the idea, pausing to hear her intuition. "Sometimes an incident that aggravates the scar is more tender than the original wound. The pain is easier to feel."

She could feel how intently every person in the room was listening. Helen took a deep breath. And plunged into vulnerable waters.

"Trust me," she continued. "I've spent plenty of nights railing against Fate, God, the universe. I wanted to blame anybody and everybody for being an orphan. But eventually you realize it doesn't make a difference. They aren't coming back. So … it's not personal. It's just your particular brand of pain."

"But you have insight, Helen," Logan replied. "Your brother does not. He has no interest in asking why these things happened to him. He wants someone else to suffer because he has suffered. He thinks, in his twisted belief system, that if he causes another person pain, he will feel less."

"It's more than that," Clarissa said. She paused as all eyes landed on her.

Clarissa had not shared this with anyone, especially not Stella. She did not want to reveal her secret now. But all she could think about was Jenna, and the fact that her sister was going to pay for a mistake Clarissa made.

She glanced at Stella. Wishing she did not have to ruin the peaceful alliance they shared since Jenna had run away. For the first time, she had her sister's respect. She lamented losing it.

Stella returned Clarissa's look with inquisitiveness. She had no idea where Clarissa was leading. But she could feel the unnerving sensation of a secret ready to unfold. The past few hours had turned her world upside-down. And now there was another surprise on the horizon.

"David is upset about those things," Clarissa began, "but he's most upset about me."

"You?" Stella asked. "Why would he be upset with you? Everything we did, we did as a team."

"Not in this instance," Clarissa confessed.

"Clarissa," Stella scolded, "don't take responsibility because you cannot help Jenna. Playing the martyr won't rescue her."

"I'm not," Clarissa insisted, as a slow blush bloomed across her cheeks. Clarissa avoided Stella's gaze. And for a woman who expressed herself with ease, she had gone breathtakingly silent.

The truth hit Helen like a bolt of lightning.

"Oh my god," Helen blurted out, intuiting what Clarissa had done. Then seeing Clarissa's startled expression, Helen covered her mouth and lowered her gaze. This was not her secret to share.

Sam, Logan, and Stella stared at Helen. Wondering what she had figured out. They looked at Clarissa. They puzzled over Helen's realization but did not say a word.

Stella turned to her sister. "What did you do?" she insisted.

"Well, to be fair," Clarissa offered, "it's more what I didn't do."

Stella looked around at the lowered eyes. No one made eye contact with either sister. This was for Stella and Clarissa to work out. Not a soul in the room was foolish enough to interfere in a fight between the Fates.

Then a light bulb went on for Stella. She stared at Clarissa. Angry. Disbelieving. Imagining what might have happened. As everyone waited for the sisters to speak, the silence grew deafening.

Finally, Stella forced herself to ask the question.

"Did you toy with that boy's heart?" Stella demanded. "Are you really going to force me to feel *sorry* for David Troy? The greatest threat this planet has known in centuries. All because *you* couldn't keep your amorous advances to your own kind? Not only did you lust after a human, you had to choose an unstable one?"

Clarissa knew her sister was furious. She wished she could accept the anger, let her sister vent, and skip telling her side of the story. For once, be the bigger immortal. But she had held the secret for so long Clarissa needed to release the truth.

"I didn't mean for it to happen, Stella, I swear," Clarissa said. "It was the year we were most worried about him. He was eighteen and so lost."

Stella turned away. Logan shook his head. So Clarissa told her story to the rapt audience of Sam and Helen.

"At eighteen," Clarissa explained, "David was lost. On the cusp of adulthood, he had no idea what to do with his life. He had always been different. He knew he couldn't take the normal path. But David was young enough to want to belong. To believe that somewhere, somehow, love might be waiting."

Sam folded his arms, doubtful that Troy had ever felt love.

But Helen sensed the honesty in Clarissa's words and leaned in.

"That year," Clarissa continued, "we took turns keeping watch. We knew he was volatile and his emotions were charged. We wanted to be sure he wouldn't strike out at the world."

"But history is filled with tyrants who have done just that," Helen commented. "Humanity is still standing."

"Yes," Clarissa conceded. "But the world has never encountered a man who could wipe out the human race in days were his full powers unleashed. We had to be ready if he showed any possibility of melting down. David didn't know the strength of his powers. I'm still not convinced he does. Though as each year passes, he seems to understand more."

"Why would you ever give a human being so much destructive potential?" asked Sam. Realizing as the question left his lips, that it sounded like an accusation. Logan stared at Sam, wondering if the young man had lost his mind.

"The simple answer," Stella interjected, eerily calm. Like a volcano awaiting the right moment to blow. "Is that we don't always know the outcome when two lovers get together. We could not have predicted every possibility of David's parents finding one another then having a child. Even with our vast wisdom, the universe is infinitely mysterious. Isn't it, Clarissa?"

"I know you're angry," Clarissa protested. "But nothing happened. It was only a flirtation."

Stella's face turned bright red. "And I should be thrilled you didn't throw yourself at him like Zeus? You broke the no romances with humans law. Which, I might add, was put in place to prevent precisely this kind of disaster. But worse, you broke the boy's heart. Did you not, for a moment, think that could be the incendiary act to turn him into a weapon?"

Clarissa knew she had broken the rules. And while she normally would have the spirit to challenge Stella on her rigid and conformist opinions, she didn't have the heart to argue now that Jenna was in danger.

"Maybe," Helen offered, an idea forming as she talked, "Clarissa thought her attention might sway David to the path of love. Not hate."

Stella glared at Helen. Her silent fury sent waves of fire down Helen's spine. Helen held her stare and prayed that Stella's silence meant she was considering the point. Clarissa gazed at Helen with such gratitude that the cool breeze of peace countered the heat emanating from Stella. Saving Helen's nervous system.

"In fact," Helen considered, "Clarissa's romantic mishap might be the advantage we need."

All eyes were on Helen. Not a single person understood. She wasn't sure herself. But Helen had an instinct and decided to run with it.

"Logan," Helen said, standing. She was energized by the first ray of hope since hearing of Jenna's plight.

"Show me David's files."

CHAPTER TWENTY-FOUR

David sat in a metal chair, across from Jenna. He had her bound and gagged in case she was able to pull magic tricks without her evil sisters by her side. David had plenty of his own tricks but he didn't need to take chances.

The room was dark and vast and verging on cliché. But David couldn't resist the impact of a dank, eerie space. The emptiness stole hope from the heart. The dampness robbed the body of heat. And the darkness made the eyes struggle and the conscious mind shut down. So many little touches he appreciated.

He supposed, like most things that became clichés, they had been brilliant the first time. Now, they looked overdone.

David shifted. He leaned forward and stared at Jenna, tapping the edge of his chair in anticipation. *Alone in a warehouse with one of the infamous Fates*, he thought. *What an incredible stroke of luck.*

Unlike the sisters, David enjoyed the notion of luck. He loved control, certainly. But he loved chaos more. And luck was an unpredictable force that threw off the best-laid plans. Never mind that it offered an intense shot of adrenalin whenever it made an appearance.

David allowed himself to imagine how much the highest

bidders would pay to take turns torturing a Fate. He must have chuckled because Jenna sat a little straighter.

He wanted to provoke her. Maybe even take off the gag to see what he could get her to say. But he was practicing restraint.

David needed to play this carefully. To weigh the possibilities of having Jenna in his possession. His baser nature wanted to cause her pain. Make her pay for every decision, every chess move the Fates made over the years. To feel the helplessness of having *her* life in someone else's hands.

And by extension, for her sisters to feel the same.

His body flooded with adrenalin. Oh, the pleasure! The amazing cocaine-like rush of causing an immortal pain. And not any immortal. The players who set up his train-wreck of a life that he — *and only he* — made worthy of the history books.

David wasn't referring to the books humans read in libraries and school. Though, certainly, his legacy would be documented there. He coveted texts that filled the great libraries unknown and out of reach to most humans. The Akashic Records. The Olympic Library. The Great Universal Web. Those were the halls worth dominating.

He calmed his urgent need to act. His perpetual desire to be in motion and cause reactions. David knew this was a moment for patience. He had tripped over an opportunity to discover what the sisters were capable of, and what they *weren't* capable of, when they were separated.

David smiled. A cruel, thoughtful smile. He surprised himself when he had a moment to slow down. To consider the full possibilities. He could not recall a single story about the Fates doing anything separately.

Were they able to run the universe when there weren't three of them? Did Jenna have any powers of her own? Did *they* know the answers to any of these questions? David had a suspicion the three sisters had rarely been outside each other's reach since birth.

The smile fell from his face.

He recalled one time they had been separated. David was eighteen. He grimaced. David did not want to think of her. He had no desire to recall Clarissa even existed.

He dug his fingers into the cold, sharp metal of his chair. Feeling the rough edge prod into his flesh. The steel pushed against the canvas of his skin. Trying to cut through to release the blood.

The pain calmed David's mind. Drew his thoughts away from the heart-crushing encounter with the youngest Fate. The brief window, fifteen years ago, when he considered giving her everything. The only time he risked his future.

He pushed his hand hard into the metal. Feeling the steel cut through skin. Releasing the pain and blood. Just enough to make him shudder and return his mind to the present.

David watched Jenna. Though she was the quietest of the sisters, she had her own charm. Not charms that tempted David. He preferred fiery women. The kind who burned at a hot temperature and expected the mate to match.

Jenna was the strong, silent type. Boring to him. Yet, he admitted, the quiet ones were often the most powerful. They took you by surprise. Usually, because everyone underestimated them. He understood. When he was young, people thought he was a mouse. Small and easily stepped on.

Now, he was the lion, ready to devour the world. That brought the smile back to his lips.

David admired that Jenna did not cower. She sat tall. She did not expect special treatment. Or anticipate his moves. She was calm. In fact, he realized, she verged on peaceful.

She should not be in a meditative state when he was threatening her with torture. Or death. The more he watched, the more he wondered what was happening. *Was she up to something? Had she transported somewhere else? Was she trying to get in his head?*

David spun out of control. The calmer Jenna grew, the more unstable he became. Like her serenity created a vacuum he filled with panic.

"Stop it," David hissed.

When Jenna did not reply, he kicked her chair. Jolting her backward. And sending a ripple of revulsion through her.

"Don't spin your mind webs around me, witch," David threatened. "I know how you and your sisters work. I also know you don't have the same strength without your evil twins. You may sustain your trickery for a short time. But you cannot outlast me. "

He pulled his chair closer. Then leaned in, so Jenna could feel the fire in his body and sense the hatred in his veins.

"Thanks to *your* work, weaving my life, I am used to working alone. I draw power from solitude. Whereas you, little sister, are nothing but a pale imitation of your far more spectacular siblings."

David saw he pushed the right button when he felt Jenna's body twitch. He knew to press that tender bruise. The concept of sibling rivalry fascinated but puzzled him. He did not grasp wanting a talent that wasn't yours. *What did it feel like to compete against your flesh and blood? To believe someone else stole your birthright?*

David had been so isolated as a child he did not understand jealousy. *But Jenna ... sweet, quiet, powerful Jenna ... she felt it,* he mused. Entertained by the shift in her energy.

David tracked the wave of resentment through her tiny body before she could restrain herself. He knew he stumbled on something precious. *A key*. An opening to the gateway of power the Fates held in their clasp.

Physically separating the Fates was one thing. He still wasn't sure whether splitting them up physically mattered, given their power.

But alienating them emotionally? David smiled. That held enormous power. He knew it. He felt it. He just needed to push the wedge of resentment between the sisters and hold it long enough.

David knew amateurs underestimated the power of emotion. His opponents even assumed he was a psychopath, unable to appreciate the subtleties of feeling. That was their error. Though he had a limited range of feeling and indeed, avoided most emotions, it did not mean he de-valued them.

On the contrary. Adored their intense and unpredictable fluctuations. He instinctively understood humans were controlled by their feelings. And the immortals?

David restrained a laugh. The same way gods launched bigger actions, they felt bigger swells of emotion.

So many people misunderstood the myths of old,

David thought, picturing running his hand over Jenna's cheek. The thought would rattle her more than the touch. She felt his intention. And spent energy hiding her repulsion.

The myths, David mused. Hovering close to Jenna. The ones that told of Zeus's exploits and Apollo's adventures. The tales of Medusa and Athena and Eris. The great feuds and battles.

David had read many texts insisting the myths were symbolic. Simple stories exaggerated to explain away the drama of early human existence. A mirror of how little control people felt.

Lies, David scoffed. *Feeble lies.*

He knew the stories were accurate transcriptions of the pursuits of gods and goddesses. What appeared as over-dramatization to humans was a routine day for the gods.

The immortals had, he conceded, learned to restrain themselves in these days of non-believers. He heard rumors they were ordered by the Board of Immortality to act with more subtlety. They could not risk upsetting the applecart of human evolution.

David eyed Jenna. *Yes,* he thought, *the immortals feel very deeply*. They've just learned to hide the feelings and control their destructive impulses.

David leapt out of his chair. The metal seat went screeching across the concrete floor, causing Jenna to flinch. She quickly regained control. But David didn't care. He possessed the power now.

He circled Jenna. Channeling his exhilaration into move-ment and clenching his hands to keep from throwing fireballs of celebration. The solution had been right in front of his nose. He had been frustrated by Jenna's composure, her flaunting of control.

"But that's it," David leaned in, whispering in Jenna's ear.

She shivered from the power and hatred in his voice. Holding strong in her upright position. The dynamic had shifted. David had discovered something that was about to change their world, her world, forever.

"You're so proud of yourselves for the control you've learned," David continued, musing out loud as he paced. "Believing you have it mastered, when really the control has mastered you."

He glanced back at Jenna, knowing she was listening. He was leading her through a doorway from which there was no return. David had figured out a riddle. She was desperate to know which one. He loved these games. Luring others down a path that led to their demise.

"You're all like domesticated cats," David said, dropping crumbs for Jenna. "You were once powerful and imposing. But who needs you now? Who even believes in you?"

We don't need their belief, Jenna shot back. Unable to keep her mind from arguing with the maniac who had held her for hours. Or probably days. She'd lost track of time.

Not that the substance meant much to her, but she discovered time had its uses. Especially as a marker. In this case, she wondered how close her sisters might be to finding her.

For a fleeting moment, Jenna doubted they knew she had been captured. Believing she deserted them for a far off beach and a life of freedom. *How ironic*, Jenna thought. *She hadn't even left the continent.*

If she were blessed with Clarissa's gift of travelling magically to another physical location, Jenna wouldn't be stuck here. But each of the Fates had her own gifts. Transporting to another place was not Jenna's. At least, not without Clarissa's presence.

She was careful not to reach out to her sisters. Jenna sensed any move on her part could give David the piece of information he needed. He was clever and fast. But he had also hit something that had him distracted.

Jenna reached deep into her heart, needing to know her sisters were safe. She got a quick pulse of their location. The Upper West Side. They must be with Logan. That meant, in all likelihood, they knew she had been captured. And there was hope.

She doubled her resolve. She needed to stay focused. Jenna was tired and thirsty. She found David obnoxious, but she could not underestimate him. Especially when his superiority grated on her nerves. She'd had enough of that quality in her peers. Arrogance was as old as Mount Olympus.

"I believe in you," David whispered in her ear. Far too close for comfort. "I believe there is something special about you, sweet Jenna. I only need to crack the code."

What? Jenna thought. Then calmed her mind. Not wanting to respond.

He brushed his fingers against her face. Causing Jenna to shudder. She reminded herself that he was a little boy, playing with a trapped mouse. Seeing what the poor animal would do when provoked.

David's fingers moved toward her lips. They tucked into the edge of the gag. Pulling the cloth gently from her parched mouth. He slid his fingers toward the knot. Taunting her with the slow motion of his skin against hers.

Jenna held still inside. Not wanting one state or another. Captivity or freedom. Touch or no touch. She knew equanimity was found only in not wanting. And she needed balance.

The gag fell out of her mouth. Releasing her lips from the strained position. Saliva rushed over her tongue. Blood flooded her lips. And sensation returned to her cheeks. As hard as she tried, she couldn't restrain the feeling. *Relief.*

David whispered in her other ear, "Doesn't it feel good?"

Jenna didn't answer. Though her mouth had been freed, she held her tongue. He didn't deserve her words.

"Tell me the truth, Jenna," David continued. "Haven't you secretly wanted that all your life?"

She was tired of him. Tired of his ranting. Tired of his insinuations. So tired, she wanted to lash out. To knock his knees hard enough that he crumpled to the cement. Then she could kick him in the stomach. Knock the wind out of him again and again. Keep him from saying one more word.

Oh Sweet Mystery, Jenna gasped. She regained her calm. But she could feel David smiling. Knowing he had won a round.

"Yes," he continued, "You've spent your entire well-behaved life secretly nursing a desire for ..."

David pressed his lips against Jenna's ear and whispered one tantalizing word that scnt chills up and down her spine.

"Release," he breathed.

Jenna inhaled sharply. And knew they were all in trouble.

CHAPTER TWENTY-FIVE

Helen marveled at the files. She stared at the multi-story room. *How did they gather so much information?* She wondered. *What was in all these files? Had they been keeping track since the first person stood upright?*

Sam was equally amazed. He gazed up and down multiple floors of cabinets. Calculating numbers that soon got overwhelming. He switched to watching the exceedingly slender women that flitted between drawers, pulling files for Logan and his staff.

"How big is this place?" Sam wondered.

"You don't want to know," Logan responded.

"He means we wouldn't understand," said Helen. "But if those are sylphs retrieving files, you can bet it's gargantuan."

"It is. And they are," Logan said, impressed.

Logan confirmed her guess but offered no knowledge, when Helen knew he could explain. Clearly, he didn't want to. At least, not yet.

"So where are his files?" Helen asked.

Logan looked far up. Helen and Sam followed his gaze to a secured floor, complete with guards, fencing, alarms, and key codes.

"Wow," Sam said. "There must be some seriously bad people up there."

"Not people," replied Logan. "David."

Logan walked to the elevator. The others followed. As the doors opened, Sam whispered to Helen, "You better have one hell of an idea."

"Thanks," she said. "Like I wasn't feeling the pressure." She felt the hope of the Fates like a weighty presence.

The elevator was tiny. Five of them crammed into a box designed to carry a handful of sylphs. Helen knew the mythical creatures were slender but this was ridiculous. Between the lack of room and the urgency of their mission, the ride was tense.

When they arrived on the top floor, everyone spilled out. Drinking in a gulp of air. Much to the amusement of the two sylphs waiting for their ride back down. The beautiful girls giggled and glanced at Sam. He nodded then locked his gaze on the brooding security guard.

Helen shook her head as the elevator carried the sylphs away. She'd met plenty of those girls in bars. Even if they were the mortal kind. She was impressed by their coy flirtation. Guys fell for their tricks hook, line and sinker. Helen also knew the consequences were rarely as innocent as the bait.

Logan strode toward the burly guard. Without a word, the man stepped aside. As Logan stood at the keypad, the guard blocked the others from seeing anything. For all Helen knew, the device was scanning Logan's eyes and testing his blood.

Within moments, the triple-layer gate looming in front of them began to unlock. A series of mechanisms crunched and popped and released multiple levels. Then opened to reveal rows of orange filing cabinets.

Logan turned to Helen. "After you," he stated.

Helen stepped across the threshold. Grappling with the exploits that must be in these files. Row after row of intelligence. All about her brother.

"Why orange?" she asked. There were probably more important questions. But she needed to know.

Logan restrained a smile. Helen's instincts were impressive. Each time she used her natural abilities, he felt a surge of hope. A rarity in his line of work. Let alone years of dealing with Troy.

"The color is for us," Logan replied. "To protect us from the contents. The pure vibration keeps the staff optimistic, while containing his darkness."

"Really?" Sam asked, puzzling over the ordinary-looking filing cabinets. Aside from their vibrant color, they looked like any other office furniture.

Logan raised an eyebrow at Sam's amazement. Then turned to Helen. The sheer volume of files unsettled her. She was unsure where to begin.

"Tell me what sort of information you are looking for," offered Logan. "And I can direct you to the right quadrant."

Helen glanced at Clarissa, feeling bad about what she needed to do. But there was no helping it. The youngest Fate had offered the information. Helen was merely putting the revelation to good use. She apologized with her gaze. Clarissa nodded, understanding.

"Point me in the direction of David's eighteenth year," Helen requested. "When he fell in love with Clarissa."

Though Stella would not look at her, Clarissa could only hope her past deeds would help Jenna.

"Love," Stella scoffed. "He's incapable." She folded her arms.

"Let's hope not," Helen replied. "Our future depends on it." Stella stared at her.

"This way," Logan said. Guiding them to the far end of the floor. They walked several minutes in tense silence before reaching their destination. Logan indicated the corner filing cabinet. "These are the ones you want."

"Is there a way to process them as fast as possible?" Helen asked.

"Of course," Logan responded. Tapping three times on the top of the cabinet.

Helen and Sam jumped as the cabinet shook violently. They saw a flash shooting out the back, as file after file shot through a highly secured portal.

Logan waited until the cabinet finished processing, and settled back into a quiet state. Then he guided the team down another hallway to a pair of immense silver doors. Sam threw a questioning look at Helen, who shrugged in response. She had a guess but decided to wait.

Logan swiped a card through a reader and punched a nine-digit code. The doors flickered then disappeared. As though they had only been an illusion.

"This place gets better and better," Sam whispered, as they stepped inside a private screening room.

Helen stared in amazement. Struck by the rooms, the creatures, and the resources at her fingertips. Part of her felt like a dazzled child at the circus. The other part knew this level of security and magic would not be required if her brother weren't equally intimidating.

They descended the small set of stairs and sat in the front row. Waiting for the show to begin. The lights dimmed and the story of David and Clarissa appeared.

David looked like a different man. One with hope in his heart. Helen could see why Clarissa was drawn to him. David still had the option of two paths at this point. He had yet to choose the dark one.

In a small seaside town, David reached out to make friends. But his secretive nature and lack of confidence caused each attempt to be rebuffed. Girls scattered when he approached. Boys ridiculed him. And neighbors whispered behind his back.

David's anger simmered and his resentment grew. The rage was palpable. Helen shifted, discomforted by the intensity of David's hatred. She forced herself to watch, knowing she needed to ready herself.

Sam offered an open hand, nudging Helen's leg in the darkness. She glanced down and smiled. Knowing Sam offered her comfort. She hesitated then slid her fingers into his. Sam's kindness relaxed her. As she turned to the screen, Helen felt the power of connection.

Helen watched with fresh eyes. She wondered whether David had been wired for destruction or if all those years of isolation drove him to madness. Either way, she could not imagine his pain. The feeling of having no other human being. *If she received his fate, would she have been like him?*

Even as the thought crossed her mind, she felt it wasn't true. Helen knew everyone contained the potential of destruction. We all harbor the sword of unkindness. She also knew there was a choice. She made her share of mistakes.

But no matter the weight of rejection or the burden of pain — fated or not — humans were responsible for their choices. She was not David. They viewed the world through very different lenses.

As Helen watched her brother seek opportunities to humiliate his torturers, she saw his choices strengthened his victimhood. He kept files on every person in the town. He lurked in the shadows, gathering details. Searching out their weakness. Testing theories with controlled hits. Wrecking relationships and causing paranoia.

David prepared for his ultimate day of revenge — a day intended to bring them to their ungrateful knees. He mapped his plot in the den of a rambling home on the outskirts of town. His obsessive planning kept him inside for days. He wanted every move to be perfect. He went over each player and scenario until he could barely see straight. He did not eat for days. And forgot to drink water.

Even as she watched, Helen wondered how no one missed the quiet, attentive young man who tried, in his fumbling way, to connect. *Were they so relieved to have him gone? Had no one wondered where he went? Or if he was alive? Why hadn't a single person shown him any kindness?*

Knock, knock, knock.

Helen jumped and watched as her brother stared at his door. Unsure what to do. He did a quick search but had no weapon. All his plans were to be executed from a far distance. He didn't have a knife or gun or even a baseball bat.

Knock, knock, knock.

David walked toward the door. Helen could see his mind whirring. She imagined him calculating his reaction with every step. Figuring out how to act based on who was on the other side. He stood in front of the door. Gathering his nerve.

Then he grabbed the handle and yanked it open.

Revealing Clarissa, hair cascading freely, gorgeous in a soft blue summer dress, and holding a basket of muffins. Clarissa wore the illusion of a tender eighteen year old. Still her beautiful self but in a form that put David at ease and sent his heart fluttering.

She played the new in town story like a song made for David's ears. And within minutes, she had coaxed him outside.

Over the course of days, then weeks, Clarissa and David grew close. Listening, laughing, and venturing out. Until the map room with David's master plan gathered a coat of dust. Helen wondered if he remembered anyone existed except Clarissa.

In her attempt to fend off disaster, Clarissa forgot that risk. David's obsessive attention moved from his destructive plan to her. Each day, his need to be with her grew stronger. She became his world. Their innocent, loving walks were no longer a joy. They became a requirement to prove she spent her time with him.

David demanded that she leave her apartment. Live with him. He didn't need anyone else. They didn't need anyone else. Clarissa's presence wiped away every slight he had endured, every rejection he remembered. And so, David insisted she be with him always. Clarissa realized in offering herself as a distraction, she unwittingly ensnared herself in the same fanatical web.

As deeply as she felt for David, the black hole of his

desperation was too much. She spent time with David based on the ruse that she was keeping a closer eye on him. Clarissa convinced her sisters they didn't all need to watch him. She would keep tabs and report back.

But her sisters were growing suspicious of the amount of time Clarissa spent. She knew it would not be long before she was discovered.

Despite her best intentions, she needed to end their affair. She could see the various outcomes her leaving might trigger, but she could not allow herself to be held hostage. She realized, too late, she had staved off destruction in the present in exchange for disaster in the future.

Clarissa told David that she was leaving town, never to return. She had no choice and he could not come with her. She delivered the news with tears in her eyes — held his hands, kissed his cheek, and departed forever. Leaving David stunned and alone.

She watched from afar as David eventually woke from his catatonic state. That night, he smashed every figurine in his map room, and tore every piece of paper he owned until his hands bled. Then, in a final fit of fury, David doused his floor with gasoline and tossed a match over his shoulder. Sending his home up in a blaze as he walked away.

The screen went black. Causing everyone in the room to pause.

"Is that everything?" Helen asked.

"Not quite," Logan replied. "Give me a moment."

Logan reached for a tablet. Typed in several commands. Then looked to the screen, waiting for the response. "My apologies for the poor quality," he said. "I had to use some rather unorthodox channels for this information."

The screen lit up. The time gap between Clarissa's departure and the present was bridged by a collage of guerrilla-style footage, security videos, and witnesses offering information if their faces were blacked out and their voices disguised.

After setting fire to his house, David went underground. Clarissa lost track of him and began to worry. She sought high and low for David, afraid of what he might be planning. His ability to avoid detection made her aware of a latent talent the Fates had not foreseen.

David was a shapeshifter. He could blend and hide when threatened. He merged with any environment, matching the frequency so completely that Clarissa could not track him. But the hiding wasn't what worried her.

She knew David had gone underground as a protective measure. But also to find out information. Something in him knew Clarissa had lied. He was determined to find out why. What may have begun as a hunt to get her back, soon turned into an obsessive desire to destroy her.

Through his dealings with the shadow-dwellers, David heard whispers that Clarissa was one of the Fates. He thought this notion laughable the first time he heard it. But each time the information was reiterated, David began to believe it.

His fury grew and his betrayal deepened. His obsessive mind made Clarissa, and by extension her sisters, the source of all of his pain. Each day, he nursed the hatred. Each day, he met another person with a grievance against the Fates.

David became a collector. Drawing toward him a network of

damaged souls who could feed his pain and believe in his cause. A world without Fate. A return to chaos. Power for everyone.

Or so he preached.

Deep in his heart, he wanted the power the sisters held. The ability to forge the fated path for any being. Not because he wanted the best for them. Not because he believed in the evolutionary ability of each person on the planet. Only because he knew no one else deserved to be the puppet-master.

David understood how the world should be ruled. And if free will was a tale the gods trotted out when they wanted humans to believe they had some say in their pathetic little lives, David wanted to be the story spinner.

He could convince anyone who had been wronged. Anyone who had a grudge to bear or an axe to grind that the time had come to take back their lives from the old ones.

As they boarded the bus to rebellion, not a single follower realized that David had no intention of relinquishing the reins of power. Taking down the Fates set chaos in motion. And in chaos great power was born. Whether that power was destructive or creative was up to the person wielding control.

And David intended to rain down destruction until the time arrived to raise his own world. One where he called the shots.

The screen dimmed and the lights went up. No one said a word.

CHAPTER TWENTY-SIX

F or several tense moments, the screening room remained silent. "Well, what good did any of that do?" Stella asked. She still wouldn't look at Clarissa but she instinctively defended her.

Helen released Sam's hand. Logan was waiting for her to respond.

Helen walked to the front of the room with no idea what to say. She used up precious time with a tour down memory lane. Logan believed in careful planning, but Helen needed to act. And act fast. Or David would gain the upper hand.

"I appreciate your misgivings, Stella," Helen began. "But I needed to understand David's motivation. Watching the footage gave me a feel for who my brother is and what provokes him. If I follow my intuition, my sense of him, then I have a chance to stop him. So I wanted to see him in action without being in danger."

"Fair enough," Stella conceded. Clarissa nodded for Helen to continue.

"I propose we lure David out in the open," Helen offered. "We ask him to come to the table willingly."

"Why?" Stella asked. "You think he's going to negotiate?"

"No," Helen replied. "But he will talk to us if he believes he holds all the cards."

"Go on," Logan said.

"We set up a scenario that he thinks he controls," Helen said. She was improvising. "Maybe a hostage exchange or a meeting on his territory."

Helen was already somewhere else, projecting her plan into the future. She had no idea how she was doing it, but she was laying the groundwork for a prospective reality. Imagining where they were headed and building the road.

Then she stumbled on doubt. "Wait," she said, looking to Logan. "Does he have territory?"

Logan addressed her real concern. "You're doing beautifully, Helen." Logan replied. "Trust your instincts. Follow the flow of where they take you —"

"We don't have time for flow," Stella objected. "David does *not* have territory. He spends his time taking over other people's hard work instead of doing his own."

"Stella, please," Clarissa said. "Let Helen figure this out. We need her."

"We don't have time," Stella shot back, standing up. "We've already spent hours in this comfortable little room, watching films and discussing theories, while Jenna is holed up in some dungeon."

"I agree, Stella," Helen said. "But we don't know where he is. Or what he wants. David is making it up as he goes."

Helen stood in front of Stella and Clarissa and forced herself to believe she was their best hope. Otherwise, she was never going to trust herself the way they needed.

"I know his improvisational instinct better than anyone," Helen continued. "I've lived with it all my life. That is why

Logan asked me here. I am wired like David but with a *very* different focus."

"So you understand him," Stella said. "That doesn't mean you can stop him."

"You're right," Helen granted. "But it does mean I can match his moves. Anticipate them. If I embrace the flow, I might even be able to figure out what he wants before he does. And like a master card player, I will use that against him."

"So why Jenna? Was it just opportunity?" Sam asked, standing up beside her. Realizing they were a circle with Helen at the crown.

"Probably," Clarissa offered. "But now he wants to unsettle us. To torture us with thoughts of what he'll do to her."

"No," Helen riffed on what Sam was offering. "He wants to figure something out. He doesn't just want to cause her pain. Or use her to get to the two of you."

Helen's excitement took over. She could feel it like a surge of electricity coursing through her veins. She looked over to Logan. *She needed something*, Helen thought. *What did she need? A surface!*

"Logan," Helen said. "We need a drawing board. Or a map. Somewhere we can plan."

Logan nodded. He typed a new set of codes into his tablet.

Inside the walls, a series of parts started moving. Clunking and sliding. Shuffling around. Then a door slid open in the wall, revealing a hidden table. Slowly, the table lowered and landed on five sturdy legs. Four on the corners and one in the middle.

A door opened on the other side of the theatre. Five sylphs glided in. Laying out markers, papers, files, magnets, a large basket with fruit and pastries, glasses, and a pitcher of water.

As they slipped back out of the room, they shot amorous glances at Sam. Blowing him kisses, they beckoned him to follow. He kept his gaze on the table.

Helen strode over to the large map already laid out. Exactly what she needed — an over-sized map of Manhattan and the boroughs. The others gathered. She grabbed a marker.

"Before he stumbled across Jenna," Helen said. "David returned to New York for a reason. "

"He was meeting with power players in Europe," offered Sam.

"David's been taking steps to infiltrate the old ruling class for years," Logan said.

"Right," Helen replied.

She reached for a button at the edge of the table and pushed. The New York map disappeared, replaced by a map of the world.

"Cool," Sam exclaimed, unable to restrain his amazement.

Helen glanced at Logan, asking for permission to draw on the map. He nodded. She proceeded to circle Amsterdam and New York City, then Saint Petersburg, Capetown, Rio de Janeiro, Istanbul, and Beijing.

"David came back with a long range plan to take over the old networks," Helen sensed. "He had no intention of collaborating. But he needed to play along to figure out how the old guard worked."

"He returned to Manhattan, his headquarters," she explained, her gaze fixed on the map's center as she received information, "ready to engage his plan. When the strangest thing happened. One of the Fates landed in his lap."

Clarissa leaned in, enthralled by Helen's talent blossoming.

Stella uncrossed her arms and closed her eyes. Logan followed suit. Sam placed his hands on the table. He gazed down and quieted his mind. Sam felt the circle bolstering Helen's gift. Though he wasn't of their caliber, he focused on assisting.

"David sees this as a gift," Helen continued, giving over to the powerful stream coursing through her. "He's not sure from whom. But on some level he believes this is a sign his time has come. So, he pauses to consider this offering."

"The obvious approach is to torture Jenna for information," Helen said, detached from the impact of her words.

"But he realizes Jenna is too strong and would take a profound effort to break with force. He's also not sure whether breaking her mind would break her gift. David's mind spins the options. Until he lands on the revelation that Jenna is a secret key. To a larger gate."

Clarissa gasped. Stella and Logan opened their eyes and shot stern looks in her direction. Unsure whether her outburst might break Helen's trancelike flow. Helen fell silent, wavering.

Then re-sourced her stream of perception.

"David sees that Jenna is a master key," Helen said. "A way through a gateway he did not know existed. She has accelerated his plan, making all alliances unnecessary. He no longer cares about them. Hasn't answered a single call. Infuriating his compatriots. Jenna changed everything."

"No," whispered Clarissa. "It's not possible."

"Shhh," Stella said to her sister, "We cannot help that he knows. We must support Helen to figure out what we can do about it."

Logan saw the bond returning between the two sisters. They

had let the upset over David come between them but were now coming to terms with the events. They were back in the flow of response — thanks to Helen.

He didn't understand why this happened. But as Logan watched Helen embrace her natural talent for leadership, he had to believe this was meant to be. Despite the perplexing fact that the Fates were the pawns, not the masters.

When the room fell silent, Helen reached out, eyes closed, and circled a small area in the farthest reaches of the Bronx. Logan puzzled over the location. A derelict warehouse district that would be abandoned in any other city. But New York real estate was too valuable not to have tenants. Even in the worst neighborhoods.

"Not a permanent location," Helen stated. "But where he is right now."

Clarissa clutched Stella's hand, as though to scream, *Let's go!* But Stella shook her head. Despite her earlier urgency, Stella's gaze was fixed on Helen. She knew the wisdom Helen spoke came from a higher source. And Stella would not act until Helen said all was ready.

Stella understood now, that they stood at a delicate moment. She watched Helen as though the young woman was a tightrope walker balanced halfway across Niagara Falls. They must hold still and not upset her equilibrium, or Helen would plummet and all would be lost.

All they could do was focus and hold their breath, supporting Helen to cross. No matter that watching each teetering move was almost more than they could bear.

Helen felt a shift in the flow. She wasn't sure why but it was like she had stepped into a different lane. Or rode a different current. Instead of a stream of words flowing though her, she saw images. Flashes of insight.

"David knows Jenna is his means to enter the halls of power," Helen continued. "He's going to take her to the portal. In Central Park, at the base of an ancient red oak. Where only Jenna knows the words to access the ancient gateway."

Clarissa and Stella exchanged glances. Each looked to the other to see if she knew of this talent hidden in Jenna. They both shook their heads. Then looked at Logan. He avoided eye contact, focused on Helen. The sisters fumed. *How was it possible that Logan knew Jenna's potential yet they didn't?*

When they shared the same furious thought, they understood. For their own protection. And Jenna's. Stella and Clarissa clasped each other's hand.

"David does not understand where the gateway will take him," Helen continued, "nor does he understand how it works. But he intends to reach Mount Olympus. Where he will provoke the greatest rebellion the world has ever seen. Knocking down the Pantheon. Stealing the power of the gods. And unleashing the Great Chaos."

She paused. The circle waited. Then Helen made her final statement. "Our only option," she said, "is to meet him by the ancient oak and prevent his crossing."

Helen slumped, exhausted. Barely aware of the words she had spoken.

"Sam, water and food. Now!" Logan declared.

Sam poured a glass of water, handing it to Logan. Logan held Helen's head up. Putting the glass to her lips to drink a long draught of water. She took the apple from Sam's hand and bit hungrily into the fruit. Helen glanced at the stunned yet impressed faces.

She gave a weak smile. "I always dreamed of a midnight rendezvous in Central Park," Helen said. "Just not with my brother."

CHAPTER TWENTY-SEVEN

D avid arranged for Jenna to be brought separately. As much as he abhorred nature and avoided being outside for longer than necessary, he knew he needed to approach the tree alone.

If the Great Red Oak did not permit him entrance, none of this would matter. Not Jenna, not the fact he had figured out a long-buried mystery, not even the fact that he had piggy backed on his sister's genius.

Helen had uncovered Jenna's hidden gift. His sister was more talented than he realized — accessing secret information from sacred annals. David sensed the surge of power and rode the wave.

Strange how everyone assumed he had things figured out ahead of them. That was the advantage of being brilliant. Half the time, he waited for others to point the way. Then he filled in the blanks.

Having a high IQ was also handy. If others broke the code, he could jump through the door and follow the clues. Many would stumble, but David had the self-confidence and intelligence to understand patterns. Weaving pieces together at lightning speed.

He pulled his coat collar up and shivered. Grumbling against the cold and the drizzle. David was relieved that the night hour kept most people away from the park. At least he did not have to suffer crowds. That might have pushed him over the edge. And the time for chaos had not ripened.

David stood at the cusp of the path, as close to the dirt as he could get without stepping off the asphalt. He wasn't sure when his dislike for nature had turned into outright revulsion. He loathed the bright greens of the grass, the feathery seeds that blew and caught in his clothes, even the fiery leaves that appeared in the fall.

David only enjoyed that the bright colors on the edges of the canopy meant the old crones would be stripped of their foliage before long. Laying their limbs bare to the fierce bite of winter. *Perhaps some wouldn't make it past the harsh frost*, he hoped. Relishing the thought.

But David knew his real resentment was that there was no mastering nature. As often as he demanded she bend to his will, Gaia seemed to revel in his defeat. As cruelly as the residents of the town where he grew up. The two were inextricably linked.

Small town people had a perverse connection to nature that he did not understand. Likely because they had nothing else. *Pathetic. To lay claim to the only thing they would never own.* Nature took everything from them in hurricanes and blizzards and tornados, yet they insisted she was their ally.

He stared at the edge between the asphalt and grass. Then gazed over his shoulder, longing for the high-rises and bright lights. He loved the metal, concrete, and brick. He preferred the controlled comfort of glassed-in walls and heated rooms. Not this barbaric expanse of dampness.

David refrained from spitting on the greenery. Resenting the city dwellers who thought green space had value. They spent their days far away from dirt and ponds, drinking martinis and clamoring for lattes. Insisting that a city needed a park was like believing a bar needed sunshine.

He was careful to buffer his thoughts. David could not risk them reaching the regal Oak. He needed her. Soon enough, however, this would be a wasteland. He would build new cities with people beholden to him. The ones who begged for their lives. The others would be a distant memory. Like every blade of grass in this park.

He eyed the Great Red Oak. Knowing she would not let him near even the outer reaches of her roots without believing he came with an altruistic purpose. How could he fool one of the oldest beings on the planet? Never mind that she shared a network few understood and spoke a language as old as the stars.

David might abhor nature but he respected her mysterious ways. She could move as slow as the glacier packs and as quick as a bolt of lightning. She spoke more languages than every dialect created by humans multiplied by one million. And though humans believed they could best her, they came out on the losing side. Every time.

Always respect your enemy, David thought, as he stared at the old tree. Never be fooled by its simple guise or clumsy ways. If a being had stood as long as this old crone, she knew more than she let on. And had figured out survival strategies that rivaled his most clever plot.

He inched his toes toward the soil. Not ready to speak her language yet. David relied on his shapeshifting abilities to sneak past most beings. As long as he matched their frequency, they either assumed he was one of their kind or did not see him coming.

This old tree was, however, infinitely wiser than his typical opponent. Otherwise, she would not have been chosen as the Great Gateway. She had come up against quicker wits and stronger physiques. But she had not battled an intuitive shape-shifter who held one of the Fates. On that, he would bet his future.

Wait until she realizes who crept past her defenses with the key, David chuckled. *That should rattle the old twig.* Even if the Oak assumed he stole the sister and forced her to the Gateway, as of course he had, the old Oak would not understand why Jenna insisted David was her friend. That was the genius of his plan.

In his travels, David had met some brilliant minds. People who worked magic with metals, neurons, electricity, even thoughts. Yet, due to their unique talents, most also accrued problems — debts or bullies or family members who prevented them from realizing their true ability.

They always needed a hand with an obstacle. And David specialized in removing obstacles. Since the day he freed himself from his past, he lived to free others. But he was a busy man. He chose who to help, and selected those who could also aid him. Still, David preferred to see himself as a liberator.

He assisted a clever Chechnyan scientist who devised an illusion serum that allowed a person to lie like a medieval Pope, yet emit the pheromones that resonated truth. Though most people would not detect such subtlety, the serum was critical to David's success with the Great Red Oak.

The serum made a person susceptible to any truth David planted in her mind. He wove the illusion, embedded the story, and the recipient believed it was true. Jenna would repeat David's fiction, fully convinced of the tale. The Oak would feel Jenna's sincerity. No matter that every word was false.

David smiled. He loved when his instincts paid off. At the time, he had no idea how the gamble with the scientist would work out. His peers thought extricating the old man from the clutches of the Russian mafia was madness. Even suicide. But David knew the serum was destined to change his life. And he was right.

Muffled cries of protest broke David's quiet reverie. He turned to see his oversized security guards carrying Jenna into the park against her will. They did not sedate her as he requested. David was far from pleased.

Fed up with her antics, they threw her to the asphalt at his feet. The guards did not frustrate easily. Jenna must have tried their patience every step of the way for them to lose their cool in David's presence. "Why is she not sedated?" David asked.

"She is," the senior guard replied. "We doubled the dose. She still fought us like a feral cat." He spat beside Jenna, searing the asphalt with his acidic venom.

"Do not damage her," David hissed, causing the guards to remember their place. They snapped into a respectful stance — hands behind their backs, heads bowed.

David acknowledged their submissive gesture with silence. The pause allowed him to gather his wits and survey the vicinity. He was relieved to see no one had noticed. The park was dark and serene.

"Did you bring the serum?" David asked. The junior guard responded with a nod then snapped a hand out in front of him.

A needle lay in his palm.

"Good," David said, seizing the needle.

At least they did that right. He could not risk the serum wearing off early. The Chechnyan's formula was still under development. The scientist did not know how long a dose would last. Let alone in an immortal.

David clutched the needle in his hand. And eyed the distance to the Great Red Oak's trunk. She was roughly five hundred feet away. Far enough to be buffered from his intentions. As long as he stayed on the asphalt. The moment he stepped onto the dirt, she would be privy to every feeling in his heart.

He looked down at the weakened Jenna. She spent a lot of energy fighting the guards. Hoping she could break free in the only time she had away from David. Lucky for him, Jenna's weakened state would improve the serum's effectiveness and make it easier to drag her to the foot of the tree.

The old crone might believe Jenna's life was in danger. That he was throwing himself at her mercy to save the middle Fate. *Yes*, he thought, *that's perfect*. The clumsiness of his brutish staff would prove handy after all.

He held the needle, wondering whether he should drag her the whole way before risking the injection. But as he paused, Jenna regained the strength to climb to her knees. She wavered on the pavement in a prayer position.

Before she could utter a sound, David made his decision. Jabbing Jenna hard in the back of her arm. Causing her to howl with pain. David and the guards jumped away. Thrown by the eerie sound as she howled to the heavens. David could not tell the difference between the Fate and the wolves of Valhalla.

Then he seized her face and locked his eyes on Jenna's, planting his tale. Willing his fiction into her mind as the chemicals took hold. David tested the formula on several humans and even a few half-bloods. But he didn't know how the chemistry — or the process — would work on a Fate.

The guards cast glances around the park, as though expecting the hounds of hell or the horses of the apocalypse. No matter what wars they had fought, immortals always sided together against mortals. So David was careful to prepare for a rescue attempt. But the park rewarded Jenna's howls with complete silence.

Jenna's shoulders slumped. As though her cry of pain was the last ounce of protest her body had to offer. David wondered whether her anguish was more psychic than physical. He was forcing a Fate to accept his illusion. A complete lie.

As curious as he was, David did not have time to waste. He nodded to the guards. They picked her up, each grabbing an arm, and slung her over David.

David grimaced as he was forced to wrap his arm around her body. Holding her up in the ruse that he was dragging her to safety and seeking the Old Oak for her aid. He had no choice but to touch Jenna — much to his disgust.

Prepped and ready for the journey, he pointed himself in the direction of the Great Red Oak. Then David took the step of destiny. Landing on the soil and knowing, in that instant, that the Oak felt him coming.

Rushes of energy and surges of information careened along her roots. Like a live wire conversation along a network of telephones. Messages went flying through the soil back to the old tree. Advising her of the people approaching, their incoming speed, and any details about their purpose.

David stepped toward the ancient tree, dragging the half-conscious Jenna. He was grateful that the serum had a temporary drugging effect. The drawback was he had not practiced carrying weight, let alone the dead weight of an immortal.

He moved slowly. David estimated he would arrive at the Gateway in seven minutes. He took his time but, in his heart, he was impatient. With each step, he tempered the edgy feeling. And quelled his aggravation with the persistent message that in a few short minutes his world would change.

David locked his eyes on her trunk. Moving in sync with Jenna. He focused on the story he must relay to the Oak. A tale of the dying Fate and her need to reach the great healers of her homeland. She was too far gone for the help of this world. She needed Chiron or Persephone or an even greater healer. The only way to save Jenna was to pass through to Mount Olympus.

As he rehearsed the story, he pulsed his hand against Jenna. Sending subconscious signals through her body to reinforce the tale. So when he needed Jenna to confirm his story, the tree could reach into Jenna's consciousness to receive exactly what David wanted the Oak to hear.

With three hundred feet to go, he felt the increasing power of the tree. She possessed a magnificent grid of energy pulsing hundreds of feet in every direction, more sophisticated than the most advanced security systems. David was impressed by the simple elegance, even as he wanted to slash her trunk and burn her roots.

Jenna surfaced. Only enough to lift her head and realize she was in a park. Someone was dragging her toward a powerful energy source. *Had she been rescued?* Her groggy mind could not figure out whether she was safe. All she knew was she was being pulled home.

She sighed. Causing a convulsion in the person who held her. Her mind assured her that she was safe. But her heart was convinced she was in danger. Whichever was true, this person was taking her home. *How could those two things go together? Why would an enemy take her home?*

Disparate images of the Trojan War flitted through her mind — Athena, Hera, Aphrodite. Scrambling to catch a golden apple. Starting a war over illusions. Eris smiling. Paris looking afraid. The thoughts confused her.

A wave of fatigue rolled over Jenna. Knocking her off-balance and forcing her to lean heavily on her companion. She felt another wave of revulsion from him. Jenna knew this person would rather cast her off and, yet, he kept pulling her home. *Had he made a promise? Had she made a promise?*

She needed to pull the pieces together but she did not have the energy. In her mind, Jenna saw images of being rescued. A knight carrying her to safety. Her bruised and tired body arriving home. The Great Halls. The Healing Waters. The Peaceful Forests. She could think of nothing else. Her body called for the calm of sleep.

The closer they drew to the source of energy, the more peaceful she became. She felt her heart match the pulse of the great being calling her name.

Jenna, it whispered. *Are you being carried of your own free will?*

Speak to me, child.

The voice soothed Jenna. And sent a surge through her that enlivened her spirit. She must be conversing with a Goddess. *Hello, Old One,* Jenna responded. *I am with a friend. He is carrying me home. Back to the Healing Waters. I need to sleep. To heal. My body is tired.*

The Old One paused.

Are you sure this is a friend? I do not recognize him. And fear for your safety. We cannot grant him entrance until we know for sure he is no threat to the Ancients.

Jenna was not sure. Her mind assured her that he was her rescuer. Yet her heart remembered pain. She could not lie to an Old One.

I do not know, Jenna confessed. *He feels compelled to take me home. Something I want more than anything else. Can you search his heart? He must feel obliged to fulfill this task. Is that not the action of an ally?*

She wanted the Old One to agree with her, though Jenna could not say why. She wanted to heal. She needed to rest. But why did she crave this with every cell in her body? Why was her mind obsessed with reaching home? Exhaustion pulsed through her and she no longer cared why. She only wanted to sleep.

David felt the electrical pulses surging back and forth between Jenna and the Oak. He did not know what they were sharing and the lack of power infuriated him. But he was confident in the serum. He knew the words and images planted in Jenna's consciousness would hold — she craved the healing waters of home. Nothing else would soothe her pain. And, most important, he was her protector.

All that mattered was that the Tree believed Jenna. He was closing in on the Gateway with fifty feet to go. He squeezed Jenna's waist, causing her to whimper. He felt the pain echo through the old bundle of wood. There was some ancient bond between these two, and David planned to use it to its full advantage.

He must convince the Oak that he was Jenna's savior. A valiant knight fulfilling the Fate's last request. David could feel the will of the Old One bending. She was swayed by a need to ease her chosen one's pain. David was close. So close he could taste it.

David carried Jenna the final feet to the base of the Great Red Oak. He placed her among the giant-sized roots. Offering her to the Gods as his sacrifice to the greater will. He stepped back and bowed his head to the Old One. Smiling underneath, but on the surface, he wore only the face of a dutiful servant.

"I am here, Old One, to save the life of this precious jewel. The one you call Jenna," David spoke with reverence.

I acknowledge your presence, young knight. What, pray tell, is your name? The Great Red Oak spoke to David's mind.

Strangely, David had not anticipated she would ask his name. Only his purpose. Should he lie? Could she tell? He assumed she could. And so, he answered simply.

"David," he replied.

And where do you come from, David?

She asked this of him with infinite patience. David knew he must be careful. And not be lulled by her affectionate, motherly tone.

"I hail from the sea," he answered. This was both true and sufficiently mysterious to cover his trail.

The Old One paused. Considering his information. Weighing how she felt about him.

And how did you come to have a Sister of Fate in your possession?

This was the true question. The one she wanted to ask all along, but needed time to assess this young man. The Old Tree ached to help Jenna but she could not, in good conscience, give access to the old world without knowing who broached the Gateway.

Even if he had a Fate in his arms. Perhaps more so because he did.

"She fell into my arms in her hour of need," David said, masterful at the art of telling the truth with his spin. "I soon realized the only way to help her was to take her home."

You knew who she was?

The Old One was surprised this man knew Jenna and where she hailed from, yet the Oak was not familiar with him. Whispers of information came up her roots offering many answers to her dilemma.

"Yes," David replied, growing impatient. But he had no other choice than to answer as many questions as the Old Crone asked.

How is it that I do not know you?

She wanted to hear the answer from his mouth. Not through the guesses of her infinite network.

"I am but a humble human, Sacred One," he replied with reverence. "I have long studied the ways of the ancients and wished to be of service to them. But as a human with no royal blood, I could not hope to reach the level of your notice."

The Old One sensed something was amiss. The man's answers were perfect. His tone was reverential. He spoke like a knight and felt like a knight. Perhaps it was the absolute perfection that caused her to wonder. No creature was perfect. And yet, he offered her everything that matched his fairy tale rescue story.

Jenna moaned with pain. Her face went ashen. Her brow broke into a sweat, then her body shook with chills. She convulsed like a victim wracked by poison. David wondered if she was suffering from a side effect of the serum. Or perhaps it was wearing off.

He needed the drug to last a little longer. He knew the serum did not have a long effect. But if it was losing its grip on Jenna, he needed to push the timeline of the tree's decision — whether the Oak liked it or not.

"Old One, I implore you," David fell to his knees beside Jenna. "She is weakening by the second. Without the healing light of her home, she will not survive. I fear she may die within minutes."

The Great Red Oak did not like to rush decisions. Her nature was to weigh information for as long as required then make a choice. But watching her poor Jenna shiver and weaken was more than she could take.

Little one, she whispered to Jenna, *say the words and I will take you home.*

Jenna's mind was a jumble, delirious with images and phrases. She was lost in a nightmare. She knew there was a string of words she needed to open the Gateway, but she could not remember them. She reached in this corner and that crevice of her consciousness. Searching for the right combination.

Desperate, David crouched next to her. And whispered in her

ear, "You know the words, sweet Jenna. Find them. Say them. And I will take you home. Then you can rest for all eternity."

The word *eternity* echoed through Jenna's body and soul. Miraculously, the combination appeared. She knew what to say. With her last trace of energy, Jenna pulled close to the ancient trunk.

She whispered,

"Oscailt an geata chun na bhflaitheas."

The Great Red Oak lit up with the brilliance of a thousand suns. Shining light across the heart of Central Park, as though dawn had arrived hours before the break of day.

As the Infinite Gateway opened, David's face lit up with the madness of power. His moment had arrived.

CHAPTER TWENTY-EIGHT

Helen saw the brilliant explosion of light and ran toward the ancient tree, her companions on her heels.

David and Jenna disappeared into the Gateway. And she screamed, "No!"

Helen knew it was pointless and still she ran, harder than ever, toward the tree. Unable to accept they arrived too late to stop David.

She saw his face light up with the knowledge that he would get exactly what he had wanted all these years. Revenge. She felt the brief pulse of David's gratification. Then, even with surge of energy from the Gateway, she sensed his signature blend of fury and resentment under the victory.

Helen picked up her pace. She had to get to the Great Red Oak before the doorway slammed shut. If she reached the portal in time, she could jump through. She couldn't let David cross alone. Helen had no idea how to stop him, but she trusted her instincts.

Her lungs burned, her legs ached. And still, she pushed harder. David was her responsibility. She may not have created the monster, but she was the only one who could stop it.

Helen saw the light from the portal retreating. The Gateway

was closing. *No!* she demanded. *Not when she was this close. One more second ...*

She lunged toward the tree. The light disappeared in a flash. The portal had closed. David was gone. And she had failed.

Helen doubled over. Desperate to catch her breath. Feeling utterly defeated. *How could they have lost? How could they have come so close, only to miss him by seconds?*

She collapsed at the base of the tree. Rested on its massive roots. Sam and Logan caught up to Helen. Silent in their disbelief. Not sure what to do.

Clarissa and Stella emerged moments later. They were unable to appear while the portal was open. The energy was too powerful for them to transport. But it wouldn't matter if Helen reached David in time.

They were stunned to see Helen alone at the base of the tree. "He's gone?" Stella asked, knowing the answer. "With Jenna?"

"Yes," Helen replied. "I'm sorry."

"No," Clarissa marched around the Oak. As though declaring her astonishment would change reality. "She can't be gone. Not with him!"

"I saw them step through, Clarissa," Helen said.

"Then go after them!" Clarissa yelled. She stared at Helen expecting answers. Action. Anything but defeat.

"There's nothing I can do," Helen said. "He took the key."

Not the only key, the Great Oak interjected.

Helen bolted up to her feet so fast she tripped on the immense roots and fell back into Sam. He reacted quickly, catching Helen. For a moment, he held her, neither of them hurrying to break the embrace.

Until they remembered what had just happened. Sam helped Helen to her feet. She whispered to him, "Did you hear that?"

"We all did," Logan replied. "What did you mean, Great One? Not the only key."

For centuries, I relied on Jenna as the key to the old world. But as the world changed and the threats to the ancient ways increased, I knew it was time to consider another. One that was less obvious to those who might seek to enter the other world.

"How do we find this key, Revered One?" Logan asked. He did not wish to sound impatient, but he shivered at the thought of David on the other side. And now they must spend time hunting a key.

You don't have to, dear Logan. She found you.

Logan pondered her mysterious reply. Then his eyes went wide. He stared at Helen. And everything fell into place.

This was the plan all along. Whether it was mapped, Logan could not be sure. Maybe the mystery was that fluid. He still had a hard time believing events could be charted so well without the Fates in charge. But clearly, a larger plan was at work. One far beyond his comprehension.

Logan knew this played out as it was meant to unravel. Everything was clear now. She not only understood David, she had the power to follow him.

Helen looked behind her and around. Expecting someone else to appear. It couldn't be her. She had let them all down. She was supposed to stop her brother, only to arrive too late.

Then the truth dawned. *Wait. No. If she was the key, she could still stop —*

She leapt to her feet. "What do I do?" Helen asked.

Place your hands on my trunk, child. Feel the pulse of my blood. Match my essence. Listen for the message of the Old Ones to come through to you. And only you.

Helen laid her hands on the ancient trunk. She could feel the slow, powerful pulse beating through the bark. A sensation unlike anything she had ever felt. The elegant flow of the natural world. This ancient being was in alignment with the slow, steady beat of the earth.

She breathed deep and quelled her mind. The quieter Helen got, the deeper she felt the connection that travelled through the roots, far below her feet. As she focused, she saw the corresponding network that reached up through the branches, high into the sky.

Helen closed her eyes. And listened. She let go. Breathed, in and out. Waiting for the ancient ones to gift her with the message. She must step out of the way. Only her open heart could receive the key.

Please gift me with this knowledge, Helen requested. *Share the wisdom of the ages, so that I might be the one to stop my brother.*

For several long, uninterrupted minutes, Helen received nothing. She breathed. And matched the frequency of the tree. Anyone who walked by would not have known she was there. She blended so perfectly with this being.

But something was still in the way. What was it? Was she holding back? Was she doing it wrong? That's when Helen noticed her impatience. Her need to know the answer. To leap to a conclusion.

Her imagination was filling the void. She could not guess.

She could not wonder. She needed only to be the receptive vessel. Helen calmed her mind. And sensed the vastness of the universe — above her, around her, below her.

Once Helen let go of everything she knew, everything she was, and everything she expected, the shift happened. Information shot through the tree and into Helen like a bolt of lightning cracking through the night sky.

The force was so strong, Helen blew backward off the tree. Landing on her backside for the second time that night. She expected to feel pain but she only felt elation.

Sam reached to help her, but Helen was already on her feet. Eyes bright. As Helen stepped to the tree, ready to speak the precious words, the Old Oak spoke first.

I know how eager you are, child. You feel this menace that entered the old world is your responsibility. First you must acknowledge that though you are being asked to stop him, you did not create him. His actions are not yours.

"But if I am the only one who can stop him," Helen replied, "he is my responsibility."

No. Your actions are yours. His are his. Though I will do everything in my power to assist you to win, you must let go of the need to win.

The world is on the brink of disaster and we're swapping riddles, Helen groaned. *I get that immortals don't have the same sense of time, but this is a little urgent.*

Not everything is as urgent as you feel, the Old Oak replied, with a hint of amusement. *You live life tackling problems alone. That time has come to an end. You may be the key, dear one, but you can only win this battle with your allies.*

Helen was beginning to feel frantic. She feared the Great Red Oak didn't know what David was capable of. This was not the time for lessons or advice. She needed to cross over. Helen could only imagine the havoc he was wreaking. By the time she got through, she might be too late.

"You don't understand," Helen pleaded. "David wants to destroy the old world so he can rule this one. If I don't step through soon, I won't be able to stop him."

I appreciate your urgency, little one. And I am grateful you are willing to risk yourself for us. But you will not stop him alone. Until you come to terms with that truth, I cannot let you through.

Helen wanted to pitch a fit. She was being stopped from doing the very thing she had been asked to do. *Immortals made no sense! What kind of idiocy was this? Was it a test?* Even though she'd been selected, did they need to make sure she was the right one? She may as well pull out a fiddle while the world burned!

And that's when the truth hit her.

Helen could not stop David with her urgency any more than Nero stopped the fires of Rome with his serenade. David was a creature of energy. She was jumping into a burning building with a case full of gasoline. David would sense her fear and panic in a second. Even worse, he would use them to fuel the destruction.

The Great Red Oak was right. Helen couldn't go anywhere near the old world until she grew calm. And, as much as she didn't want to admit it, she might get spooked when confronted with David. She could not be sure. She would need her team to distract him or buffer her feelings.

Almost, the Old Oak replied, startling Helen. Since they aligned, the ancient one could read everything going on inside her.

You forget, dear Helen, that your allies bring gifts of their own. You can never truly know how things will go in the moment. You must trust that your team will bring what you need, regardless of whether you plan for it.

Helen glanced at her small yet powerful team. They had risked everything on her. Believing in talents she didn't know she had. Helen marveled at how she had grown to love each of them in such a short time.

But trust? Trust was strange new territory. She didn't know how it worked. Love was much easier. Love she could give away without expectation of anything in return. She felt magnanimous with love. Whatever she got back was a bonus. Trust meant she had to count on them.

Precisely, the Old Tree replied.

I don't know how, Helen admitted.

Acquaintances described Helen as a risk-taker. Even a daredevil. They saw her willingness to jump into new scenarios as brave. But she knew that the courage the Great Oak requested was much greater.

Helen jumped off cliffs with her own parachute and her eyes locked on the target. Now she was being asked to close her eyes and fall backwards. No parachute. Only a prayer that the people she loved would catch her. She couldn't believe the fate of the world had come down to her ability to let go.

Helen wasn't sure she could.

That is the beauty of trust, little one. Be willing. Then take the step.

Helen turned to face Sam, Logan, Clarissa, and Stella. She was more frightened than she had ever felt in her life. She stared at these people she had known for only a few days and wondered whether she could let them hold her.

She honestly didn't know. What she did feel — curled up like a shaking animal in the corner of her heart — was how deeply she cared. How much she wanted them to catch her. Helen understood now that she could not truly claim to love them unless she was willing to jump.

Helen took a deep breath, reached out a hand, and uttered three words that terrified her more than the specter of death.

"I need you," Helen said.

Sam stepped up, wrapping her hand in his. Logan strode forward and took Helen's other hand. The sisters closed the circle, connecting Sam and Logan then each other. Stella gazed at Clarissa with forgiveness and Clarissa looked on her sister with deep gratitude.

Once the circle was closed around the Great Red Oak, Helen felt the power of her loved ones. She saw that the ancient words were useless without the surge of energy that must accompany them. Helen knew she would never have been able to open the Gateway on her own. She felt the Oak smile.

Connection is the Great Mystery. Speak the message, child.

Helen closed her eyes and bowed her head. Her heart grew calm and her mind was very still. She whispered the words gifted from time immemorial.

"Oscailt an geata chun na bhflaitheas," Helen said.

The immense tree lit up like a blinding star. Rays of light shot up through her branches and out across her roots. Inside her trunk, opened the sacred Gateway between worlds. The intensity blew Helen's hair back. And the light took her breath away. Helen stood stunned by its unmatchable beauty.

Then Stella and Clarissa shouted, "Jump!"
And the five of them took the greatest leap of their lives.

CHAPTER TWENTY-NINE

Helen landed on a hard surface. By the bumps and bruises on her body, she swore she had rolled across pure marble. She reached out to touch the cold stone beneath her. *Oh my god,* she thought, *it is marble.*

She rubbed her head. Helen's eyes travelled up a cavernous marble room. Beautiful tapestries hung on the walls. And carved doorways appeared on every side.

Helen wondered where she had landed. The height was immense and the ceiling was a beautiful, lifelike rendition of the night sky. She recognized some of the constellations but most were foreign to her. If she stared long enough, she swore the stars moved.

She rubbed her eyes and focused back on the room. *Wait,* she thought. *Where is Sam? Where are Logan and Clarissa and Stella?* Helen looked around but she was alone. How could she arrive without them? Could they have been separated in the portal? Helen tried to remember what happened after they jumped.

She recalled the blinding light. So powerful she closed her eyes. Then felt a pull like she was being sucked through space and time. She tried to hold on to Sam and Logan but the force of the energy in the tunnel ripped them apart. And she couldn't see or feel the Fates.

Helen had panicked then recalled the wisdom of the Great Oak. Trust. She had to believe that whatever happened in the portal was part of the plan. So she calmed her mind. Then held the single thought that she and her loved ones would be guided to their destination. She would land exactly where she was meant to be.

But how could this be where she was meant to land? Helen wondered. *Stranded in a hall without Sam and Logan? Or the sisters?* She didn't even know where she was.

"Only one way to find out," Helen said, and forced herself to her feet.

She swayed, dizzy from the effort. The room spun. Helen stumbled forward and caught herself on the edge of an ornate fountain at the center of the room. She puzzled over a water effect inside, but then who was she to question the decorating choices of the gods?

"Wait a minute," Helen said, gazing at the woven tapestries with lions that seemed strangely familiar. The flourishes in the marble that she swore she had touched somewhere else. And the warm rosewood doors that looked remarkably like —

The coincidences were only hints, like the glint of a light that appeared in the darkness but does not burn long enough to confirm its presence. But Helen knew these visual echoes. They were as familiar as her hands.

"What is going on?" Helen called out. She didn't know who would answer but she no longer cared. "I leapt into the portal to follow my brother. Not to land back in New York City!"

As her voice echoed into the far corners, she heard the faint return of laughter.

"This isn't funny," Helen insisted. "I have to find him."

Who says you have not? a female voice replied.

Helen looked around but saw no person to match the voice. *Great. More tricks and riddles.*

"Well, based on what I see," Helen declared. "It sure as hell looks like I've landed in some hidden room in the New York Public Library. *Not* Mount Olympus."

Very good, the woman replied.

Very good? Helen wanted to yell back. Then a chill shot down her spine. *Very good,* she thought again. She assumed her brother made it through. But if she was here in New York then he was here in New York!

"David never made it through," Helen said.

Exactly, the wise voice replied. *Like you, he made a large assumption that in leaping through one side of the portal, he would automatically gain entry to the other. But every Gateway has its own guardian and its own rules. David may have opened one doorway, but he did not have permission to pass through the other.*

Helen gazed around the room. Taking in the doorway. She had assumed the portal was a one-way ticket. But now she understood that there were many doors.

Then she remembered the Fates. "Does he still have Jenna?" Helen asked. "If he does, I need to find him."

Her head spun again. Whatever that portal did to her, the effects were not wearing off. She could barely stand.

Do not worry, Helen, the voice said. *Jenna is healing in the sacred lands of her birth. Her sisters are tending to her wounds.*

That's why she couldn't feel the Fates, Helen thought. *They made it through. Just none of the mortals.* Or so she assumed.

"Wait," Helen said. "Where are Sam and Logan?"

Peer into the waters, the voice replied.

Helen gazed into the fountain. Not quite sure how the fountain flowed yet the waters in the basin remained still. She marveled as an image of Sam and Logan appeared on the surface. They stood outside the library, gazing around as though searching for someone.

"They're looking for me," Helen said. "They need to know I am safe."

Now that you have said the words, the voice stated. *Logan will know.*

And in that instant, Logan touched Sam's arm. He said something that brought relief to Sam's face. They walked together down the steps, between the Sacred Lions.

"I need to go," Helen said. "I must join them in the hunt for David. He'll be angrier than ever. And hell bent on revenge."

No, Helen, the voice replied.

Helen grew agitated by the voice that both calmed and infuriated her. This room that seemed to be inside, yet outside. That she was somewhere in the New York Library, but nowhere she had ever seen.

Every thought made her head hurt. Every contradiction caused her world to spin. She had landed in the physical manifestation of a paradox.

The voice chuckled. Amused, yet impressed.

"Where am I?" Helen asked, awestruck. "And who are you?"

I, dear one, the woman replied, *am Sophia. Goddess of wisdom.*

Holder of the great paradox of truth. I see into many realities and I hold the possibility of many outcomes.

Helen felt the profound urge to kneel and hide her eyes. *No need,* the voice chuckled, entertained by the idea of supplication. *I brought you here to offer myself as teacher.*

"Teacher?" Helen asked. "Isn't that Logan's job?"

Ah, yes, Sophia replied. *Sweet Logan. He does know a great amount. And he will teach you in the ways of his world.*

The room fell quiet. Helen wondered whether she had offended Sophia. Then she noticed a ripple wave through one of the tapestries. A beautiful woman, clothed in a flowing gown, stepped out of the fabric. And walked toward Helen.

Helen simultaneously wanted to run and embrace this figure headed her way. The woman must be an illusion. A spectacle to comfort. Yet her flawless beauty and glowing presence unnerved Helen.

"Fear not, child," Sophia said, as she leaned against the fountain at her side. "I don this appearance to make our conversations easier. My essence lives in the walls of this edifice."

"The library?" Helen marveled. The goddess nodded.

"Library. Sacred hall. Portal to the ways of wisdom," Sophia smiled.

"Portal?" Helen gasped, not sure she was physically ready for another journey.

Sophia laughed. "You are staying here with me. No sudden travel required."

"But David —" Helen began.

"Is the reason you are now in my care," Sophia responded. "You are right in assuming that your brother is enraged and doubly motivated to seek revenge. You have much to learn, dear Helen. About your brother. And about yourself."

Helen stared at Sophia. She was silenced by the sheer number of questions dancing through her mind. She wasn't sure where to begin.

"Worry not," Sophia said, as she smiled and touched Helen's hand. "That is my job. Suffice to say, David will be bringing the fires of hell to our doors. And you, my dear student, must be ready."

END OF BOOK ONE

GRATITUDE

So many people make this beautiful offering possible. A huge, heartfelt thanks to:

My lovely beta readers who gave sage and generous insights when this story was a mere framework — Cynthia, Elizabeth C., Elizabeth K., Kathryn, Kyle, Sam, Sherri, Siv, Stephanie, and Vanessa.

My talented final draft readers: Kathryn Cottam and Vanessa Mayville. Your patience and enthusiasm were fuel for my creative fire.

Roberta Cottam for the stunning cover design. Your genius is unparalleled and inspiring.

Laura Wrubleski for the gorgeous cover and inside book layout. You are forever gracious and delightful.

Siv Klausen for your clear and careful editing. Your exacting eye is a remarkable gift.

Cynthia Mayville for your kind heart and thoughtful final review.

Kathryn Cottam, my dear sister and friend, for your faith, love, and delightful ideas.

Kevin Corkum, my powerful and insightful husband, for your support and love.

My beautiful family and friends who offer encouragement for each triumph on this ever-winding path.

Every wonderful reader for your generosity and support.

And the sacred Divine for trusting me with this tale.

ABOUT THE AUTHOR

K.M. Tremills is the author of the *Great Lands* and the *Fated* series. She built her writing career in the film industry, receiving support from the National Screen Institute and Telefilm Canada and screening a film at the Cannes and Toronto Film Festivals. Kate also contributed articles to Elle Canada and Moving Pictures. She was lured back to her first love — novels — when *Messenger* came calling.

While writing her series, Kate collaborates with the brilliant Kathryn and Roberta Cottam. They have written two collections together: *Three Short Tales of Red* and *Fabled*. Kate is currently writing the sequel to *Blue Moon* and has plans for the sequel to *Messenger*. She gathers inspiration by speaking at conferences and travelling to lands near and far. Kate is always delighted to hear from readers at **www.kmtremills.com.**

A GLIMPSE INTO

BLOOD MOON

BOOK TWO IN THE FATED SERIES

David sat in a café with a view of the Seine. On the outside, he looked relaxed, even patient. He was a refined man sipping a cappuccino.

On the inside, David roiled. He was furious. Humiliated. And determined to have his revenge. But he must wait. His plans went beyond the immediate need for punishment. David's first attempt at power was foiled by his sister's allies. More impressive companions than he had supposed.

David sipped his coffee. He was not ready to smile but he felt a glimmer of change in his prospects. Helen's fortune could be his providence. She was growing in power. He wondered how long it would take before she was a worthy adversary.

Now, he smiled. Helen's influence was a tool he could use. She believed herself impervious to his charms. A confidence he would encourage. But David knew her weakness. She longed for a family.

There was only one person who could deliver on that promise. Him.

AN EXCERPT FROM THE NOVEL BY
K.M. TREMILLS

My world is dying. And I am on the run. The others cannot see it. In fact, they are fighting for the very world they need to let go. But my father could see it. He knew that life was about to get tenuous and I had to be hidden.

When life gets frightening, people act out. They take their fear and they send it into the world. They burn. They rape. They pillage. They chase away the very thing that holds hope in the tender palm of an open hand.

I cannot blame them. It makes me angry. But I cannot blame them. People have forever crushed the things that scare them most.

And nothing is more frightening than a thing not understood.

This is what has brought me to the church. A tiny church. Filled with kind, brave souls who understand what I feel. They do not speak the words out loud. For to do so would call the monsters to their door. But they know. They know I am what these times need. What they have prayed for over many decades.

And they have agreed to give me shelter until the time comes that I must leave.

They know I am a Messenger.

I see it in their eyes. They understand that a Messenger, by her very nature, cannot stand still.

She can wait. She can rest until the Message is ready … but once she has received it, she cannot hide anymore.

To do so is to forsake the gift of the Message.

That would be the most dangerous thing of all for her. And the World.

The church where I am hiding is far on the edge of my father's lands. Others call it his Kingdom. Though my father would never claim ownership. He believed he was a steward. A guardian of the land. Appointed by the Divine to care for those within the reach of his authority.

There was a time when this was the common opinion. When all believed that the land was a shared gift that no one owned.

But this is not the view anymore. In their fear, people want to own things. To lay claim and carve their names into buildings and archways.

In their fear, they grasp, they clutch, they hold.

They became infected by the suspicion that spread across the land. A fear that was less palpable as the years wore on. But even then, it was making its way across all the Kingdoms.

By the year when I was born, Queendoms had ceased to exist. People could not comprehend a woman on a throne alone. Or with a King as her consort.

The fear had taken root. Pushing out the old ways.

I cannot lay the impetus of this change at the feet of the Great Prince. For no one remembers the source. Or what brought the fear to our shores.

What I do know is that the older the Prince became, the stronger the winds of hatred and suspicion grew.

The more the idea spread that, instead of many smaller Kingdoms, there should be one Grand Ruler. A single man who knew what was best for all. No matter how foreign their ways or how remote their villages.

A truly strange notion. And a dangerous one.

For placing power in the hands of one man has only ever left all at the whim of one man's thoughts. Fears. And every strange notion.

Power is balanced in the sharing. In trusting that others are as capable of holding your heart with care. A notion now deemed perilous.

Trust has become that foreign to us.

As suspicion spread from village to village, and Kingdom to Kingdom, lands were closed to one another. Neighbours became guarded. And the slightest difference was perceived to be a threat.

Life went from a beautiful mystery to a beast that must be wrestled, conquered, and kept safe in a stockade.

This is why the church where I am hiding is precious.
The wise ones who were once the gateways to mystery became gate-keepers. Clutching the key to a magical realm that is no longer deemed safe for the average being. In fact, they deny the mystical unless it suits their needs.

Amidst fear and uncertainty, anything that challenges the rule is heresy. Treason. And something that must, immediately, be extinguished.

That includes me. You see, I have always been different …

Wait. That is not true.

In truth, I am like everyone else. Yet this truth has been lost. Buried. Crushed under the burden of suspicion and doubt.

Kept from the common person in order to keep the wheels turning.

So that now, the very thing we all share, has become the thing that stands me apart. That marks me as different.

Different. Frightening to some, and special to others. A line in the sand that draws people into two camps.

When all it means is one thing is not like the other.

And this difference that I must hide? I feel the connection to the Gods and Goddesses. I am their hands on this earth. I know that the very things I touch, say, do, need – are extensions of the Divine Ones.

This is true of us all.

And this, I am told, is heresy. Except … I know in my heart of hearts, that the Great Prince also knows it is true.

He denies it. Sending his minions to strike the thought from history.

Cutting the words from people's mouths. Burning it from their bodies. But this does not negate the truth. In fact, it makes the truth stronger.

For the truth is like a whisper on the Wind. Living on forever and carrying for miles. No one knows when that whisper may turn the corner and whirl back into her life.

Like the Wind, a truth has many seasons. And stands the test of time. A truth is carried by many. And owned by none.

And when a truth has been forced to lay dormant for too many years, the whisper awakens in a being asked to make this truth her essence. Her mission. Her reason for walking this earth.

For a whisper does not exist unless it is shared.

This is my whisper to you.